RICH GIRL

Joy Ruble

Rich Girl
Joy Ruble

Published February 2020
Little Creek Books
Imprint of Jan-Carol Publishing, Inc.

ISBN: 978-1-950895-30-4
Library of Congress Control Number: 2020934012

You may contact the publisher:
Jan-Carol Publishing, Inc.
PO Box 701
Johnson City, TN 37605
publisher@jancarolpublishing.com
jancarolpublishing.com

To my husband, Sam. To express my gratitude to you would fill the pages of a much larger novel. I owe you everything.

To our boys, Zach and Jacob. You are my greatest treasures.

Now unto God and our Father be glory for ever and ever. Amen.
Philippians 4:20

Author's Note

So many of us are looking for that perfect life, you know, the one that doesn't exist. Don't let life pass you by while you're searching for the perfect one. That doesn't mean you have to settle. It just means you have to be awake and open to possibilities.

Prologue

Ah, the early '80s. Times were simpler back then. We'd never heard of gluten, and didn't know carbs were bad. We had no idea that fat would be a bad thing for a while, but then suddenly become good again. We just enjoyed our carbed-up, gluten-filled doughnut, complete with super fatty buttercream inside, like there was no tomorrow. Twinkies were more prevalent than apples in school lunchboxes, because processed foods were delicious, period. We were conservatively dressed, from our preppy, Oxford-cloth shirts tucked into our Levi jeans down to our matching socks and penny loafers. Our hair was big, (*really* big) and our cars were even bigger.

Only businesses owned computers, except for a few geeks. We didn't have smart phones to waste all our free time either, so we read books or watched one of our three network television channels, which usually consisted of reruns of *Gilligan's Island* and new episodes of *Dallas*. Some lucky people in metropolitan areas had cable and could watch MTV (which was actually almost entirely music videos back then) and HBO. The good old days, we might call them. We listened to Journey, Boston, and Foreigner (the best of the best) on our cool, new cassette tapes in the boom boxes we carried around on our shoulders. We talked to each other in person, on a pay phone (look it up), or on the land line that we still simply referred to as our phone.

But the good days weren't all good. We didn't have the advances in medicine that we have today, out-of-state phone calls were long-distance (think data overage, if you're too young to remember), and people who lived in rural areas had often never even met anyone of a different race. Ignorance was bliss in many ways—but sometimes it was just plain ignorant.

We are all given a space in history, a time to be born and live our lives. People say that life is what you make it. That may be true, but I believe that where and when we're born can make a vast difference in the quality of life. To be born in Salem, Massachusetts in 1692 would be much different from being born in Boston in 1992. But no matter when or where we were born, each of us is given a hand breadth of time to create our own, unique story. Here's mine.

Chapter 1

PRESENT

"If you don't like the road you're walking, start paving another one."
–Dolly Parton

Me

All I ever wanted to do was marry a rich man. It had been my only goal in life since I was twelve, when I told mama that I wanted to live in a big house on the beach with a pink door and a maid. Mama just rolled her eyes and told me I had better marry a rich man. Some people didn't consider marrying a rich guy a legitimate goal—like getting a college degree, or becoming a doctor, or a mother—but marrying into wealth was actually hard work. The biggest obstacle was finding someone rich. Rich men didn't exist where I lived in Possum Valley, Tennessee, so my job was to track one down like a bloodhound. Daddy always said we could learn a lot from animals, and I had learned a valuable lesson from our bloodhound, Rockefeller (yes, I named him). Daddy said when Feller (as we called him for short) was tracking a deer, he wouldn't give up until he either found the source of the scent or reached the end of the trail. I knew I had to be relentless like Feller to get a rich guy, so I determined that I wouldn't give up until I found the source of my desire...or died trying.

When adults asked my girlfriends and me what we wanted to do when we grew up, my friends always recited the usual "female" professions like teacher, nurse, secretary, to which every girl growing up in the '70s aspired. My friends always received an uninterested reply of "That's great." When I responded that I wanted to marry a rich man, I always got a robust laugh and a "Now, *that's* an ambitious young lady." It was ambitious, but Daddy always said that anything worthwhile takes effort. And then there was the voice inside my head. Ever since I could remember, there was a voice that spoke to me: not audible, of course, but a gut feeling that told me things like who my friends should be and what I should or shouldn't be doing. The voice had clearly told me I was going to marry a rich man, and it had never let me down before.

My goal became increasingly important as I got older and realized that if I didn't get out of the small, rural town in Tennessee where I lived with my parents on a fifty-acre farm, I would end up stuck in a doublewide trailer on a rocky piece of land for the rest of my life, like almost everyone I knew. Because of all the hills in East Tennessee, there were many valleys named after indigenous critters in the region. We were "lucky" enough to live in Possum Valley. Did you catch my sarcasm there? That's right. Try telling someone from out of state you live in Possum Valley, Tennessee sometime. The looks you got were priceless, and it was certain to be a topic of almost offensively fascinated conversation. "Are possums like rats?" "Do you *eat* possums in Tennessee?" Yep, being from a town named Possum Valley was downright humiliating.

But not everyone agreed with me about our town's unique name. In fact, Possum Valley residents were generally very proud of their little town and its name. They were poor, but most of them didn't seem to even know it. Maybe it was because being poor was all they had ever known. My best friend Jenny had one of the nicest houses in Possum Valley, but the majority of people lived in old, run-down trailers like ours. Most were content though, never questioning if there was more to life, because Possum Valley was a quaint little town with friendly people, mostly farmers, and spectacular views of the Great Smoky Mountains. We even had a big welcome sign as you entered town:

Welcome to Possum Valley (Where Roadkill Rules)

Population 3,710 (more or less)

Home of Prize-winning pigs and strawberry-rhubarb pies

The "where roadkill rules" phrase (with a small, animated image of a possum's grinning face and one paw made into a fist raised in the air) was added to the sign by our new mayor, Randy Fisher, two years after he took office. Mayor Fisher, a Possum Valley native who was a fiscal conservative (like everyone else in Possum Valley), had a unique sense of humor. Over the years, a few citizens had petitioned to change the name of the town because of the negative connotation that it held for some. But Mayor Fisher liked the name, and felt we should embrace it and even capitalize on it. Everyone in town liked him, so they were willing to go along with his idea for facetiously making our town name a novelty for tourists—not that Possum Valley was a big touristy area by any means, but we did occasionally have some vacationers stop in on their way to the Smoky Mountains. The shops, stores, and our two bed and breakfasts in town sold stuffed possums of different sizes and coffee mugs that had *Possum Valley, TN* or *Roadkill Rules in Possum Valley, TN* printed on them. Sales were good for the souvenirs. In fact, our two convenience stores couldn't keep them in stock. Most locals had bought at least one, and they were very popular among tourists that stopped in for gas or a cup of coffee.

Mayor Fisher had several ideas for boosting the economy in Possum Valley, and he had big plans to build a new library and a park with the tax proceeds. At the time, our library consisted of a few donated books (the locals weren't avid readers) in a storage room in the Town Hall. He wanted to encourage children to read more because he thought reading books would improve the low high school graduation rate. Many high school dropouts were a result of parental apathy, I believed. The parents hadn't graduated high school themselves and didn't see the need for their children to graduate either, since most were just going to end up being farmers or farmers' wives anyway. Others dropped out because they were needed on the farm to make ends meet. The mayor believed that improving the graduation rate began with our youth reading books, learning about the world and all it had to offer them. Most people thought he was crazy, but they would say, "Bless his heart; you gotta give him credit for trying."

The prize-winning pigs mentioned on our sign were mostly from our farm. Daddy took pigs to the Tennessee Valley Fair in Knoxville every year to be judged. His pigs had won the previous eight years in a row, and as a result, he was treated like a celebrity in Possum Valley. "No use in even tryin' to beat Larry Fillmore's pigs," townspeople would pridefully say. "He treats those pigs like part of the family." And it was true. He loved those pigs, and they loved him back. I fed them most of the time, and they usually ignored me, but when daddy walked into the pen, they would run up to him and eat right out of his hand. They followed him around like puppies, dropping onto the ground and rolling on their sides for belly rubs. Daddy said his pigs were smarter than most people he knew.

Miss Myra Pepper made prize-winning strawberry-rhubarb pies. Miss Myra was 85 years old, but she still grew her own strawberries and rhubarb in her back yard. Her secret recipe was handed down to her from her great-grandmother. She wouldn't even give the recipe to her daughter Jeannie, but she kept a copy of it in her safe deposit box at the bank; Jeannie would inherit it when Miss Myra died. Although no one had been able to replicate the pies, we assumed she used Crisco for the crust because several people had seen her buying it in six-pound cans at the IGA. Miss Myra might have been stingy with her recipe, but she was very generous with her pies. She made four of them every year for homecoming Sunday at Possum Valley Baptist Church, and smart congregation members (some might say selfish, but those were just the ones that didn't get their slice of pie) always got a slice of her pie with their meal on their first trip through the line, because they knew the pies would be gone if they waited until they went back for dessert. She also made one or two every time there was a birth or a death in the community. They became known as the "hail and farewell" pies.

* * *

I knew it wasn't going to be easy for a pig-farming girl from Possum Valley such as myself to marry into wealth, so I had studied rich people since I was thirteen. I took copious notes that I kept in a large three-ring binder that Mama had bought me for school. We learned very little useful information at school, as far as I was concerned, so I wrote the words *How to Marry a Rich Man* on the cover of the binder with a black marker and made a big pink circle around it. I didn't know any rich people personally, but I had resources: namely TV shows, books, and magazines. Mama subscribed to *Redbook*, so I got most of my fashion and make-up tips from its pages. I watched old movies on TV with actresses like Aubrey Hepburn and Grace Kelley so I could learn how to walk and talk like a sophisticated lady who belonged on the arm of wealthy man. I knew I certainly wasn't going to land a rich guy with my Southern accent and clumsy, awkward gait that I inherited from Mama. She leaned forward and hunched her shoulders when she walked, like she was about to break into a full sprint. She was always in a hurry, trying to keep everything done on the farm. She worked hard and never had any time (or money) for going to the mall, getting her hair done, or worrying about things like walking like a lady.

I was determined to have a different life from Mama's, so I used words like "fabulous" and "darling," and practiced walking in mama's one pair of high-heeled shoes, which she only wore to church on Sundays. I read books about the Kennedys (we had two in our library, thanks to Mayor Fisher) to get an idea of what rich people cared about and thought. I was an avid reader and a straight-A student, breezing through school with very little effort. My 9th grade teacher, Mr. Howell, said I had potential. Now I know that he meant I had potential to go to college and have a good career as a teacher or a nurse, but at the time, I thought he meant that I was pretty enough to find a rich husband and move away from Possum Valley. It was a compliment either way, though.

I never cursed or used slang words, because Mrs. Starry, my Sunday-School teacher at Possum Valley Baptist Church, told me once that only uneducated people cursed because they didn't have a good vocabulary. I studied vocabulary words and grammar every day for years. I learned five new words from the dictionary every week. I went alphabetically, so I knew words like *abdicate, adept, aloof, and amiable.* Of course, no one in my circles ever used these words, so people usually gave me a blank stare when I practiced saying something like, "I try to be amiable to everyone, including aloof people." I never made it past the letter N in my studies. I quit at *nepenthe*, but my vocabulary was still exemplary, (one of my words) especially for letters A through M. We didn't learn much vocabulary or grammar at Possum Valley Elementary School. It seemed pointless, since even my English teachers used double negatives, dangling participles, and *ain't* on a regular basis. It was as if they assumed we poor, rural kids would never have any use for proper English or geography, since we would probably grow up to be poor, rural adults that never went anywhere or did anything that would require more than a basic knowledge of math and reading. Due to my self-education, I knew to respond that I was "well" when someone asked me about my health, and my extensive vocabulary prompted some of my *colleagues* (another vocabulary word) to ask if I was "a rich kid." They meant it as an insult, of course, but it was the ultimate compliment to me.

* * *

Mama and Daddy had lived on our farm in the same trailer ever since they married 21 years ago. The farm belonged to Papaw Fillmore, Daddy's father, when Mama and Daddy had first married; when Papaw died suddenly of a heart attack, Daddy inherited the farm. Mama and Daddy were content in the trailer and never bothered to save up for a house. Instead, when Daddy got a little extra money, he used it for more farm equipment or more livestock (usually pigs). He said that adding to our investment was the best way for us to "get ahead." I waited my entire childhood for us to get ahead, but we never did. Instead, we just had a yard littered with plows, manure spreaders, wheelbarrows, and lots of pigs. Although we had chickens, a few cows, and a pond stocked with fish, we were pig farmers. We typically had anywhere from forty to sixty pigs, which was more than enough for people to smell our farm long before they could see it. Daddy was a butcher as well as a farmer, so he slaughtered all his pigs right on the property. Manure and Daddy's slaughtering business gave our farm the distinct aroma of manure mixed with freshly-slaughtered animal flesh. The smell was so dense, it seemed you should be able to reach out and grab a handful; it was so strong you could taste it. On the rare occasion when we went out of town, the odor followed me in my luggage, just like cigarette smoke follows a smoker. It was in my clothes and my hair, as a constant reminder of my lot in life. It seemed to leave a grimy film on me that I couldn't wash away, no matter how hard I tried.

Farm life had never agreed with me, to say the least. I always thought it was wrong for people to judge me about hating the farm until they had tasted the constant aroma of animal feces and flesh for themselves. I had been feeding the pigs since I could remember, and I started hauling manure from the stock barn in town as soon as I was old enough to drive. These were not glamorous jobs by

when my neighbor Mike Ledbetter just happened to drive up beside me in his black Chevy Silverado.

"Hello, darlin'. Looks like you could use some hay-ulp," he said in a syrupy voice as he put down his window. He pulled up in front of my truck and got out, towering over me as he looked down at me and then at the continuous stream of smoke pouring from the engine with his pale blue eyes. Mike and I were in the same grade at school, and everyone liked him. He was a star basketball player and an honor student, but his real passion was music.

"It's a girl, my Lord, in a flatbed Ford, slowin' down to take a look at me," he sang, in his best Glen Frey voice as he lifted the hood on my truck. Mike had this annoying habit of singing lyrics from a song to fit every occasion. If it was sunny, he would break into John Denver's "Sunshine on my Shoulders;" a couple of times when I had complained of being hot, he sang "Hot Blooded," by Foreigner. He had a song for rain, snow, trucks, cars, dogs, cats...you name it.

"I don't have a *flatbed* Ford, and even if I did, I wouldn't slow down to look at you," I scowled. I knew I should've been grateful that he stopped to help, but I was embarrassed and annoyed and certainly not in the mood for his stupid songs.

Mike

Mike played the guitar, and he loved to write songs. His uncle Paul had given him a guitar for Christmas when he was ten, but his parents couldn't afford to pay for lessons, so he taught himself to play. Mike was just one of those people who were fascinated with everything and looked at challenges, like playing the guitar or working on cars, as opportunities. He read books from our small library as often as he could, and I admired him for trying to better himself—even though he had no ambition to *use* his knowledge, as far as I could tell.

Mike was an only child, and lived with his parents on a small farm down the road from ours. His daddy was a construction worker for Homebuilders of Possum Valley. They had a small but adorable Victorian house with pale yellow siding and ornate white trim that gently curved around the windows; Mike's daddy, Bill, had built the home himself. The house had a wrap-around porch that gave it a dollhouse effect with detailed wooden brackets that curled into the posts like snails. The front porch was adorned with white wicker chairs and hanging baskets overflowing with purple and white petunias in the summer. The front lawn was just as impressive, manicured boxwood hedges enclosing the porch and leaving an opening just large enough for the stairs that led to the front door.

I always thought his mama, Angie, was the perfect fit for their sunny dollhouse in her knee-length floral skirts and solid blouses covered by a ruffled apron. She reminded me of Mrs. Cleaver on *Leave It to Beaver*, and everybody in town liked her. Every time I went to visit, the house was filled with the aroma of cookies, brownies, or whatever else Angie was baking that day. I always told Mike that I would be enormous if my mom baked as much as Angie did, but he and his parents were pictures of health. Bill and Angie were in their early forties, and both were very attractive. Mike had definitely inherited their good looks, with his dad's blue eyes and his mom's thick, dark hair. Mike was very content with his small-town farm life. He had told me on many occasions, as we sat by the pond on my property skipping stones and talking about the future, that he could never imagine leaving Possum Valley. I think he would have been content living on his dad's farm and working with him in the construction business for the rest of his life. Reading books like *The Great Gatsby* inspired him to write more songs, but he didn't seem to care about living the glamorous lifestyle described in the novel. To him, getting up to the rooster's crow and living the simple life, with plenty of open sky, fresh air, and green grass, was all he needed. Most of the girls at school had a crush on him, with his tanned skin, dark hair, and sky-blue eyes. But Mike had been in love with me since third grade. He used to write me notes in class. *Do you like me? Check YES or NO.* I always checked *NO*, but he had never given up—no matter how many times I rejected him. I admired his persistence, but there was no future for the two of us. He and I had known each other all our lives, so he was like the annoying brother I never had. We grew up playing cowboys and Indians and riding bikes together, but he was usually better at everything than I, and it annoyed me. He could run faster, stay underwater longer, skip stones farther, and sing better. When I complained to him about it, he would say I shouldn't worry because I was so pretty, I didn't need to be good at anything. He meant it as a compliment, so he couldn't understand when I got angry and went home. I had gotten a mood ring for my twelfth birthday; it was always black when Mike was around, so I had decided he was toxic for me.

"I always said FORD stands fer 'found on road day-ud,'" he smirked.

"Could you just go find my daddy, please?" I asked, trying to stay calm. I had pressed my fingernails into the palms of my clenched fists so hard I was sure they were bleeding.

"I can take a look at it fer ya, darlin,'" he grinned. He called most all girls darlin', because of his Conway Twitty obsession, and I was certain that he tried to talk with more of a Southern drawl than was natural just to annoy me. It worked.

He looked around under the hood for no more than a minute and closed it. "I need to go git ya some water fer your radiator to git ya home. I'll be right back," he said, as he opened his car door.

"Thanks, Mike," I said reluctantly, wishing I didn't need his help so often. He had been the one to help me win homecoming queen the year before by buying forty boxes of Krispy Kreme doughnuts for the fundraiser. I still have no idea what he did with all those doughnuts. He was also the one that went and got Daddy when I wrecked my bike and broke my arm in sixth grade. I always felt needy around him, and I hated it. Sometimes I felt like I was destined—or doomed—to end up with a backwoods guy like him with no aspirations. I got back in the truck, rolled down the windows, and turned on the radio. "It's a girl, my Lord, in a flatbed Ford, slowin' down to take a look at me" were the first words I heard, the Eagles echoing over the air waves. I changed the channel, even though the Eagles was one of my favorite bands. Mike had ruined the song for me that day—possibly forever.

I was singing "Chains," along with Fleetwood Mac when Mike got back. I quickly turned off the radio so he wouldn't start singing, and ruin yet another favorite for me. Mike had a beautiful voice, and everyone said he should go to Nashville, but I wasn't in the mood to hear him. He got out of his truck with a big can of water and poured it into the radiator. I watched his bicep muscles flex. *What a waste of a fine specimen of flesh he is*, I thought. *What if I don't deserve any better than someone like him?* The thought made me hate him, almost as much as I hated the manure-filled truck he had just repaired for me.

"All fixed up, so you can keep on a-truckin' with that nice load o' manure you got back there," he said with a grin. That made *me* think of a song as the flies swarmed around my truck. "Why Me, Lord?" by Kris Kristofferson.

* * *

Rain started falling before Daddy and I could finish unloading the manure off the truck that evening. *Could this day get any worse?* I wondered. I started shoveling faster, scooping up big loads and throwing them on top of the enormous pile on the ground so that I could try to avoid standing in soggy manure. As I started to shovel my next heap, I heard Daddy whistling. The only thing Daddy loved as much as cow manure was rain. I don't recall ever having a dinner conversation that didn't include precipitation. "We *have* to get some rain," he would tell us, as if we could make it rain on command. It could rain for two weeks straight, and he would still say we needed rain. It was like a worn-out recording that he couldn't stop playing, "Needmorerainneedmorerainneedmorerain."

Daddy wasn't a churchgoer, except on two occasions. One was when we were in a drought. "Pray for rain for the farmers in the valley," he would stand and request, in his best shirt and the only tie he owned with a farm scene printed on it, complete with a barn and cows (I assumed he couldn't find one with pigs) enclosed in a white fence. The other time was when we had dinner on the grounds. He never turned down a free meal. "They always have a good spread over there at the church," he would say, giving his girth three hearty slaps while simultaneously unbuttoning his pants. You can probably see why I had to get my culture from books and movies.

Daddy was a big man, well over six feet tall and nearly 220 lbs. When he didn't have on his white blood-stained apron and work boots, his hair sticky with sweat, he was handsome with thick, dark hair and dark eyes that sparkled when he talked about butchering an animal, rain, or manure. He always smelled metallic, because he couldn't seem to ever get all the dried animal blood from beneath his fingernails. It was an art, he said, to be able to slice the bacon and cut the meat leaving just the right amount of fat so that all the flavor came through. He was good at what he did, so farmers from all over the county came to have their pigs, cows, and an occasional sheep slaughtered. Admittedly, I was proud of him on some level, but I still hated farm life. He had a smokehouse and a meat locker, so he cut up the meat and smoked or froze it for his customers. Because it was the early 1980s and we were way back in the country, he didn't have a license; no one ever inspected Daddy's slaughtering and packaging operation.

Our home was about a quarter mile off the road on a rolling hill with a newly-painted red barn that made the farm appear rather charming, from a distance. Daddy took pride in our barn, and always made sure it looked nice. Of course, you couldn't see our 21-year-old doublewide trailer erected on cinder blocks, or its peeling redwood deck, from the road. I had never lived in a house, but they seemed so much sturdier than our trailer. It rocked during a thunderstorm, and I always felt like it might tumble over and roll down the hill if we all stood on one side at the same time. Rita and I had our own rooms, though, and our kitchen had a big bay window that overlooked the pig pen, which was Daddy's pride and joy. I'm sure he would have chosen the pig pen view over an ocean view, if he'd had the option.

You also couldn't see the old, worn-out smokehouse from the road. The tired little building leaned to one side so far that I was certain I could knock it over with a little shove, and thought about doing it on many occasions. Then there was Daddy's collection of junk, which was scattered all around the farm like manure piles in the field. A tire here and an old kitchen sink there. Here an old broken-down car that hadn't run in ten years, and there a rusted plow that could be used on any one of the three old tractors that happened to be running at the time. Daddy knew I despised the farm, and he told me that I'd never be happy if I didn't accept who I was. "You can be one of two things, Kathy," he used to tell me. "You can be your true self, or you can be your church self. Before people walk into the church house, they might be as mean as the devil himself," he would say, "but as soon as they walk through the church doors, they transform into angelic beings, walking around smiling from ear to ear, saying stuff like, 'Bless your heart, sister.' They might have a few people fooled, but they ain't foolin' me." Of course he was right, for the most part. Everyone knew that "Bless your heart" in the South was usually synonymous with "you're a loser," at best. And I knew some people in the church well enough to know that they didn't act the same way on Monday as they did on Sunday. But I hated the farm every day of the week, so I *was* being my true self, I thought.

Daddy didn't have anything bad to say about our pastor, Preacher Charlie Brown, though. Daddy said bad-mouthing God's man would surely get you in trouble with God himself. Besides, our preacher was one of the most genuinely decent people I knew. Preacher Brown probably heard the phrase, "Good grief, Charlie Brown," at least once a day, but he had a good sense of humor. He always said that at least he had more hair than the other Charlie Brown, and he actually got the little red-haired girl. He was referring to his wife, Miss Judy, who had beautiful red hair and milky white skin. Mama said she got that skin from clean living, which was one of the reasons I never took up smoking—that, and I hated the smell of cigarettes. Preacher Brown was a nice man in his early fifties, with a full head of grey hair and a big belly. His belly hung over his pants, which were held up with suspenders. I knew he wore suspenders because he always took off his suit coat when he started preaching, sweat dripping from his brow and staining his starched white shirt. Congregants at Possum Valley Baptist Church often joked about how even the deacons didn't want to sit on the front row, fearing they might have sweat or spit slung on them, possibly both if the preacher was feeling really spiritual. Daddy said it was like sitting too close to our dog, Feller, who could sling spit for several feet. Everyone in Possum Valley liked Preacher Brown though, because he always visited the sick and afflicted, never missed a funeral, and was always willing to help people with anything, from digging a ditch to unclogging a sink. He had been a construction superintendent in Oak Ridge before being called into the ministry, so he was very good with his hands. Another reason people loved Preacher Brown was Miss Judy. She was technically Mrs. Brown, but people at church put Miss in front of her first name to show both respect and familiarity. (It's a Southern thing.) Miss Judy always had a sweet smile on her face, and she loved to bake coconut cakes for the sick. She was known for making the best coconut cakes around. They were light and fluffy like eating clouds, and Daddy said he thought some people pretended to be sick just to get one of her cakes. Even though Daddy didn't attend church, he had a lot of respect for Preacher Brown and Miss Judy. "I don't know *when* the man sleeps," Daddy would say. Daddy respected people that worked hard. He loved God and knew all the church hymns, but Daddy always said he didn't have time to take off work for church. He quoted scripture about an ox being in a ditch. He said the verse meant if you had work to do, God understood if you stayed out of church to get it done. It sounded reasonable enough to me, but Mama said Daddy was good at finding a Bible verse to support whatever he wanted to do.

I liked Preacher Brown because he seemed to genuinely care about people and their problems. When someone asked him to pray for something, he would stop right then and pray. He said he did that because he didn't want to risk forgetting later. I knew it was true because I had asked him to pray that God would send me a rich man. He stopped, put his hand on my shoulder, and said, "Let's bow our heads and pray for your future husband right now." As he prayed silently, I had a good feeling that his prayer would be answered, since he was a preacher and all. Daddy probably would've told me my prayer was too selfish, and I shouldn't bother the pastor about it. But Preacher Brown had told us many times that if we asked, we would receive. So, I was asking for a rich man. Was that wrong?

The Neighbors

Daddy was never an organized person by nature, but he did have a very organized method for slaughtering animals. First, he shot them in the head while they were in his cattle truck; then he cut off the convulsing legs and head before he strung them up with a rope on a tree branch to skin. The legs bothered me the most. They kept jerking long after the animal was shot in what seemed like a last, futile attempt at fighting for life. After the skinning was complete, Daddy cut the animal down and removed the insides. Cleaning up wasn't his specialty, though. A couple of times after he'd had a long day and couldn't clean up before dark, we found the blood-encrusted, decaying heads a day or two later on the road in front of our house; Feller or some wild animal had carried them down the hill. Well, once it was actually our neighbor Ted who found a head, but he definitely let us know about it.

Ted lived next door to us in a small Jim Walter home; he had hit a cow's head, and it got stuck underneath his bright red 1982 Pontiac Firebird Trans Am, complete with T-tops and luxury reclining bucket seats. He was obviously proud of his muscle car, which served as a redneck chick magnet for men whose hairlines were receding along with their youth. Ted was muscular with big, brown eyes, and had probably been good looking and used to attention from the ladies when he was younger. Most men in our neck of the woods had trucks, and the women had station wagons, Impalas, or some version of that body design. Ted had moved to Possum Valley from Chattanooga when he was hired as the fourth-grade teacher at Possum Valley Elementary. He was a nice guy, but I didn't think he really liked living in Possum Valley much. Daddy said he didn't think he'd last long, but he seemed to like his job at the school, and all the kids loved him. He walked up our driveway that day as I was feeding the pigs, carrying the mangled cow head with a shovel. I had never seen him so angry. He dumped the cow head in front of me and said, "I think this belongs to your daddy. Tell him if there is damage to my car from hitting it and dragging it down the road with me, I will send him the bill."

"Yes, sir," I said, struggling to keep a straight face. If it hadn't been so funny, I would've been really embarrassed.

Ted had two children: a girl named Christine, who was five and had just finished kindergarten, and a boy, Teddy, who had just turned three. His wife, Sandy, was a stay-at-home mom, but I never saw her outside much. They were normally very nice neighbors, but Sandy occasionally complained about the flies and about Daddy shooting the animals where her kids could see him do it. I loved Daddy, and I knew he worked hard to keep us clothed and fed. But secretly, I was embarrassed about the way we lived, which made me more and more desperate to find a way out.

Our neighbors on the other side, twin brothers named Heath and Henry, were not as nice as Ted and Sandy. Their big, old house with the rusty tin roof was probably white at one time, judging from the barnacles of cracked paint clinging to the decaying wood; the place probably hadn't seen a coat of paint in the past fifty years. The dilapidated structure appeared uninhabitable even to Possum Valley residents. The front porch, which they obviously used as a storage shed, had caved in from the weight of a rusted washing machine and refrigerator that had been positioned on it for at least a decade. Most of the windows were broken, with pieces of shutters dangling beside them like broken ladders. The kids in the neighborhood were sure the house was haunted. Even though I didn't believe in ghosts, I was afraid to go near it too. At a minimum, it looked like the perfect haven for spiders and snakes. Mama said it needed to be torn down, but nobody was brave enough to confront Heath and Henry about it. They became belligerent when they drank, which was most of the time. Heath went into violent fits and would sometimes chase Henry around the neighborhood with things like hatchets and hammers.

One summer afternoon when I was about ten, I was watching Heath chase Henry through our field when he suddenly looked over and stared right at me. When his eyes met mine, I immediately knew I was in big trouble. As he headed for me, I sprinted barefoot across the yard and into the trailer, locked the door, and ran to my bedroom. I went barefoot all the time in the summer. It was just what we did, in Tennessee. I was proud of my toughened feet, which could run across the gravel in our driveway like I was running through a soft meadow. In fact, gravel was preferable over the field on our farm, since the field inevitably had more than a few cow piles distributed through it like chocolate chips scattered throughout a cookie. As Mama was interrogating me regarding the commotion, Heath banged on the door while yelling, "Where's 'at girl that's been snoopin' around out here?" I warned Mama not to answer because it was Heath with a hatchet, and she grabbed Rita and joined me in my bedroom. We could hear him yelling and threatening us while we hid behind the bed, warning us to leave him alone or he would cut us up in bite-size pieces and feed us to the buzzards. I asked Mama if he was really going to cut us into bite-size pieces, as I considered the nightmares that were forthcoming. "Be quiet," she whispered. Mama wouldn't let us play outside for a week after that, but I didn't care. I was too afraid to go out anyway.

Heath and Henry weren't all bad though. They usually felt bad after one of their drunken incidents, and sometimes brought Mama gifts to make amends. One time, after one of their rampages just before Thanksgiving, they came over with a live turkey that looked malnourished and close to death. They said they had bought it at a turkey farm the week before, and put in the trunk of their car to bring home. (They had an old beat-up Mercury that went perfectly with their house.) The turkey looked better, they said, when they first bought it, but they had forgotten about it and left it in the trunk of their car all week. Daddy nursed it back to health though, and it tasted pretty good on Thanksgiving Day. Mama had invited Heath and Henry to join us for Thanksgiving dinner that year since they had given us a turkey, but they declined because they were going to their sister's house in Georgia for Thanksgiving. We were all relieved.

* * *

"Life itself is the proper binge." –Julia Child

It's probably pretty clear by now why I wanted to get out of Possum Valley. Most women in the valley dreamed of a better life when they were young, just as I did. But then they got married to a local guy after high school, and became what they would later describe as "stuck" there, after having three or four kids and settling down in their doublewide on a rocky little piece of land. Some of their husbands were able to buy their own land; others just put a trailer on their family's property and took it over when their parents died, liked Daddy did. These families were often referred to as clans, like the Jenkins clan that lived down the street from us. There were three generations of them on the same property.

Most women in the valley seemed to cope by line-dancing the night away to Billy "Crash" Craddock on Friday nights at the Valley Barn Dance Hall, going to church on Sundays, and collecting things. Mama's best friend, Jolene, collected crystals that were supposed to bring her good luck. This was ironic, I thought, because she had about the worst luck of anyone I knew. She had set her trailer on fire when she fell asleep with a cigarette in her hand. She sustained burns on 25 percent of her body trying to save her crystals, which were in the bedroom closet. More recently, Jolene was in a car accident and broke her collarbone. In her defense, maybe her luck would be even worse without the crystals. I didn't want to find out, though.

Mama collected Elvis Presley memorabilia. Not for good luck, but because of her undying love and devotion to the king of rock and roll. We really couldn't afford it, but she had all his albums and everything she could get her hands on related to Elvis. Her favorite collectible was the "I Love Elvis" Precious Moments figurine, complete with blue suede shoes, that Daddy had gotten her for Christmas one year. The king had been dead for almost five years, but this was a small detail Mama chose to ignore. Elvis was still alive and well, in her mind. Daddy drove her by Graceland in Memphis once before Elvis died. She didn't see Elvis, of course, but she did see one of his Cadillacs leaving the house. She was sure Elvis was in it, and it was the highlight of her life to date.

Of course, everyone remembers where they were on August 16, 1978, the day Elvis died. I was in the kitchen with Mama when we heard the news on TV. At first, it didn't seem real that somebody like Elvis Presley could actually be dead. Mama broke down and cried, more than I had seen her cry since her daddy had died two years earlier. She just sat there in the living room, holding her favorite picture of Elvis. It was a black and white photo taken around 1960, with his hair slicked back and his skin perfectly smooth. "Like a baby's bottom," Mama always said. Mama loved that photo because she said his eyes pierced right through her soul. Rita and I did all the chores and cooked dinner that night, because Mama went to her room that afternoon and we didn't see her again until the next morning, her eyes bloodshot and puffy from crying.

Mama announced that same morning that she wanted to be cremated when she died so that her ashes could be spread around Graceland. Daddy told her he didn't think that was something they did at Graceland, but Mama said it was her dying request, so we had to honor it. We all thought she was crazy. Not because she wanted her ashes spread around Graceland, per se, but because nobody got *cremated* in Possum Valley. I didn't have a problem with it, though, especially since traditional funerals in Possum Valley could be outrageous, even violent at times. Fights often broke out at the Last Stop Funeral Home, over everything from pets to costume jewelry. It had almost become a form of entertainment, and I was pretty sure that many people attended funerals just in case a "good" fight erupted. When Jolene's mother, Francis, died, Jolene and her sister Candy got into a fist fight over who loved their mother the most. Candy lived near the high school with her husband, Rick. She was in her early thirties and worked as a palm reader in their doublewide. Candy had been saying she was clairvoyant since she was a little girl, and she could usually tell her clients with a fair amount of accuracy if something exciting or new was going to happen to them in the next year. She read Mama's palm once and saw that Mama was going to have a rocky relationship with a loved one in the following days. Candy was right, too; when Daddy found out Mama had spent money on Candy's "Satanic soothsaying," as he called it, they fought about it for nearly a week. Candy always had big hair, and wore long fake fingernails and tight mini skirts. Daddy called her a witch in harlot's attire. He didn't know much Bible, but Mama said he knew just enough to identify the wicked. Candy did look a little trashier than most, but she definitely got lots of attention, so I didn't see a problem.

The fight started when Jolene accused Candy of not loving their mama because she was eating Cheetos while their mama lay dead in the casket. Candy had just come back from the vending machines in the back of the funeral home with a Dr. Pepper and a big bag of Cheetos. Candy told Jolene that she hadn't eaten anything since breakfast, but Jolene continued with her accusations, saying that Candy only visited their mama so she could ask her for money, and had probably even stolen from her. At that point, Candy decided she'd had enough. She kicked off her stilettos and pushed Jolene toward the casket. Jolene lost her balance and fell over a wicker basket of pink and white carnations on the floor. "You never loved Mama like I did, you Jezebel!" Jolene screeched. She jumped up and grabbed Candy's hair, trying to pull her down. Their lack of respect for their dead mother left me wondering if either daughter could have really loved her much. Randy, Jolene's ex-husband, broke up the fight and carried Jolene outside kicking and screaming. "I predict your funeral's gonna be next, Jolene!" Candy yelled, as she plopped down beside the casket and put her stilettos back on. Her black fishnet pantyhose had a hole the size of a softball in them, but she had somehow kept from ripping her skin-tight leather mini skirt. Her mama wouldn't have approved of her choice of attire for the funeral home, and that was another fact that Jolene had pointedly mentioned before Randy showed up. Other than the ripped pantyhose, Candy had some scratches on her face from Jolene's long, candy apple red fingernails, which was her signature color. Jolene had told me once that it was important for a woman to have a signature nail polish color and a signature cologne to express her unique personality. Jolene's cologne was Avon's Unforgettable, which was truly hard to forget; it always lingered in the room long after she was gone.

Jolene fared much worse from the fight than Candy, though, and she had a black eye when I saw her at the Seek & Find Market the next day. I had stopped in to buy a Mountain Dew, and Jolene was there to get a pack of Virginia Slims. I wanted to ask Jolene if she had taken one of her lucky crystals to the funeral home with her, but I didn't want to offend her. She was always nice to me, and had actually encouraged me to get out of Possum Valley and follow my dreams. "You're so smart, Kathy," she would say. "Find a way out of here for all of us that can't." She even gave Rita and me Christmas gifts every year. Mama had started opening them for us though, after Jolene had given us sexy lingerie one year; I had just turned twelve, and Rita was eleven. I received a black teddy with matching undies, and Rita got a pink transparent gown with fur trim. They didn't have tags on them and looked gently used. Mama screamed and told us to go wash our hands after we had pulled them out of the boxes and held them up in disbelief. Jolene frequented flea markets and yard sales all over East Tennessee, so we assumed she had picked them up for us during one of her shopping sprees. "Her intentions might have been good," Mama told us, "but you don't buy lingerie for girls your age. And you never buy *used* lingerie, period." Mama said it as if she needed to make sure Rita and I knew that used panties were not OK, *ever*. We were young, but some things you're probably just born knowing. We couldn't help loving Jolene, though. She was a good person, and we knew she didn't mean any harm. Mama said Jolene had gone a little crazy since she and her husband Randy had split up. I'm pretty sure she was always a little crazy. You don't start giving preteens lingerie just because you get divorced. She did seem happier when she was still with Randy. He was a nice guy, and Jolene probably should have held onto him, but Mama said women like Jolene were never satisfied. Mama was right that Jolene wasn't satisfied; I felt it was my duty to make it out of Possum Valley for myself, for her, and for all the other women like her.

Chapter 2

MAY 1982

"Failure is not an option."
–Gene Kranz, Flight Director, NASA

The sun shone through my bedroom window as I opened my eyes and swatted at the fly on my arm. Flies. They were ubiquitous on our farm. Mama hung yellow sticky strips from the ceiling all over the trailer, like party streamers at a high school dance. Despite Mama's efforts, the cows in the field, along with the fragments of animal carrion laying around, made it impossible to control all the flies. I often woke to them crawling on me, and it usually put me in a foul mood. But not today. Nothing could spoil this day. Today was my eighteenth birthday, and I was giddy with excitement. I had a checklist to complete, and the first item on it was to write my ad for *New York Magazine*'s "Strictly Personals." I had long awaited the moment that I was officially old enough to take out a personal ad. From this day forward, my life was my own, and I was going to make it good. I grabbed my *How to Marry a Rich Man* binder and turned to a blank page in the back. The binder was fat with information, plans, and ideas that I had been compiling for years; now it was time to start implementing my life's work. "Just a small-town girl, living in a lonely world," (Journey was one of my favorite bands, so I hoped my dream guy would appreciate my clever song reference) "looking for a city boy to take me anywhere," I carefully penned. I reasoned that guys liked girls who were a little needy and dependent on them to enhance their lives, while still being witty and interesting. I thought this truth transcended socioeconomics. My simple ad should work perfectly. I had studied other ads in the magazine, and I wanted mine to be different from the usual trite, and probably half-fabricated, "Tall, beautiful blonde with a sexy French accent seeking good-looking smart guy with a great sense of humor." Of course, I *was* blonde, and everyone told me how pretty I was all the time, but I had to set myself apart from the others to attract the kind of guy I was seeking.

I had asked Mama and Daddy for a short black dress with shoulder pads that I saw in the JC Penney catalog for my birthday. The dress was sooo sophisticated, and would be perfect with black lace tights for my first date with my wealthy dream guy. When Daddy finished cutting up the two cows he was slaughtering, we were going to have cake and ice cream and I would get to open my gifts. Mama made my favorite Mississippi Mud cake, and she had bought some rocky road ice cream to go with it. One could never get too much chocolate and marshmallow, I thought. Mama knew how much I loved chocolate. She was trying to make this birthday special for me, even though we didn't have enough money to have a proper party, with guests, or go out to a nice restaurant and celebrate. I was never the girl who had the pony or clown for her birthday. Daddy always told us if we wanted entertainment, we could go out and chase the chickens around the coop. One could never tell if Daddy was serious or not, which Mama said was part of his charm. Prince Charming Daddy was not, but as long as I got my new dress, I didn't care. Someday (hopefully soon) I would have a whole closet full of dresses from Macy's and Nordstrom and other places that I'd only heard about. *Today Is the beginning of something big*, I thought, and I was dripping with enthusiasm. When Daddy finally finished gathering up the scraps from the cow he had been carving into select cuts on the kitchen table, I scrubbed it down and we started setting the table for dinner. One of my jobs (along with the Manure Monday festivities) was to clear off the kitchen table when Daddy finished carving up an animal carcass. Yes, Daddy cut and sliced raw meat on our kitchen table. As a result, our table had a permanent greasy film on it that couldn't be removed with the toughest of grease cutters. Believe me, I had tried. Cleaning off a table with blood, gristle, and fat scraps was enough to turn some people against meat, but Daddy would disown us just for having the thought. Daddy liked to call what he did sculpting, because he believed his butchering was a work of art. Daddy's warped sense of humor and twisted way of thinking made life interesting, and he was one of those people you couldn't dislike, as much as I wanted to sometimes. Most people didn't want the "bonus parts" from the slaughter, as Daddy called them: the feet, ears, and tongue. He saved those "delicacies" for the four of us. Daddy said cow tongues tasted like roast beef, and with a little imagination and some salt, he was right. Our house might have been peppered with flies and permeated with a pungent odor, but we never wanted for food.

I set the bowl of mashed potatoes on the table. We were having my favorite meal, roast beef (*actual* roast beef, not tongue), mashed potatoes, fresh peas, and corn on the cob. Mama was a good cook, and could work wonders with just about any cut of meat. She believed that food could solve any problem and cure any ailment we might have. Any time Rita and I were sad, angry, or sick, Mama offered to make us a hot dog. Daddy made up his own sausages and hot dogs, and they were the best around. I assumed that when I married into wealth I would be eating caviar, escargot, and other delicacies, but I hoped I wouldn't have to give up hot dogs entirely, because there was nothing like a good hot dog when I was feeling down. As many hot dogs as Rita and I ate, it was a good thing we worked on the farm, or we would have been as fat as the pigs out back. As we bowed our heads, Daddy prayed, "Lord, bless our beautiful daughter as she becomes an adult, and grant her the serenity to accept the things she can't change, the courage to change the things she can, and the wisdom to know the difference." I knew these words were not daddy's, but he meant them all the same. I had read this prayer before, and I hoped that I could change most everything about my life. Since it was my birthday, and I had been doing my Jane Fonda aerobic video every day that week, I allowed myself to have a second helping of mashed potatoes. Mama's mashed potatoes were perfect: a bit lumpy, with no shortage of butter. Mama cut the cake as I finished my last bite of potatoes and served us each a slice with a scoop of ice cream as they all sang happy birthday. We didn't have dessert often, so we tried to make it last a few days when we did. The cake was delicious, as always. Mama wasn't afraid to be liberal with butter and sugar, so most of her desserts were restaurant quality—or better.

Rita wanted me to open her gift first. She handed me a small package neatly wrapped in newspaper with a pink ribbon tied around it. I carefully untied the ribbon, so I could save it for my hair, and tore open the newspaper. It was a bottle of Vanderbilt perfume, the perfect gift. I had saved up money from selling tobacco that we had grown on the farm and bought a pair of Gloria Vanderbilt jeans about a year before, and now I had a bottle of her new signature fragrance. I couldn't wait to wear it with my little black dress.

But the dress wasn't meant to be.

As Daddy handed me a narrow, rectangular box covered in leftover Christmas wrapping paper that was red and white striped but could be construed as multi-purpose wrapping paper since there were no Santa Clauses or other Christmas images on it, my heart sank into my stomach. My eyes began to burn, but I was determined not to cry. I ripped off the paper and saw the picture of a rifle on the box. I couldn't believe my eyes. *Maybe it's just a rifle box, and my dress is stuffed in here to surprise me.* I slowly opened the box, afraid to look inside. When I got the nerve to peek inside, I was surprised, all right. *A rifle... They got me a rifle for my eighteenth birthday.*

"Kathy, you're an adult now," Daddy quickly interjected, "and this is a practical gift that will keep on giving." *Another gift that would keep on giving. Make it* stop *giving.* "I'll teach you to hunt, and you'll never want for food," he nervously continued, as he obviously noticed the disappointment on my face. I tried hard not to show my frustration, but a tear trickled down from one of the pools in my eyes that were prepared to flood my face at any moment. I didn't want to seem ungrateful, but I was. I really was. Unlike Daddy, I had no interest whatsoever in cleaning and dressing animals. Nor would I eat vermin, such as squirrels and possums, unless I was truly starving to death; even then, I wasn't sure I wouldn't choose starvation. I didn't want one of his "gifts that kept on giving." I just wanted a *dress*. That was the story of my pathetic life: I always seemed to get the exact opposite of what I wanted. I thanked Mama, Daddy, and Rita for the party without making eye contact, picked up my rifle and perfume, and walked to my room, warm tears streaming down my cheeks. It was going to be one of those cries where my nose got so stopped up that I couldn't breathe all night, and my eyes stayed red and swollen for hours. I turned on my radio to drown out my sobs and convulsive gasps, the tears soaking my pillow while I lay on my bed listening to "Wild Horses," by The Rolling Stones. "Faith has been broken, tears must be cried," I sang loudly with Mick Jagger. I'd always thought the song was dark and depressing, and it was perfect for my current mood. I'll admit I was being dramatic, but it *was* my eighteenth birthday; Daddy could have granted my one and only request.

Rita

When my nose was too stopped up to breathe through, I got up and grabbed some toilet paper from the bathroom to blow my nose and dry my tears. As I walked back to my room and flopped down on the bed, I started thinking about how I could earn the money to buy the black dress myself. As Mama always said, "Where there's a will, there's a way." Desire is a great motivator. Plus, I was an eternal optimist; I had to be, to survive in that environment. Each day that I remained wallowing in the Possum Valley mud with the pigs would only make it harder for me to pull myself up out of the mire, so I would find a way. "Life is what you make it," Rita often told me when I complained about the farm. She was just like Mama, with her perpetual proverbs.

Rita and I were as different as night and day. She was only one year and three days younger than I, but she loved farm life and actually wanted to have a chicken farm someday. I was certain she had inhaled too much manure over the years, because if anything could be worse than a pig farm, it was a chicken farm. We passed one every day on our way to school, and I could smell it long before I could see it. Maybe I was just accustomed to our stench more than the chicken farm aroma, like someone with body odor being unaware that he reeks because he's used to his own scent. But the intense ammonia from the chicken poop mixed with urine always made me regret whatever I had eaten for breakfast that morning. I couldn't understand why Rita didn't want more out of life. Even though Rita didn't consider herself pretty, she was. She and I looked similar with thin, medium frames, blonde hair, and blue eyes, but I liked to dress up and experiment with hair and makeup, while she was perfectly content in a t-shirt and jeans, her hair pulled back in a ponytail. In high school, Rita hung around the farm girls, while I was friends with the other cheerleaders. I was captain of the cheerleading squad all four years of high school and was voted

Miss Possum Valley High the last two years. Rita and I got along, though. We would lie awake at night and share our dreams about the future. She would talk about how she wanted to stay in Possum Valley and marry her boyfriend Clyde, and I shared my dream of fleeing the life I detested and never looking back. It's not that I didn't love my family, though. Mama and Daddy meant well, and Rita was a very loving and thoughtful sister. I just didn't think I belonged in my family. I felt like Mork, the alien from that TV show *Mork and Mindy*, who had been sent to earth from Ork to observe human behavior and had no clue how to assimilate. I was certain that a rich man was the answer to all my problems. I envisioned my knight in shining armor as a tall guy, a Richard Gere type, with dark hair and piercing eyes rescuing me from this alien planet I had somehow landed on.

"Kathy, can I come in?" Rita asked, as she quietly tapped on my bedroom door.

"Sure, Rita," I said, wiping my eyes again and trying to suck up all the mucus still clogging my air passages.

"I told Daddy you wouldn't want a rifle," she said, walking over to hug me. "You know he loves you though, Kathy." She wrapped her arms around me and let me cry on her shoulder.

"Yes, I know," I sobbed. "I can't stay angry with him, but I just wish he would try to understand me. He's trying to mold me into what he wants, instead of letting me be who I am."

Rita looked at me and smiled sympathetically. I knew she didn't really understand me either. She had told me in an argument once that I just needed to accept who I was, and stop trying so hard to be someone else.

"Well, I know you will find a way to achieve your dreams," she said, hugging me tightly. "You're a woman now. A smart and beautiful woman. You can do whatever you want."

"Thanks, Rita," I said, as Mama walked into the room.

Mama had just turned forty on January 19, and was still pretty. She had always been proud that she shared a birthday with Dolly Parton. She believed she and Dolly were kindred spirits because of their shared birthdays and because her middle name was Rebecca, just like Dolly's. Mama told Rita and me once that when she felt inferior or was afraid to do something, she would just think of Dolly and all her accomplishments. "What would Dolly do?" she asked herself. She said it always gave her the confidence she needed. Mama even looked a little like Dolly, with her petite figure, blonde hair, and big blue eyes. Daddy called her his Dolly sometimes, which always put a grin on her face, even though she would say, "Oh, hush, Larry. Flattery will get you nowhere." He told her all she needed was Dolly's big "udders." "You are 'udderly' ridiculous," Mama would tell him, laughing. Of course, only Daddy would refer to women's breasts as udders, but he had a one-track mind when it came to farm animals.

Mama tried to dress nicely for someone who lived on a farm with nowhere to go. She usually wore floral skirts and pretty blouses that she found at yard sales in Knoxville. She never bought new clothes for herself. She said it was because rich people in Knoxville just wore their clothes a time or two, and it was a shame to let them go to waste when they were still in perfect condition. But Rita and I knew she wore used clothes so she could buy something new for us occasionally. Mama was the kindest, most generous person I knew. She was a hard worker, too, which was one of the things Daddy loved about her. She tried hard to keep a clean house, amidst all the flies and raw meat. When she had free time, she loved to read magazines about Dolly and her career, and watch her favorite soap opera, *Another World*. I've often wondered if she would like to escape to another world, if she had the chance. Maybe she related to Jolene more than she was willing to admit. But I knew she loved Daddy and could never hurt him. When I got rich, I planned to buy her a big, beautiful house near Graceland.

"Kathy, someone is here to see you," Mama said in a sweet, hesitant voice.

Great. The last thing I wanted was to have company. I looked up to see Mike peering over Mama's shoulder, his guitar strap on his shoulder.

Chapter 3

Mike (again)

Happy, happy birthday baay-by," Mike handed me a bouquet of yellow roses and began strumming his guitar as he sang the tune that he knew I liked to hear Dolly Parton and Willie Nelson sing. I had told him once when we were riding our bicycles to Joe's Pharmacy in town that yellow was my favorite color, because it reminded me of sunshine. We couldn't have been more than twelve at the time, but he had never forgotten. Mike had always been the romantic type, which would have appealed to me on some wealthy guy in a Mercedes, but I found it loathsome on Mike.

Joe's Pharmacy was about two miles from where I lived near the high school. When we were younger, Mike and I used to ride our bikes to Joe's any time we got some money to buy a fountain soda or some candy. If we had a dollar or more, we would get a milkshake. Joe had the best chocolate milkshakes I had ever tried. He always gave me an extra cherry on top because he knew how much I loved them. We'd usually sit around and talk to Joe, if he wasn't busy, while we drank our sodas or shakes. Joe was probably in his forties, although I never gave it any thought. Anyone over twenty-five was old, and someone thirty might as well be seventy, as far as I was concerned. They were ancient either way. Joe had jet black hair, (looking back, it was probably dyed) and a warm, friendly smile. I used to think he liked us better than the other kids because he often gave us Tootsie Rolls or a piece of Juicy Fruit gum, but one day when we walked in, we saw him handing Ray Turner, a boy from school, a piece of Juicy

Fruit. I knew Ray didn't buy it, because Joe didn't sell individual pieces of gum. Joe had a table in the back that had a checkerboard painted on it and checkers in a drawer that pulled out from the table. Sometimes we would play a game or two of checkers (more if I hadn't won a game yet; I was very competitive). Other times, we would just sit and listen to the music coming from Joe's intercom system. We knew all the songs on his playlists. He must have liked Frank Sinatra and Elvis best, because we heard them nearly every time we came in.

Mike and I both loved music, so we enjoyed singing along when Joe didn't have customers. We knew the words to every song, and when a duet came on, like "I Got You, Babe," by Sonny and Cher, we sang the parts and danced around. The only time I didn't enjoy our sing-alongs was when Joe played Percy Sledge's "When a Man Loves a Woman." Mike declared it "our song" the first time we heard it. Every time it came on, he would pretend to serenade me, often dropping to his knees as he sung, "Baby, please don't treat me bad," as if he were begging me. I had informed him countless times that *we* didn't *have* a song, and I would rather kiss a frog in the mouth than to be his woman. Joe would just laugh. "You have to admit," he would tell me, "the boy can carry a tune."

One day, when I didn't have any money, Mike used his own money to buy me some Jolly Ranchers, my favorite candy. "These are fer Kathy," he told Joe as he laid them on the counter. Joe looked at me and smiled. "This may be true love, Kathy. He's spending his hard-earned money on you." I blushed as Mike held out the candy. "I'm still not going to let you beat me home," I said, as I grabbed the candy and headed for the door. We often raced home on our bikes, and even though I was pretty sure Mike could have beaten me every time, he usually let me win. "She's a feisty one, Mike, but don't give up, because I have a feelin' you're gonna win her heart one of these days," I heard Joe whisper on my way out. Men are not good at whispering. Their voices just get deeper and raspy, but still completely audible. "I'm gonna marry her when I grow up," I heard Mike reply. *Mike will need a lot more than Jolly Ranchers to win my heart*, I thought. I wanted to throw them at him when he walked outside, but the watermelon flavor was already calling my name.

I breathed in the scent of the roses as I took them from Mike. I loved roses. Mike knew that, of course. "Thanks, but you really shouldn't have gone to any trouble for my birthday," I said. Honestly, though, I was glad *someone* had gone to the trouble. My eighteenth birthday was supposed to be special, and so far, it had been anything but. "The purtiest eighteen-year-old in East Tennessee deserves some purty flowers," he replied.

I felt a little better as the aroma from the roses filled the air. I noticed how they brightened my drab bedroom as I placed them on my dresser. I decided I needed fresh flowers more often. My room was small, with one tiny window above my bed. Mama had made some yellow curtains for it when I was a little girl. They were a shade of dingy white now, and I had a faded pink, yellow, and blue quilt on my bed that my granny made when I was ten. Granny told me she made it for me so that I would always remember her. Obviously, I wouldn't have forgotten her, but the quilt was still special. The old dresser where the flowers sat was in the corner by my bed, and I had a small closet across from the bed. I was glad Mike had brought the flowers in a vase, because I didn't think we owned one. Nobody had ever given me flowers before. Mama and Daddy thought flowers were an unnecessary extravagance, and most people in Possum Valley would have probably agreed. Life was simple, and pleasure consisted of sitting on your front porch with some iced tea after working hard all day. *Someday, I will have fresh flowers in every room*, I thought, as I remembered my want ad.

"Have you been cryin', sunshine?" Mike asked, as he examined my face. His concern was genuine, but nonetheless irritating. "I'm just so happy that I'm finally an adult and have so much to be thankful for," I lied.

The last thing I wanted to do was to tell Mike about the rifle. He would agree with Daddy, as he always did; he probably would have offered to take me hunting to prove how "fun" it was. All guys in Possum Valley hunted and fished. It was like some sort of rite of passage at puberty. Boys were raised to know how to survive, and most of them had killed, dressed, and eaten just about every kind of animal in the region by the time they were thirteen, including squirrels, catfish, rabbits, deer, raccoons, groundhogs, and yes, our town's namesake, possums. *Ugh*. Besides, I knew how to shoot a rifle. Daddy had made sure that Rita and I could shoot when we were around ten years old. We hadn't been hunting with Daddy yet though, because Mama had forbidden it. Nancy, one of Mama's friends, lost her eleven-year-old daughter, Anna, in a hunting accident when she had gone raccoon hunting with her daddy and her nine-year-old brother. Anna's brother was trying to shoot a deer when he heard a sudden noise, turned quickly, and accidentally shot her. This tragedy didn't deter men from taking their sons hunting in Possum Valley, though. A man wasn't a man if he didn't know how to hunt and chew tobacco, so accidents and teeth stains were things you just had to try to prevent through careful training and good oral hygiene. The tragedy did, however, cause a lot of mothers to keep their daughters at home when their husbands went on a hunting trip. I didn't want to go hunting with Daddy, Mike, or anyone else. The only thing I was interested in hunting was a rich guy. When I got out of there and moved to a big city, I would have no need to hunt anything else.

"You are a lucky girl," Mike agreed. "Lots of girls would love to be as purty and smart as you. Why don't you let me take you to Kay's to get some ice cream?" Kay's was my favorite restaurant. It was known for its ice cream and banana splits, but I loved the burgers too. Mike knew I loved Kay's, just like he knew everything else about me.

"Oh, I'd love to, Mike," I lied again, "but you have done enough, and I am still full from the big birthday dinner we had." Mike was sweet, and just about every girl in Possum Valley would love for him to bring them flowers and take them out on their birthday. But Mike and I were just friends—and that's all we would ever be, as far as I was concerned. I was determined not to end up trapped in Possum Valley, collecting Elvis records and watching *Another World* while wishing I was *in* one.

"Whatcha gonna do, now that you're eighteen and out of school?" Mike asked.

"I desperately need a job, Mike," I said.

"I can prob'ly git ye on at the Seek an' Find Market, if you're interested," he said. "They're lookin' fer a new cashier." The Seek & Find Market was a new convenience store near the interstate, about four or five miles from our farm. Mike had gotten a job there as a grocery clerk when it had first opened.

"Oh, Mike, that would be great!" I said. I jumped off the bed and hugged him before I even realized what I was doing.

"Well, darlin', if I'da known I'd get a hug out of the deal, I woulda told ya as soon as I walked in the door," he joked.

"You're the best, Mike, really," I flashed him my sweetest smile. "Thanks for the song and the flowers. Mike, you could make it big in Nashville if you wanted." I meant it. He was good-looking and talented, which seemed to be the recipe for success in the music business.

"And give up all this?"

I hoped he was joking, but I wasn't going to argue with him since he was helping me get a job at Seek & Find. I needed a job to buy my black dress and anything else that would help me get out of there. With any luck, this would be the last birthday that I was stuck in this trailer, in this town, with this guy.

Chapter 4

MAY, 1982 AT THE WORLD'S FAIR

Jenny

I'm gonna stop and check the mail on our way out," I told Jenny as we climbed into my pickup truck to go to the World's Fair in Knoxville. Jenny Johnson had been my best friend since seventh grade, when she moved to Possum Valley from Boston. Her clothes and hair were much more stylish than everyone else's in the valley, and her speech was foreign to all of us. She may as well have been from China.

"I like yuh ha-uh," she told me when I introduced myself to her on her first day of school. She had to tell me she liked my hair three more times and actually touch my hair when she said the word *hair* before I understood her. Our teacher referred her to the speech therapist on staff at the school, so she could learn to speak so that we could understand her. She had trouble understanding us too, of course. Robert, who sat behind her in class, told her there was a "skeeter" on her arm one day, and I had to translate for her. "He means a *mosquito*," I explained. "He knows how to say it correctly; he's just being an idiot," I said, giving Robert a mean look. She smiled and thanked me as she flipped the mosquito off her arm. We were inseparable after that. Jenny and I naturally hit it off because I tried hard to minimize my Southern accent, since I didn't think it sounded sophisticated enough. (How could I possibly land a rich guy saying words like *skeeter* and *tater*?) She could understand me better than the others, and I wanted desperately to understand people from places like Boston and New York, where a lot of rich people lived. Her daddy was an engineer and had been offered a position at the nuclear lab in Oak Ridge. He and her mom wanted to live in the country for some reason, so they chose Possum Valley. They said they wanted to breathe fresh air, but with all the livestock around, the air was more ripe than fresh.

Jenny wasn't anything like the other girls in Possum Valley. I felt cool just hanging around her. She was pretty, with short, dark hair and pale skin peppered with freckles around her nose. Jenny's appearance wasn't important to her, but she had a sort of natural beauty that made fussing about her looks unnecessary. It wasn't the Southern way, though. The Southern idea of beautiful was big, blonde hair with lots of makeup, and everything overdone. Think Dolly Parton. Dolly was the prototype for us all. Because Jenny was ordinary by Southern standards, she wasn't the most popular girl in school. She definitely wasn't the cheerleader type, but she had plenty of class and had actually been places and seen things. I thought this more than made up for her simple appearance. She had been to Broadway musicals in New York City, to the Smithsonian in Washington, D.C., and she had even been to California once. I had never even flown on an airplane, or been out of the South. People in Possum Valley dreamed of going to a beach in Florida or South Carolina for vacation, but most of us only made it as far as Pigeon Forge or Gatlinburg because it was much closer and cheaper. "The pigs aren't gonna feed themselves," Daddy would always say when I mentioned a long trip. We could have easily gotten Mike or someone to feed the pigs for us, but the truth was that Daddy never saved up enough money for a real vacation. Jenny had already lived much of the life I had only dreamed about. Even though I was always a straight-A student, Jenny was much more knowledgeable. I had *read* about the Erie Canal, the Boston Harbor, and the Great Lakes, but she had *seen* them. She desperately wanted to leave Possum Valley too, but she was going to do it via college. Unlike most people in Possum Valley, Jenny's parents had some money; they were sending her to the University of California, Berkeley to study physics. She had been trying to get me to apply for scholarships so I could join her in California, but I told her I would make it out there *without* having to go to school for four more years. She thought my goal to marry a rich guy was crazy. "You need a career of your own," she would tell me. "Why do you want to be dependent on some *man*?"

she asked. Jenny was one of those women's lib types. And I agreed with her for the most part, but I didn't feel the need to push the issue too much. I mean, I liked having guys open doors for me, carry things for me, essentially treat me like a princess. Why would I want to give up all of that? No man was going to tell me what to do or treat me like a doormat, but if he wanted to get the car for me in the rain, or pay for dinner and a movie, I wasn't going to stand in his way. Jenny said I let guys treat me like I was weak and helpless, but I was getting them to *do* things for me that I didn't want to do. I called that being smart. I told her that she would end up marrying some rich Berkeley guy and becoming a lady of leisure just as I planned to do, I was just taking the "path of least resistance." I knew she would appreciate the physics reference. Maybe I wasn't as cool as she was, but sometimes I thought I might be a little smarter.

I had checked the mail every single day since sending my personal ad almost two months before. I knew the response would take a while, since the ad had to be published in the magazine and distributed to readers before anyone would get a chance to respond, but I was so excited that I started checking the mail the day after I sent it. My heart began to pound as I opened the mail box, as it did every day. I pulled out the mail and looked through it quickly. A phone bill, a letter for Mama from her friend Nancy, who moved to Nashville from Possum Valley a few months ago, and a sales catalog from JC Penney. Nothing for me yet. But that was OK. Do you ever have those feelings where you just *know* something good is going to happen soon? I had that feeling. It had started about a week before, when I was unloading manure. It was a nice, cool morning, and a well of hope seemed to spring up in my chest out of nowhere. The voice inside my head told me, as I shoveled the crap out of my truck, that I wasn't going to be doing that much longer. I had a good feeling, and it was as real as the flies swarming around me.

"Are you expecting something in the mail?" Jenny asked, as I climbed back into the truck. I hadn't told her about the personal ad. I know, I know; best friends are supposed to share everything. But she would try to talk me out of my plan. In fact, she would think it was completely absurd. But when I ended up dripping with diamonds on the arm of a fabulous guy driving a convertible Porsche, she would understand. It's not that I was really *that* materialistic. OK, maybe I was, but can you blame me? I would look really good in diamonds and a Porsche.

"Not really." I shrugged. Just thought I might have a late birthday card from an aunt or something," I lied.

"By the way, did you get that dress you wanted for your birthday?" Jenny asked.

"Uh, no. I didn't. Daddy decided I needed a rifle instead," I said.

"A *rifle?*" Jenny shook her head. "Are you kidding me? What are you supposed to do with that?"

"Well, Daddy says it's a gift that keeps on giving, and I will never want for food," I said.

"Wow. Your dad might be the weirdest man I know. Are you going to sell it and buy the dress? You could probably use the money to buy some nice shoes and a purse to go with it," she said, suddenly getting excited.

Jenny loved to go shopping. She would jump at any chance to go, even though we had to drive to Knoxville to the closest mall, and she said it wasn't nearly as nice as the ones in Boston.

"I can't sell the rifle," I said. "Daddy bought it for me, and his intentions were good."

"But it's a *rifle*," she said. "Are you ever going to use a rifle? Did he really even think about you and what you wanted for your birthday? Come on, Kathy. You asked for a *dress*."

Jenny always said exactly what she thought. That's another reason she wasn't very popular in high school. Southern girls were expected to sugarcoat everything they said. Most girls from the South talked about you like you were a worthless piece of trash behind your back and then treated you like their best friend when you were with them. "Bless your heart," they would say, but the kindest version of what they really meant was "You are an idiot." That's just the way it worked in the South. Girls here *never* said what they meant. It was an unwritten rule. But Jenny wasn't willing to play the game, and I appreciated that about her. In fact, I found it very refreshing. Before Jenny, I had no idea that there were people who just said what they really thought. It was bold. It was cool.

"You're right, Jenny," I said. "But Daddy would be crushed. And the truth is that I could never get rid of a gift he gave me. We have a strange relationship, for sure, and I know he wishes that I was a boy. But he works so hard, and he really did mean well. I could never disappoint him."

"It's your life," Jenny said. "It just seems like he doesn't mind disappointing you. And now you're stuck with a pickup truck and a rifle you don't want. Your next gift will probably be a gun rack for your truck." Couldn't she just say, "Bless your heart?" Just this once?

I decided not to tell her that I already had a gun rack. Daddy had given me his extra one. I hadn't put it up yet, thankfully.

I got off the interstate at the Kingston Pike exit and drove past the University of Tennessee campus. Knoxville was bustling with activity. I had never seen the city so busy with cars, people, and buses everywhere.

"Look at that guy!" Jenny pointed to a tall man with blonde hair in shorts and a tee shirt crossing the street in front of us who looked around twenty. "I wonder where he's from. Maybe he's British. I love the accent," she said, in her own version of a British accent. "Hope there are lots of gorgeous guys like him to choose from at this fair. We could sure use some interesting guys around here."

Regardless of his origin, I was glad the guy distracted Jenny from our conversation. I criticized Daddy all the time, but I didn't like it when other people did.

"Me too," I agreed. "Preferably wealthy ones." I knew deep down that if it weren't for Daddy, I wouldn't even be at the World's Fair. Season tickets cost $100, and the only way that I could afford to go was because Daddy let me keep some of the money from the tobacco we had grown on the farm and sold last year. It was a dirty, hot job that Jenny said I shouldn't do, but she didn't understand being poor. Money wasn't a big deal in her family, since her dad had a steady job as an engineer. For us, Daddy just got paid when people brought their livestock to slaughter, and when he sold a pig or tobacco from the farm. Just about everyone I knew grew tobacco, and because it was such a part of our lives, most people smoked or chewed it. Mama and Daddy both smoked two packs a day each. They said it was their way of supporting the industry. It didn't make sense to me, since buying cigarettes just exacerbated our poverty; but I knew a lot of poor people, and it seemed that the less they had, the more they smoked cigarettes and drank beer. I think they had just given up. Maybe they believed smoking and drinking helped them survive by numbing their senses to the world around them. It seemed to be how they coped. Not a way I wanted to live, though. And it was a cycle. Many kids in our town started smoking and drinking before high school because it was all they had ever known, but I hated cigarettes and beer. I hated the way they smelled, and I hated how people sat around all evening and drank and smoked and laughed with that raspy smoker's laugh that always led to a croupy cough that most everyone over the age of twenty-five in Possum Valley had. Jenny would never understand the life that I grew up in and how much I wanted out. That's why she couldn't understand the importance of my marrying someone wealthy. I didn't want to sit around a mobile home dulling my consciousness with cigarettes and beer for the rest of my life. No child dreamed of growing up and living that life, I was sure of it.

I readjusted my shirt as we walked toward the entrance gate. I had worn my favorite pale pink shirt with my Gloria Vanderbilt jeans. I wore the shirt out with a big, white belt around it that perfectly matched my white sandals. Jenny had on a bright yellow tank top tucked into tight Levi jeans. Everyone had big hair, and I was no exception. My big hair made me at least an inch taller, and it had so much hairspray that it felt like one of the scouring pads we used at home to scrub the pots and pans. I didn't have to worry about it moving in anything less than a tornado. Perfection.

It was crowded inside, so Jenny and I were glad we had chosen to buy season passes so we could come back as much as we wanted. Plus, we wanted to meet guys. Good looking guys. Guys who were not from the South. Guys who didn't drive pickup trucks and haul manure. *Rich* guys.

I wanted to go the French pavilion first because I was dying to meet someone from France. The French seemed very sophisticated, with their sexy language and their incredible style. I wore L'Oréal makeup because I wanted to be more like them. My goal was to one day be able to afford to wear Chanel makeup and cologne, because I didn't think it could get much classier than that. When we made it through the line at the pavilion, a tall woman with short, dark hair and a beautiful accent walked up to us. "Are you interested in knowing more about France?" she asked in perfect English.

"Yes," I said enthusiastically. She began telling me about the history of France, which wasn't any more interesting than it was when I learned about it in my world history class in high school. I wanted to hear about fashion and French men, not history. She must have noticed we were getting bored after a few minutes, because she stopped abruptly and asked us if we would like to learn any French words or phrases. I blurted out the first thing that came to my mind, "How do you say, 'I am rich' in French?" She looked at me strangely for a second, probably thinking about how weird Americans were, and said, "Of course. It is 'Je suis riche.'" I tried to repeat it, but obviously not to her satisfaction, because she laughed and repeated the phrase, asking me to try again. I carefully repeated what she said, trying to use her accent. She said that sounded better and that I should visit France sometime before she started to move on to the next visitor. As we were walking away, she said, "Puisses-tu etre riche! May you be rich!"

"One day I will." I laughed, but of course, I was quite serious.

I looked at Jenny as we walked out, and she rolled her eyes at me. "Really?" she said. "'I am rich?' Very sophisticated, Kathy. I can't take you anywhere." She flung her purse at me and hit me on the back. "Let's get in line to go up in the Sunsphere next," she said, as she looked at the directory we were handed when we walked through the gate. Jenny had visited much taller buildings than the Sunsphere, including the Empire State Building and the World Trade Center, but she knew this was a big deal for me, as a lifetime resident of Possum Valley. As we turned to head toward the Sunsphere, Jenny was still looking at her map when she collided with a tall, good-looking black guy.

"Where are you lovely ladies headed?" The guy beside him asked. He was an equally handsome white guy with short sandy blonde hair accentuating his chiseled facial features and blue eyes.

"We're on our way to the Sunsphere," Jenny replied with a big grin, showing her perfect teeth.

"What a coincidence," he said, looking straight at me with his pale blue, Paul Newman eyes. "So are we. I'm Kevin, and this is Chris. Mind if we escort you over there?"

"Sounds good to me," I said, trying to remain calm. "I'm Kathy, and this is Jenny."

Chapter 5

Kevin

On our way to the Sunsphere, Jenny announced she needed to make a rest-room stop. "I'll go with you," I said, just because I didn't want to be left out there with the two guys we'd just met.

"We'll be here," Chris said, with a grin.

"Oh my gosh," Jenny said, holding onto my shoulders and jumping up and down, "Chris is so gorgeous! I have to get him to ask me out."

"Yeah, Jenny, but would your parents be OK with your dating a black guy?" I asked quietly.

"Why wouldn't they?" she asked, moving toward a stall. "They aren't racist like everyone in Possum Valley."

"I'm not racist, Jenny," I said.

She turned and smiled, "I wasn't talking about you, Kathy. But most everyone else is."

I couldn't argue with that. The majority of people in Possum Valley weren't fond of strangers. Mama said a black family looked at the property where Ted and Sandy now live, but when some of the neighbors on the other side of the property saw them looking, they went over with rifles in tow and assured them they weren't welcome. I felt it was really fear of the unknown that made our neighbors behave that way. Most people in Possum Valley, including me, had never even met a black person. Possum Valley was comprised of all white people, and our idea of diversity was owning cows *and* pigs. Really diverse people had cows, pigs, and chickens, like us. I didn't understand why people thought skin color mattered. My skin got really dark in the summer from being out on the farm so much. People always complimented me on my good tan. I guess it was OK to be dark in our town, just not *too* dark.

Kevin and Chris were waiting on us when we returned from the restroom.

"So, where are guys from?" Jenny asked, as we continued walking toward the Sunsphere. Chris said, "I'm from Philadelphia, and Kevin is from San Francisco. We graduated from the Air Force Academy together."

OK. Uh, wow. Not only had I met a black person for the first time, but I had also met military guys for the first time ever. How cool was that? Maybe people in Possum Valley would accept Chris since he was in the Air Force. Most everyone in Possum Valley was patriotic. In fact, many carried around a big American flag in the backs of their pickup trucks. How could they not like Chris, since he was obviously patriotic? *Perhaps because many carried around even bigger Civil War Battle flags in the backs of their pickups*, I remembered. Still, if they met Chris, I just knew they would like him.

"Where are you and Kathy from?" Kevin asked.

"Well, Kathy is from around here, and I'm originally from Boston, but my parents moved near here a few years ago," Jenny said, skillfully avoiding the name of our town. Possum Valley even got made fun of by people in neighboring towns with similar names, like Groundhog Ridge and Beaver Brook. It was easier just to avoid it. "How long are you here?" she asked.

"We both just finished training and have a few weeks before we report to our duty stations, so we're planning to hang out for a while with my aunt and uncle," Kevin looked at me and smiled. "My uncle is a biology professor at the University of Tennessee."

We rode the elevator to the observation deck of the Sunsphere. It was a clear day, so we were able to get a nice view of the city. Knoxville was exploding with color, from the dogwood trees with their clusters of pink and white blossoms to the vividly purplish redbud trees that lined the streets and punctuated the lush green parks. On the south side, we could see the Tennessee River as it snaked through town with the Smoky Mountains in the backdrop. Of course Neyland Stadium, one of the largest college football stadiums in the U.S., was visible from the Sunsphere as well. Nearly everyone in the state was a Tennessee

Volunteers fan, so the stadium was one of the most beloved landmarks in town. During football season, most of Knoxville was either at the game, watching it on television, or listening to it on the radio as it was broadcast by the one and only John Ward. I loved Knoxville, and I felt a surge of pride as I looked out the windows of the Sunsphere. Possum Valley was an hour away, so getting to visit Knoxville had always been a treat. There were two shopping malls in the city, one on the east side of town and one on the west side. They were both beautiful and full of stores with all the things I wanted but couldn't afford—yet. Kevin was definitely good-looking and in amazing shape, but military guys weren't rich, were they? It was now my life's mission to find out.

"Air Force, huh?" I smiled at Kevin. "Sounds exciting."

"Yes, well, it's a living, I guess," Kevin shrugged modestly. "I'm off to see the world. First stop, my home state of California," he laughed.

"That's cool! We'll be neighbors," Jenny said. "I'll be at Cal Berkeley this fall."

"We really will be neighbors," Kevin said. "I'll be stationed at Travis Air Force Base, which is just about an hour from there."

"Small world," Jenny said, smiling. "What about you, Chris?"

"I'll be out in California with all those nuts and fruits, too." Chris said with a sly grin. "I'll be in Southern California, though."

"Hey, west coast, best coast, dude. You're just jealous." Kevin laughed.

I loved the way Kevin talked. No one around here said "dude," and even if they did, it wouldn't sound half as cool as when Kevin said it.

I tried to hide my enthusiasm as Kevin maneuvered himself beside me as we walked toward the Japanese Pavilion. "What will you be doing this fall, Kathy?"

I was afraid he would ask the question, and I had no good answer. I couldn't tell him I'd be looking for a rich husband. It had never sounded stupid before, until I thought about saying it to Kevin. He was so perfect, and for the first time in my life, I felt like I had no ambition, even though I had been working hard for years to groom myself for marrying into money. Kevin and Chris were military officers, and Jenny was going off to college. What could I say that sounded half as impressive?

"I just got a job at Seek and Find, which is a convenience store around here, and I'm saving up money to go to college," I lied. I don't know why I lied. I just didn't want to sound like I had no plan and was just sitting around waiting for some *guy* to sweep me off my feet. The truth is I *wasn't* doing that. I was very aggressively seeking a husband, and I had the binder containing years' worth of information and the magazine ad to prove it. But it didn't seem right to say those things out loud to Kevin. I cared what he thought about me. There was a quality about him that seemed to expect excellence from himself and others, and I didn't want to disappoint him. Maybe it was his military training. My eighth-grade science teacher had been in the Marine Corps, and he was like that. He expected the best from his students, and even though science was my worst subject, I had the highest grade in the class that year simply because I didn't want to let him down.

I could feel Jenny's eyes on me. "Well, Kathy, you know you can get scholarships for college, as smart as you are. I will help you fill out the applications this weekend," she smirked.

I wanted to crawl into a hole. Jenny had been after me forever about college, and I was so certain that my plans made much more sense. Now, for the first time, I wasn't sure. I felt embarrassed that my only ambition was to marry for money. I had been in the top five of my class in high school, and I was successful at everything I had tried, so why did I suddenly feel like a loser?

"I know, I know. I'd love for you to help me with the applications, since you have some experience." My words surprised me. College had never been in my plans. No one in my family had been to college. What would I even do there?

A beautiful hand fan sprinkled with cherry blossoms caught my eye as soon as we walked into the Japanese pavilion. As I picked it up to examine it more closely, I could feel Kevin moving closer to me.

"Sakura," Kevin said, as he looked at the fan in my hand.

"What?" I looked up at him, startled.

"The Japanese word for cherry blossom," he smiled.

"I never knew that," I said, admiring the pink blooms. I have always loved cherry blossoms, though."

I thought about Heath and Henry's house beside us, with the three cherry blossom trees in the front yard. They were the first trees that bloomed each spring, and their soft pink blossoms looked out of place in front of that old, decrepit house. They had always given me hope though: hope that a beautiful life could emerge amidst the worst of circumstances.

He took the fan from my hand. "I'm not surprised," he smiled. "They are almost as delicate and beautiful as you." I had never been compared to a cherry blossom before, but I liked it. I liked it a lot.

"Smooth talker," I said, looking away as I felt my cheeks burning.

He walked toward the front carrying the fan. I just stood there in a daze, wondering what it was that made him so different from other guys I knew.

Jenny walked over wearing a blue silk kimono covered with white dragons. "What do you think?"

"You're not the geisha type," I laughed. "Way too insubordinate and opinionated."

She threw back her head and straightened her shoulders, her black hair falling perfectly in place. "Yeah, I'm more of the Emperor type, for sure," she declared, smiling.

We walked around for hours, looking in pavilions and observing new developing technology. We were shown new concepts that would allow customers to pay for fuel at the pump using their credit cards and make phone calls from their cars. Chris and Kevin were both fascinated by these possibilities, but there was no way these things would ever happen in our life time, I thought. Kevin and I rode the Ferris wheel together, which was supposed to be the biggest one in the world. I was terrified when we were on top, and grabbed Kevin's arm before I even thought about it.

"Are you OK?" he asked, putting his hand on top of mine.

"Oh, I'm fine," I said. And fine was not the word, as he held my hand in his.

We stopped and got Petros for dinner after we realized we hadn't eaten lunch. The time had flown, we were having so much fun. "Fritos topped with chili, cheese, and sour cream. Now *this* is my kind of meal," Kevin said, referring to the World's Fair debut of the concoction served up in a Fritos bag. "Anything in a Fritos bag has *got* to be good," Chris chimed in.

It was the kind of day that was surreal for me. My typical day was filled with feeding pigs, hauling manure, and cleaning freshly-cut animal flesh off my kitchen table. We stayed for the parade and the fireworks show. It was late, but I didn't want still didn't want the day to end. I wanted to be this girl, the one that experienced the world and its different cultures and ate Petros with Air Force officers. Everything was exciting and new and the opposite of my reality. For the first time in my life, I was confused about what I wanted. Did I want a rich guy, or just a better life? Or was a rich man necessary for a better life? My head was spinning from all the excitement.

* * *

"I think I'm in love!" Jenny fell back in the seat of my truck as we drove back to Possum Valley.

"With *whom?*" I asked, surprised. She hadn't mentioned a guy, and Jenny always tells me everything. She had never been interested in any of the guys in Possum Valley before, so this caught me completely off guard.

"With *Chris*, of course," she laughed.

"Are you joking? Chris is wonderful, just like Kevin, but you can't be serious."

"Why not, Kathy? He's gorgeous! I totally want to go out with him."

"That's impossible," I felt my heart pounding as I thought about how people in Possum Valley would react to her dating a black guy. "You know I always support everything you do, but there is no way you can live in Possum Valley and date a black guy."

"I'm going away to college in a few months, and he doesn't even live here, Kathy," she said. "I'm beginning to think it's you that has the problem with Chris."

My cheeks felt hot, as if she had just slapped me across the face. "I can't believe you said that. I don't have a problem with Chris. I just know people in Possum Valley. And your parents live here. It's a small town. People would find out, trust me."

"Let them! It's my life, and nobody is going to tell me how to live it."

Jenny had always been a free spirit. That was one of the things I admired about her most.

"I get that," I said in a soothing voice, trying to calm her down. "Just be careful. You know it took people forever to accept your family when you first moved to Possum Valley because you're considered Yankees around here."

When Jenny's family first arrived in Possum Valley, most people didn't like them simply because of their Boston accent. You would've thought they spoke a different language, and most people didn't even try to understand them.

"A Yankee dating a black guy isn't going to be well-received around here. I am just letting you know as a friend, Jenny."

"I know you mean well, but I think I can handle a bunch of ignorant hillbillies. Present company not included, of course," she smiled. "The people in Possum Valley did finally accept us after they got to know us, and they will accept Chris too. Don't be such a worry wart."

I was glad to see she wasn't angry with me, and I dropped the subject, but I knew that Jenny dating a black guy wasn't going to be as easy as she thought.

* * *

It was almost eight a.m. when I walked into the kitchen the next morning. I was still on cloud nine from yesterday, and I wondered if I had just dreamed the whole thing—until I saw my commemorative Coca-Cola cup that Kevin had bought me after I had mentioned I wanted to try the Coke with extra vanilla flavoring that Coca-Cola was testing for the first time.

"I thought you were going to sleep all day, Kathy," Daddy said, as he grabbed the keys to the tractor. "How was the World's Fair?" he asked, half interested. Daddy didn't get excited about much of anything that wasn't related to the farm in some way.

"It was really great, Daddy," I said enthusiastically. "You should go and take Mama."

"Eh," he sighed. "I don't have the time or money for fooling with that, honey. I'm glad you liked it, though. You young'uns need to enjoy yourselves some." Daddy really was one of the kindest people I knew. His heart was always in the right place. He just had trouble relating to anyone that didn't love pigs and farming like he did.

I was normally up by six a.m. on Saturdays, but I couldn't get to sleep the night before I was so excited. I had spent half the night thinking about Kevin and how perfect he was. Not only was he super cute, he was doing something with his life that was bigger than himself, something that meant more than just money. Maybe I needed to do something more meaningful with my life besides marrying a rich man. Or perhaps I could just date someone that was doing something meaningful. That should count.

Daddy cleared his throat. "I fed the pigs for you. We're gonna need some more feed, though. You can go to the Co-op and pick up some after you eat breakfast. Your mama left you some sausage and biscuits on the stove."

Pigs. Taking care of them had been my responsibility since I was nine years old, and it was one of the things that a rich man was supposed to rescue me from. I hated pigs. Hated everything about the mud-splattered, smelly animals with their lucid, pink skin exposed under their bristly hair. I wanted to put some clothes on them so they wouldn't look so sickly and naked. *Yorkshire pigs sounded way more sophisticated than they really were*, I thought. I only got attached to a pig once when I was about six or seven, before the pigs became my obligation. I named her Petunia after the Looney Tunes cartoon character. Petunia was a runt when she was born, and Daddy let me feed her with a bottle. She made cute little grunting noises when I fed her, and I felt a special bond with her. When she got older, she followed me around and ate out of my hand. Daddy didn't believe in lying to his children though, so he never tried to guard Rita and me from the truth. "There are no big lies or little lies," he would say. "They're all just lies." For as long as I could remember, he had told us that there was no Santa Claus, and that we might as well name the pigs Bacon, Ham, and Sausage, because that's what they would be when they got big enough. Some people might have thought he was a little harsh, but Daddy was just Daddy; at least we always knew we could trust him to tell us the truth. After Petunia's demise, I still ate pork, of course (bacon is delicious, hello!), but I never had another pet pig. I grabbed a sausage biscuit and sat down at the table. Yep. Delicious.

"Daddy, do you think people around here would be OK with Jenny dating a black guy?" I didn't want to tell him about Chris yet, but I needed an opinion from someone who I knew would tell it to me straight.

"What do you think, Jenny? I believe you know the answer to your own question." Daddy looked deep into my eyes the way he always did when he tried to get me to figure something out on my own.

"OK. I know, Daddy. But why?"

"Kathy, most people around here are good folks." Daddy put down the tractor keys. He was a busy man, but he always made time for Rita and me. "But they ain't been around black people. Most of them have never been out of the state of Tennessee, and they have trouble accepting anybody that ain't like them."

"What do you think, Daddy?" Daddy didn't go to church much, but I knew he loved people. He was the type that never knew a stranger and could talk to anybody. I couldn't imagine that he was racist, but I needed to be sure.

"I reckon God made us all, honey. We're no better than anybody else."

"Thanks, Daddy. I'll stop and pick up some feed for the pigs on my way to work later." I got up and grabbed the other sausage biscuit as I headed out the door. I got so annoyed with him sometimes, but right now, it felt pretty good to be his daughter.

* * *

I found a message from Mama that Jenny had called when I got back from Seek & Find Market that evening. I could tell Jenny was excited about something as soon as she answered my call. "Guess what?"

"What?" I plopped down on the bed and removed my shoes from my aching feet.

"Chris and Kevin want to take us to see *An Officer and a Gentleman* tomorrow!"

My first instinct was to tell Jenny that it wasn't a good idea; but after yesterday, I didn't want to risk upsetting her again. Besides, it had been a while since the incident with Ted and Sandy's property, so maybe more people felt like Daddy now. "Sounds great. You know I've been wanting to see that movie."

"We'll meet at six tomorrow at my house, OK?"

"See you then." I hung up the phone. I still couldn't help but wonder what Jenny's neighbors would do if they saw Chris and Kevin pick us up. *Oh, well; what's the worst that could happen? No one's going to shoot us. I hope.*

"Wanting to see what movie?" Rita was standing at my door when I turned around.

"Eavesdropping again, Rita?" I smiled.

She rolled her eyes. "What are you going to see?" She asked.

"If you must know, *An Officer and a Gentleman.*"

"Cool. Can I go? Clyde has to work tomorrow, so I have nothing going on."

Clyde worked at the Farmers' Co-op in our county and was hoping to someday become manager, so he put in as many hours as he could.

"Not this time, Rita. Jenny and I are going out with a couple of guys we met at the World's Fair yesterday," I said. I gathered some fresh underwear and headed for the shower, attempting to avoid more questions from Rita.

My attempt was futile. "So, you picked up some guys from the World's Fair? What do they look like?'

"Wouldn't you like to know?" I raised my eyebrows and smiled as I closed and locked the bathroom door.

I wasn't used to keeping secrets from Rita, and I would tell her later, but right now, I just had to focus on keeping Jenny out of trouble.

* * *

When I arrived at Jenny's house, Kevin and Chris pulled in right behind me in a big, white Cadillac. Jenny and her parents lived on ten acres in one of the biggest and nicest houses in Possum Valley. It had huge windows in the living room with stunning views of the Smoky Mountains, and the living room and kitchen alone were as big as our entire doublewide domain. Her bedroom was the coolest I had ever seen, with its own bathroom and a king-sized waterbed. Seeing her house again reminded me that my goal to marry into wealth was not a crazy, frivolous idea. It really did make perfect sense.

"Hi, Kathy." Kevin walked over to greet me as I opened my door. "Is this your truck?"

The evening air was very pleasant, but I still wondered if I had worn enough deodorant as I began to break out in a sweat. He must've thought I was such a redneck. I was hoping to get here long before they did, but Daddy needed me to move some manure from the barn over to the garden area for planting this coming week, which reminded me that my truck probably smelled like manure. I looked back at the bed and there were already flies swarming around it. Perfect. I definitely needed more deodorant.

"Yes," I said, as I tried to subtly move away from the truck and the flies. "Is this your Cadillac?" I attempted to draw attention away from my miserable pickup. My cheeks were burning as I looked at Kevin in his perfectly-fitting Levi's and baby blue Izod shirt that matched his gorgeous blue eyes. He was so good-looking. Lord, why did I have to have an old beat-up truck that attracted flies and smelled like a barnyard?

"No. The Caddy belongs to my aunt." Kevin smiled and gave me a wink. "Nothing's sexier than a beautiful girl in a pickup truck, by the way." After shoveling manure, I barely had time to shower and put on my floral sundress that I'd had my senior picture made in last year. I was having a good hair day, and I looked pretty good when I checked myself in the mirror, so I could buy the beautiful girl part, but no way the rust bucket I drove made me look sexy.

"Gee, thanks, but I think I would look a lot better in a Corvette, don't you?" My heart raced. I wanted to make sure he knew that I would drive something better, given the choice.

He walked up to the truck, his eyes still on me. "That's impossible."

"It is right now, but I will have enough money someday." I felt a twinge of defiance building up inside me. I didn't like anyone telling me that my dream was impossible. Not even him.

"Impossible that you could *look* any better," Kevin explained. "Not impossible that you could own a Corvette."

"OK, Prince Charming," Chris said, as he went to knock on Jenny's front door. "Enough sweet talking. We're going to be late for the movie."

I was grateful to Chris for rescuing me from myself. Kevin was just trying to be nice, and I got defensive because all I could think about was money, or the lack of it. *But poverty does that to you*, I thought.

As we slid into the car, I noticed Johnny Parson, Jenny's neighbor, standing in his yard staring at us. I suddenly wished we had planned to see the nine p.m. show, so it would have been dark when we left. Johnny had caused problems for Jenny's family ever since they moved in years ago. When Jenny and I were little girls, we used to play in the creek that ran between the two properties. One summer day when we were out wading in the creek, Johnny came running over and started yelling at us to get out of *his* creek. Jenny's parents insisted the creek was on their property and even had the survey from the deed to back it up, but he wouldn't listen to reason, and said he wasn't going to have any Yankees taking his land. Because the Johnsons didn't want to cause trouble, they conceded, and we weren't allowed to play in the creek anymore. I tried to tell myself that maybe Johnny was just curious as he stood there looking at us, but the churning in my stomach didn't subside until we arrived at the theater in Knoxville.

* * *

We sat near the back of the theater in the center of the row. I felt so cool seeing *An Officer and a Gentleman* with actual Air Force officers. Kevin said the officers in the movie were in the Navy, and were losers compared to the Air Force. I didn't know the difference, nor did I care. This date was like a dream. It *was* a dream. I had never imagined what a military officer might look like, but if I had, Kevin would've been it. He was tall and muscular and looked so perfectly clean-cut, with his short, blonde hair and preppy clothes. I wanted to know everything about him. What he thought, what he did, what he liked. But could he ever be interested in a country girl like me? The movie made me question this more and more, as the officer candidates were warned to avoid the local girls that were trying to escape their lives of factory work in a small town by marrying a "rich" officer. Did Kevin know that I wanted to escape my life? Was I like these girls that planned to use a man to get what they wanted? No, my situation was completely different. I was smart and pretty. Everybody knew that. I wasn't just some factory worker looking for a way out. OK, so I was a pig farmer looking for a way out. But these women wanted to marry a military pilot. I didn't care if my future husband was a pilot. In fact, he could be a dog food taster so long as he was rich...and used lots of mouthwash. Kevin reached over and took my hand. My palm was sweaty. Yes, sweaty like a pig. Daddy always said pigs didn't sweat, but the comparison seemed to fit.

The movie seemed to go on forever, as one officer candidate committed suicide after his girlfriend ditched him when she found out he had given up his opportunity to become a pilot to marry her, because she had pretended to be pregnant with his baby. I hated this movie and wanted it to end. Why did it have to portray women as evil gold diggers? I would never try to trap a man by pretending to be pregnant, and I didn't need any guy to come and *save* me like the other needy girl played by Debra Winger.

"What an awesome movie," Jenny said, as we finally walked out of the theater. "I bet you guys look even better than Richard Gere and David Keith in your uniforms."

"That we do," Chris said, smiling. "I think you and Kathy are after our sexy good looks instead of our money like the girls in the movie. We get that a lot, you know."

"Of course," Jenny elbowed me. "We don't care a thing about money, do we, Kathy?"

"Hey, my aunt says we have to try Krystal hamburgers while we're here." Kevin made a welcome change in the subject. "Is there one nearby?"

"Oh, yes," I said cheerfully. "I love Krystal. Turn left at the second traffic light."

Chapter 6

I was up and out early the next morning feeding the pigs. Since I had graduated high school, we mostly used feed for the pigs since I wasn't at school to bring home slop buckets in my truck on Fridays any more. Yes, slop buckets. I was sure that Daddy sat around at night thinking of ways to embarrass me sometimes, and his agreement with Possum Valley High School for me to bring home the lunch leftovers in buckets that Mike helped me seal with lids and load in the back of my truck every Friday was one of the more humiliating tasks Daddy had created for me. The buckets sat in the cafeteria on either side of the window where we returned our lunch trays for students to deposit uneaten food. Since school lunches were not well-loved by most of my peers, there was no shortage of fodder for our pigs. I wasn't alone, though. After word got out (and it did rather swiftly) about daddy's ingenious plan for me to start a slop shuttle, other pig farmers had their truck-driving teens get in on the action. I was the only girl "lucky" enough to do it, but at least Daddy had asked Mike to help me. Mike got on my nerves some, but I wasn't sure I would have survived high school without him. The other girls actually envied me because he spent so much time with me. They would come watch as he loaded my truck with the heavy five-gallon buckets that made his tan biceps bulge underneath his t-shirt. They pretended to be there to talk to me, but I knew better.

The air was hot and humid, a clear sign that summer was on its way. Summers on the farm seemed to last forever. The days were so hot sweat dripped off your eyelids and made your hair damp and sticky against your face. It seemed like things were always sticking to me on the farm. Beggar's lice, cockle burrs, snails, ticks... My bath water always had a variety of things floating around in it when I came in at the end of the day. One way or another, this had to be my last summer on the farm. But right then, I didn't feel very optimistic. I had no prospects for any kind of a future. Everyone seemed to have a plan except me. Jenny was going away to school in the fall. Rita had a husband lined up, as pathetic as he was. Kevin and Chris had their lives completely mapped out. And then there was me. I'd thought I had it all figured out, but that darn movie made me feel like a complete gold-digging loser. A rich husband was supposed to come and sweep me off my feet. But let's face it, rich guys weren't knocking down doors for a pig farming, part-time convenience store worker, no matter how clever and pretty she was. How could I not have seen it before? I didn't have much to offer. There were lots of pretty girls out there. I was just one in a crowd.

Just then, I realized that I was throwing all the pig feed in one spot. Pigs had surrounded me, greedily snorting up the food and fighting each other for every morsel on the ground. (There's a reason the simile "eats like a pig" is used so often). As I tried to maneuver my way through the chaos, one of the big sows bullied her way through and pushed me against the pigs on my right side. I lost my balance and fell on top of a small pig, causing him to squeal and take off running. My shoulder hit the ground as my long hair swept through the mud. I pushed myself up quickly to avoid getting trampled by a herd of muddy pigs (not how I want my obituary to read) and tried to push my muddy hair out of my face. It was then that I realized that the mud in my hair was mixed with pig manure. *I love my life. I love my life. I love my life.* I didn't think I could say it enough to make myself believe it at that moment.

As I started to walk toward the house to wash off the mud/manure mixture and change into some clean clothes, I saw George, the mailman. George had been our mail carrier since I could remember. He drove a brown 1974 Pinto, and he had walked with a limp after he was attacked by Killer, Heath and Henry's German Shepherd, a couple of years ago. Killer tore several ligaments in George's leg; he was on crutches for a while after the attack, but George never missed a day delivering the mail. Everyone liked him. Well, everyone except Heath and Henry. Some people say they commanded their dog to attack him because he delivered bills to their house. Henry and Heath were definitely the type to shoot the messenger, so I didn't doubt the rumor.

"What happened to you, honey?" George asked, as he handed me our mail.

"Oh, I've been rolling around with the pigs, George," I laughed. "Better to laugh than cry, Mama always said."

"You're too pretty to be hanging around with pigs, Kathy," George said with a smile.

"Thanks," I replied, and he drove on to the next stop. I shuffled through the mail as I walked back up the driveway. Same old stuff: a bank statement for Mama and Daddy, a mortgage statement, and...a letter. A letter for me! There was no return address, but the postmark said Jersey City, New Jersey. Someone had written me from *New Jersey*! I was so excited I tore it open before I reached the house. But then I was afraid to look. There was no guarantee that it was a response to my personal ad. And did I still really *want* a response? Kevin was incredible, and I really loved spending time with him. But this was my dream. I had to follow it through. I slowly unfolded the white notebook paper.

The short letter was printed in blue ink, with several quotes I recognized instantly.

"Just a city boy, goin' off to see the world."

"Climb aboard. We'll search for tomorrow on every shore."

"Come sail away with me!"

He not *only* referenced the song I had used by Journey, he also referenced another favorite of mine by Styx. This was obviously manifest destiny.

Let's begin our adventure. Can I meet you in Knoxville next month? the short letter continued.

OK, he *must* be wealthy, right? I mean, he was obviously from New Jersey, and he wanted to come here to meet me. You couldn't just travel all the way from New Jersey to Tennessee to meet a girl if you didn't have money. This could be it. Come sail away. It might have sounded trite, but maybe my ship had finally come in!

"Why are you smilin' so big?" Rita's eyes followed me as I skipped into her bedroom, beaming, unable to hide my enthusiasm. "And why are you muddy?"

"Oh, who cares about a little mud?" I skipped in circles around her room making the trailer shake. "I just got an answer in the mail to my want ad. A guy from New Jersey wants to meet me!" I exclaimed.

"That's great, Kathy. Really great. You know I want the best for you, but aren't you afraid to meet this guy? You don't know anything about him."

"Look at this letter." I ignored her. "Aren't the song lyrics clever? He sounds perfect."

She took the letter and scanned it. "Clever, but still, you don't know what he's really like. You don't even know his name."

I snatched the letter back and sat down beside her on the bed. "Rita, I have a pickup truck with a gun rack hanging in the back window. Do you really think some guy from New Jersey is going to mess with me? In fact, I'll probably scare him away when I drive up."

Rita gently pushed the muddy hair out of my eyes in a motherly way. "I just want you to be safe."

I knew she was genuinely concerned; despite my enthusiasm about my knight in shining armor, she was making me feel a little uneasy. "OK, why don't you go with me to meet him? There's safety in numbers, right?"

"How about I go with you *and* bring Clyde?" she suggested. "We could make it a double date. And if this guy isn't willing to do that, you'll know he's probably up to no good."

My sister... Why did she have to be so practical and sensible all the time? I knew she was right, but I didn't want Clyde tagging along with us. Talk about cramping my style! I would have to look *really* good in my little black dress and high heels to avoid scaring this guy away.

"All right." I glared hard at her. "I'll think about it, but I'm not paying for you and Clyde." Meanwhile, I hoped I could come up with a better idea that didn't involve her tobacco-spitting, overall-wearing boyfriend.

"Now you're acting like the smart sister I know. Let me know when you plan to meet. And go take a shower. You smell horrible."

I rolled my eyes. "Yeah, whatever."

* * *

Rita hadn't given me the positive reaction to my good news that I wanted, so I decided to call Jenny. A friend was the one person you could count on for support when family gave you grief. My family meant well, but they thought everyone from outside the state of Tennessee was a child of Satan. I remembered my aunt and uncle from Nashville took a trip out to Las Vegas a couple of years ago, and my mom actually asked everyone at Wednesday night's prayer meeting to pray for her sister because she was in "sin city." I definitely didn't want her requesting prayer for me about meeting a guy from New Jersey. I could just hear her describing him as a Mafia member or a gambler.

"Did he send a photo?" As I'd hoped, Jenny was much more enthusiastic than Rita. One of the things I loved about Jenny was her sense of adventure. Most of the people in Possum Valley feared the unknown and had no desire to experience new things—or new people, for that matter. But Jenny was always eager to explore the unknown. She added so much to my uninteresting life, and she made me believe that anything was possible.

"No photo," I said, "but he sounds awesome, and he wants to come all the way here to meet me."

"What about Kevin, though?" she asked. "He's pretty darn gorgeous, you know."

"I know. I know. I go for years with no prospects, and now there are two. Just my luck."

Jenny laughed. "When it rains, it pours, and luckily for you, it's raining men!"

"Hallelujah!" I sang. Along with every other girl our age, we knew all the words to the new song by The Weather Girls. We sang, referenced, and quoted it often. I got the results I wanted from Jenny. I felt much better about meeting my personal column guy as I hung up the phone.

I had just put the phone down when it rang again. I got it on the first ring, assuming Jenny had forgotten to tell me something. "Hallelujah! It's raining men," I belted out into the phone.

"Kathy?"

It's not Jenny. Oh. No. It's not Jenny. Hang up. Hang up the phone.

"Uh, yes, this is she." I tried to recover by using good English and making sure I used the predicate nominative after the linking verb. It was a guy's voice, but maybe it was for Daddy. Men were always calling here asking him to slaughter animals. But the accent... It didn't sound like a Southern accent.

"Kathy, this is Kevin. How are you?"

He didn't mention the song. Maybe he didn't hear it. Maybe the reception was bad when I picked up. I had just hung up with Jenny, and sometimes the reception was bad when you'd just hung up the phone because the lines got crossed or something. I thought I'd heard of that happening. I really hoped that had happened.

"I'm well, Kevin. Thanks."

"Chris and I want to do some hiking in the Smoky Mountains while we're in Knoxville. Are you interested in joining us on Saturday? Kevin asked." "Chris has already spoken to Jenny, and she's in."

I didn't want to tell Kevin this, but I had never been hiking. Mama and Daddy just weren't the hiking type. They weren't the boating type either, even though there were lakes all around us. They were more the all-work-and-no-play type. It was rare that we ever even left Possum Valley. A few years ago, we went to Pigeon Forge for the weekend during the autumn season and stayed in a motel along the highway. I remember driving through Cades Cove and getting out to look at the barns and farmland there. The beautiful scenery was captivating, with the Smoky Mountains bursting with color against the bright blue sky. People with license plates from all over the country were stopping in their cars along the loop to take pictures of squirrels, deer, and other wildlife. They seemed to be more interested in the deer and squirrels than they were the mountains. I couldn't understand what the appeal was, since I saw plenty of wildlife just walking in the woods on our property, and Daddy had even brought deer home to dress for dinner sometimes. These people had probably never seen a deer up close; they probably hadn't seen an animal slaughtered, either. They weren't like us. Kevin and Chris weren't like us. To be honest, I didn't want to be like us, either.

"That sounds like fun."

"Great! How about I pick you up at your place around eight a.m., and we can meet Chris and Jenny at her house?"

My place?! I couldn't let him see where I lived just yet. I knew I would need to completely win a guy's heart before subjecting him to our doublewide resting on cinderblocks, Daddy's old junk scattered all over the place, and manure piled up a mile high. At a glance, we probably appeared to be the quintessential "trailer trash" that you heard people talk about. But I didn't believe we were trashy—not really. I'd often wondered if trashy people were aware they were trashy, though, because people with body odor didn't seem to be conscious of their problem. Perhaps when you're used to being around something, it becomes imperceptible to you, like the smell of raw meat. Jenny couldn't stand to visit me at home because the odor was so offensive to her, but I barely noticed it. Well, I might have been in denial about *being* trashy, but I knew without a doubt that our place *looked* the part. So, I did what any girl in my position would do. I lied.

"I was planning to spend the night with Jenny Friday night anyway, so you and Chris can just meet us at her place," I said. "That will be easier."

"Oh," he said. "Chris didn't mention you would already be at Jenny's house, but that sounds good. We'll pick you girls up on Saturday around eight."

Whew. That was close, but my reputation was still intact, thanks to my quick thinking.

"By the way, how's the weather there?"

"The weather? It's nice, I guess. Why?"

"Just wondering if it's still raining men."

Hmm. So much for my reputation. I attempted a feeble laugh. But the future was looking pretty bright as I hung up the phone, letter in hand.

Chapter 7

"Darkness cannot drive out darkness; only light can do that.
Hate cannot drive out hate; only love can do that."
–Martin Luther King, Jr.

Jenny and I woke up early Saturday morning to get ready for our hiking trip. Jenny had hiked a lot in New Hampshire and had all kinds of cool gear. She let me borrow her extra pair of hiking boots, and I had brought my jeans to keep the briars and bugs off my legs, a hot-pink shirt, and my black Members Only jacket in case I got cold. Jenny said I might ruin my jacket, but it was a chance I was willing to take; hiking or not, a girl's gotta look good.

Jenny's bedroom was upstairs, but I could still smell the aroma of bacon and apple-cinnamon pancakes wafting through the air. Breakfast smelled so much better at Jenny's house. I was sure it was because the other layers of odors that enveloped our trailer were absent in her big house. I hoped we had time for breakfast while I pulled my hair back into a ponytail with my hot-pink scrunchie. The doorbell rang just as we were putting on our boots, and Jenny's mom, Peggy, answered the door.

"I guess punctuality is something you're taught in the military," I heard her say as she invited them in.

Peggy was tall with short, dark hair. Unlike most mothers in Possum Valley, Peggy worked outside the home as a physical therapist, so she had this confidence about her that was foreign to me. She had an athletic build and was in good shape for her age. Jenny had told me she was a star basketball player in college. Peggy had perfect posture, so I always felt the need to push my shoulders back and stand up straight around her. I loved her poise. She let people know exactly what she thought without apology. Southern women were good at talking about you behind your back, but Peggy wasn't afraid to say it to your face; Jenny had obviously learned that from her mom.

"You could certainly learn a thing or two from them, Jenny." Peggy rolled her eyes and smiled at Jenny as we walked into the room.

"Oh, please, Mom! Don't pretend you're ever on time," Jenny laughed. Jenny and her mom had more of a friendship than a mother-daughter relationship. They laughed, talked, and did things together. It was yet another thing I envied about Jenny's life. I loved Mama, but she was always very serious, and *very* tired. Her life and Peggy's life were completely different, even though they lived in the same town.

Kevin and Chris were both dressed in t-shirts, jeans, and hiking boots. Kevin's blue t-shirt had the words *AIR FORCE* across the chest in white. He filled out the shirt nicely, his broad shoulders and muscular arms bulging with every movement. He was definitely eye candy.

Peggy insisted that we all have breakfast before we left, and it was wonderful. Kevin and Chris were perfect gentlemen, and the food was just as delicious as it smelled. One of Peggy's friends who lived on a farm in Vermont sent fresh maple syrup to her each spring, and it was the best syrup I had ever tasted. We always had the store brand imitation syrup when we had pancakes at home. I vowed to myself that one day I would have the real thing, just like Peggy.

* * *

The sky was clear, and I breathed in the fresh morning air deeply as we walked along the trail to Abrams Falls, a waterfall in the Smoky Mountains that had a long, deep pool at its base. The oak and maple trees blended in with the pines, providing a perfect backdrop for the colorful redwood and dogwood trees. The sight was so beautiful I couldn't believe I'd never hiked in the Smoky Mountains, since they were only an hour and a half away from me. The trail was rocky and sometimes slippery, and Kevin must have told us to watch our step ten times. When we reached Abrams Falls, we found a spot to rest and have lunch. Jenny and I had packed a picnic lunch for us the night before, and the guys carried it in their backpacks. It felt magical to suddenly reach a hidden waterfall after walking for miles through the scenic woods. The volume of water rushing forcefully over the falls was stunning. We stayed at the falls and ate our lunch, just enjoying our surroundings and the soothing sound of the water. Everyone seemed to be having a good time, but I was literally having the time of my life. I didn't get out of Possum Valley nearly enough, I was certain. The nearly three-mile trip back was not as fun as the trip there, though. I was looking at the landscape instead of the ground when I slipped and fell on a wet rock, landing hard on my right hand. The ragged edge had cut my hand open and sharp, tiny slivers of rocks were lodged inside the wound. It burned terribly, and I wanted to cry—not so much because of the pain, but because I had ripped my Members Only jacket. The fact that Jenny had cautioned me against wearing it only made it worse. But I did look great, at least until I fell. After that mishap, I was covered in dirt with a ripped jacket and a bleeding hand. Kevin knelt beside me and gently took my hand in his. *Dial soap*! I thought suddenly. I had been trying to figure out the fresh scent that I always smelled when Kevin was near me. I was certain it was Dial soap, and decided it smelled great on him.

"Oh, baby, you're bleeding a little. We need to get this cleaned up," he said. "Are you hurt anywhere else?" He called me *baby*, and I didn't hear anything else after that.

"Does it hurt anywhere else, Kathy?" Jenny bent down to look at me.

"No, guys," I said. "I'm fine." Kevin's concern for me was so endearing that I forgot all about my hand, as I looked into his attentive (and gorgeous) eyes. I started getting up to prove that I was OK, and Kevin helped me to my feet. The touch of his hands made my skin tingle. Growing up, Mama and Daddy were never the tender, gentle type. We were taught to be tough and just deal with little scrapes and bruises. All this attention was new, and rather nice.

"Take it easy, Kathy." Kevin put his arm around my waist. "Let's get you back so we can take care of this cut. I can carry you, if necessary. I've carried packs heavier than you on our marches."

"Now the secret's out. Kevin is actually Clark Kent, aka Superman," Chris laughed.

I was surprised at Kevin's gentleness, knowing he was an Air Force officer. He must have been capable of being very tough when duty called—and that was a definite turn-on—but this tender side of him was very sexy, too. He was like a knight in shining armor: capable of protecting his damsel in distress and saving the world, simultaneously. How could I not be impressed? I still felt a little like an idiot for falling, but it was almost worth it to have Kevin dote on me. Chris might have been joking, but Superman had nothing on Kevin, as far as I could tell.

"You're so sweet, Kevin, but It's just a little cut on my hand," I assured him.

"We passed a visitors center on our way here that isn't too far away. We'll stop there so you can wash your hand. Maybe they will have a first aid kit we can use," Kevin said, continuing to take charge of the situation.

Jenny and I went into the restroom when we arrived at the visitors center while Chris and Kevin checked about the first aid kit. "He is so into you, Kathy. You must see that," Jenny smiled. "And he is so good-looking."

I almost screamed out in agony when the water hit my open wound. "Oh! Gee, that hurts." I held out my hand and blew on it to try to stop the burning.

"What about Chris?" I tried to take my mind off the pain. "He seems pretty interested in you." I was still afraid of what might happen if people in Possum Valley knew she was dating a black guy, but I also knew Chris was great; people just needed to give him a chance.

"Oh, I'll be seeing more of Chris." She grinned. "He's perfect."

Kevin was waiting with antibiotic cream and bandages when we came out of the restroom. He pointed to a bench in front of the map display. "Sit here, and I'll bandage you up," he said. I jerked my hand away as he started to apply the ointment. "You can trust me, Kathy," he assured me. I held out my hand, believing I could.

The day was full of romance and adventure, and Jenny and Chris were obviously feeling it too. On the way home, I couldn't help but notice them sitting close and stealing an occasional kiss in the back seat. Kevin hadn't tried to kiss me yet, but every time he put his hand on the small of my back or touched my hand, my stomach turned flips. I wasn't sure if I was nauseated because of the curvy roads, or if I was falling for Kevin and a bundle of nerves. I just knew I wanted him to kiss me. A part of me wondered if he felt the same way, since Chris had already made a move on Jenny, but there was an electricity between us that was undeniable. I knew he felt it too.

* * *

By the time we got back to Knoxville, my hand was feeling much better. We stopped at the Western Sizzlin' Steak House for dinner, and that's when I first noticed the stares. Chris and Jenny were snuggling up to each other across from us in the booth, and people were giving them looks and whispering as they walked by our table. Maybe no one was staring at the World's Fair and on the hike because Jenny and Chris weren't sitting close to each other, so it wasn't as obvious that they were together as a couple. I didn't know if Chris and Jenny noticed it, but if so, they didn't seem to mind. It really bothered me though, and I couldn't be quiet.

"What are those people looking at?" I asked in a louder voice than normal.

"Don't worry about it, Jenny," Chris reached across the table and gently took my left hand, careful to take the one that wasn't injured. "I'm used to the stares. In case you haven't noticed, black people are in short supply around here. Plus, look at me. I'm so good-looking, I'd probably stare at me too, if I were them." Chris squeezed my hand and gave me a wink. "Besides," he smiled. "If they don't like my color, they'll have to take *that* up with my painter."

I loved how Chris seemed so cool about being in the minority everywhere he went in East Tennessee. I wondered how he really felt, though. I tried to imagine how it would feel to be the only representative of my race in a restaurant, or a church, or anywhere, for that matter. I thought Chris must have felt lonely. Even we, his friends, couldn't really understand how he felt, being stared at and treated differently because of his skin color. Chris was smart, funny, and polite. He was everything a girl could want in a guy—but around here, he was considered a threat because he didn't look like the rest of us.

Dusk had settled over the valley as we walked out to the car. We left the restaurant without incident, after Kevin had assured me that he and Chris would handle the situation if anyone tried to mess with us. I knew we were in capable hands, and I was on cloud nine when Kevin took my hand in his as we drove back to Jenny's house. Daddy had made sure I could drive a pick-up truck, shoot a 12-gauge shotgun, and sing all the words to Hank Williams, Jr.'s, "A Country Boy can Survive," but I still liked the idea of having a strong, confident man by my side. If only he were rich, I would cancel my date with the personal ad guy.

When we drove up to Jenny's house, Kevin came and opened the car door for me. I got out, and we walked to the front porch together, while Chris and Jenny stayed in the car. "I'm sorry you hurt your hand today, Jenny, but I hope you still had a good time." He pushed my hair away from my face and looked deep into my eyes until I felt like he could hear my heart pounding in my chest. I wanted to tell him that I had never had so much fun in my entire life unless I counted the other times I'd been with him, but I knew that sounded too pathetic.

"Today was wonderful." I smiled. "You and Chris are so much fun to be around."

"Chris is a good guy, but I was hoping just the two of us might go out next time."

"Sounds good." I couldn't breathe as he pulled me close to him and kissed me softly, then passionately as I gave in to him a little more. I was on fire inside when he pulled away, as Jenny's footsteps became audible on the porch steps.

"Better get goin' bro, before somebody comes out here and runs us off," Chris said.

* * *

Jenny and I stayed up half the night evaluating Kevin and Chris. Tall, check. Good-looking, check. Smart, check. Good kisser, check, check, check. We tried to think of flaws, but we were at a loss up to this point. I mentioned to Jenny that I still didn't know Kevin's financial status, which was still an important box for me to check, but Jenny just rolled her eyes at me.

"A military officer makes a very decent living," she hissed. "Who cares if he isn't rich? What would you do with all that money, anyway?" Did she want the short list or the long one? She knew how important money was to me, but I let it go for the time being, since Kevin truly *was* an excellent kisser, and that's worth something.

* * *

Jenny's mom was waiting for us when we came downstairs the next morning. "Jenny, we need to talk." Peggy was usually very calm and easy-going, but the look on her face made it obvious that something was wrong. I tried to think of what we might have done to upset her. We weren't out late last night, and even though we stayed up late talking, we were very quiet after she and Jenny's dad, Don, went to bed.

"Come sit down, and we'll discuss it over breakfast," Peggy said, as she placed a big platter on the table.

Peggy always made breakfast on the weekends. Back in Boston, she had worked full-time as a physical therapist, so she was used to being busy during the week. Since they had moved here, she only worked two days a week in Knoxville, but she still limited the big breakfasts to the weekends. Today was breakfast pizza with sausage, eggs, cheese, bell peppers, onions, and black olives. It smelled just as delicious as it sounded. Eating with the Johnsons was always a treat, because Jenny's mom made gourmet meals that were completely different from anything I had at home. The first time I told Peggy what a good cook she was, she was very gracious, saying that I was welcome to eat there any time, and mentioned how she wished she could make gravy and biscuits like my mom. Mama was known around Possum Valley for her biscuits and gravy. Daddy loved gravy on just about everything, so Mama always made it for breakfast—and we often had it for dinner, too. Daddy smothered his mashed potatoes, dinner rolls, and meat in gravy. Last time he went to visit Dr. Bailey, he told Daddy he needed to cut out the gravy due to his high cholesterol and blood pressure. "I might cut back," he told the doctor. "But mark my words, I ain't givin' up the gravy." Gravy and biscuits were staples in most Possum Valley homes, but personally, I didn't know why it was so appealing. It was grease, flour, and milk. I would rather have breakfast pizza and apple cinnamon pancakes any day.

Peggy began slicing the pizza as Jenny and I joined Don at the table. "Good morning, girls," Don said quietly. He didn't seem as upset as Peggy, but he wasn't his usual jovial self, either.

"Hey, Dad." Jenny poured herself some orange juice. "What's going on? You two are acting like someone died."

We passed around the pizza in silence, and I began to wonder if someone *had* died. I nervously cut my slice and took a bite. It was so delicious, I hoped I could at least finish it before we got the bad news. *What could we have done to make them act so strangely?* I wondered.

"Jenny, Kathy," Don began, "someone burned a cross in our yard last night. I've called the sheriff, and he should be here soon."

"*What*?!" Jenny threw down her fork. It bounced off the table and hit the floor. That really happens?"

"It did really happen, Jenny." Don picked up her fork and laid it on the table.

"Do you have any idea who did it, and why?" Jenny asked.

"We have no idea who would do such a thing, but we have a good idea of why," Peggy said.

"I hate these ignorant people! How could they be so cruel? They don't even know Chris! How can you hate someone you don't even know enough to do that?" Tears were streaming down Jenny's face.

I knew people in Possum Valley would have a hard time accepting Chris, but even I was shocked that someone would burn a cross in Don and Peggy's yard. "We saw some people staring at us last night at the Western Sizzlin' in Knoxville, but no one we knew," I said, trying to think of who it could be.

"I can't wait to get out of here," Jenny sobbed. "We should have known a place like Possum Valley, Tennessee would be the armpit of the universe, full of racist rednecks."

"Jenny, you're no better than the person who did this when you talk that way," Don said.

I had mixed feelings. I felt like I did when someone said something negative about Daddy or Rita. I might completely agree with them—and I might even say the same thing about them myself—but it was hard to hear someone else say it. I knew Jenny had a right to be angry, and I was angry too. I was ashamed to be identified with a group of people who were so narrow-minded and judgmental. But deep down, I knew that the people in Possum Valley weren't all bad. Most of them were very generous with what they had, and were always willing to help their neighbors whenever there was a need. Anytime Daddy's tractor broke down, our neighbors were there to help Daddy fix it. Daddy always said there was good and bad in everyone. The bad was definitely overshadowing the good that day, though.

"What are we supposed to do now?" Jenny was shaking. I had never seen her so upset.

"We'll wait on the sheriff and go from there," Don said calmly. "Don't worry;

everything is going to be fine." His eyes told a different story, though. I could tell he was concerned.

"We can't let them get to us," Jenny pushed away her plate. "They can't dictate who our friends are."

Peggy brought in the coffee pot from the kitchen. "We'll straighten all of this out, Jenny. Let's try to stay calm and enjoy our breakfast."

I had been looking forward to the breakfast pizza since the aroma had drifted into Jenny's room earlier that morning. Now, the thought of eating another bite made me feel nauseous. Before I met Chris, I had no idea how I felt about black people. I'd never given it much thought. Now, it was obvious to me that they were no different from us. Chris was right. God made him the color he was. We don't question Picasso or Van Gogh's color choices in their paintings. Why would we question God's creation?

Sheriff Turner arrived just as we were finishing cleaning up the dishes from the mostly uneaten breakfast.

Bobby Lee Turner had taken over for Sheriff Moore when he retired five years previously. Sheriff Turner was in his mid-thirties, and tall, dark, and handsome in a rugged law man way that was irresistible to the women in Possum Valley. He and his wife, Bella, had recently divorced, so he was probably the most eligible bachelor in town. Sheriff Turner had lived in Possum Valley all his life, so he knew most everyone, and most people liked him.

"Come in, Sheriff." Peggy led Sheriff Turner into the living room, and he sat down on the sofa.

"Thank you for coming out so quickly," Don said.

"I got a look at your back yard before I came in," Sheriff Turner said. "This is my first experience with a cross burning," he added. "They ain't common around here. O' course, we don't see many minorities around these parts. But you said there was a young black man named Chris with Jenny yesterday?"

"Yes," Don replied. "His name is Chris Cox. Jenny and Kathy left with him and a white boy named Kevin Murphy yesterday morning around nine a.m. and went to the Smoky Mountains. They got back around ten last night."

Sheriff Turner looked at Jenny and smiled, revealing the dimples in his perfectly-chiseled face. "Where did you meet this young man, Jenny?" He asked.

"At the World's Fair the other day," she replied. "He's a really nice guy. He's in the Air Force."

"I'm sure he's very nice." Sheriff Turner said. "The problem is most people around here will judge him long before they get to know him."

"That's what I hate about these people," Jenny said. They are so judgmental. What makes them think they're better than everyone else?"

"It's more complicated than that, Jenny," Sheriff Turner said. "People around here live in a tiny, little world of their own. It's easier for them to just exclude people that aren't like them than it is for them to get to know someone who is different. They're afraid of what they don't understand, so they cover up their fear by assuming the role of superiority."

In addition to being good-looking, I thought Sheriff Turner was smart, too. We were lucky to have a sheriff who knew racism was wrong, but could still get along with the people in Possum Valley because he was from here. He knew that they were acting out of fear more than hatred. I thought he tried hard to keep the peace and get along with everyone. He had always been very gracious to our family when the neighbors complained about Daddy's cow heads getting in the street. "Now, you know Larry can't do much about these stray dogs and wild animals dragging those heads around the neighborhood," he would explain. "Those animals can turn over the trash cans and find them." If the truth were to be told, it was usually Daddy's fault for not cleaning up when he was dead tired after a slaughter—but what they didn't know wouldn't hurt them, I guess.

The sheriff's questions were thorough, but we weren't much help since we didn't hear or see anyone on the property when the incident occurred. I told him about the stares from people at the restaurant, and we assured him we'd let him know if we remembered anything else.

"Daddy says racism is mostly fear of the unknown," I said.

"Your daddy's exactly right, Kathy," he replied. "The best thing we could do is have some minorities move into town, so people could get to know them. I'm hoping it will happen eventually. Meanwhile, I'm going to find who did this, and make sure people know this behavior will not be tolerated in Possum Valley."

Sheriff Turner got up to leave when I remembered Johnny Parson. "Wait!" I yelled a little louder than I intended, making Peggy jump a little. How could I have forgotten such an important detail? "I just remembered something. I saw the next-door neighbor, Johnny Parson, before Jenny and I went to the movies with

Kevin and Chris a few days ago. He was just standing there in his yard, staring at us. He didn't say a word, he just sort of...*glared* at us. I should've mentioned it before, but I had forgotten all about it until just now. It could've been him!"

"Oh, I wouldn't be surprised," Jenny chimed in. "That guy gives me the creeps! He's always staring at me when I'm outside. I've seen him pulling back his curtains and peeping out his window."

"Good job, Kathy," Sheriff Turner smiled, displaying those dimples again, and nodded in approval. "I am planning to question the neighbors, and this information may be helpful. But we need to get the facts straight before we lay the blame on anyone, of course."

* * *

News travels fast in Possum Valley. Bad news travels even faster. Everyone at the Seek & Find that evening was talking about the cross burning in the Johnsons' back yard. Most people hadn't heard about Chris before, but suddenly he was the talk of the town. The doorbell rang to let me know we had another customer. I looked up to see my neighbors, Ted and Sandy.

"Hey there, girl." Ted had always called Rita and me *girl*. We wondered if he knew our names.

"Hey, Ted. Hey, Sandy. What brings you in today?" I smiled.

"Just grabbin' some dinner." Sandy picked up a family-size bag of Doritos.

"What I'd like to know is what you're doing hangin' around with a black boy, Kathy?" Ted asked, as he grabbed eight corndogs and put them on the counter.

"Ted, it's not like *she's* the one dating him." Sandy tried to take up for me in her own unique way. "She can't help what her friends do."

"Truthfully, I don't have a problem with it, Sandy." Mama wouldn't have liked my being confrontational to my elders, but I decided to go with my heart instead of Mama on this one. "Chris is a great guy, and any girl would be lucky to date him."

"Well, you see the kind of trouble he's already caused, Kathy." Sandy didn't seem to be on my side anymore. "This isn't going to end well for anybody."

"*Chris* hasn't caused any trouble," I said, as I rang up their order.

"That Yankee girl has influenced you too much. I wonder what your daddy would think about all this." Ted grabbed his bag and turned to leave.

I wanted to yell after them and tell them that Daddy was a Christian and that meant he loved everybody, but I thought better of it when I saw my manager, Billy, walking in from the storage room. I was very angry, and I wanted to let them know they weren't acting like the Christians they professed to be—but I needed this job, if I ever wanted to get out of this town.

"Have a good evening, guys." I smiled when I said it. Mama said you always look and sound friendlier when you smile, and I needed all the help I could get at that moment.

"Ya handled that like a pro, Kathy." Mike suddenly appeared beside me. He had been quietly stocking shelves while I was talking with Ted and Sandy. I wondered how he felt about the whole thing, but I was afraid that even he wouldn't be on my side this time.

"I was ready to step in if I needed to," he said. And I knew he meant it.

Ted was right about one thing. Jenny *had* influenced me, and I was glad. What if Jenny had never moved to Possum Valley? Would I be racist too because of the pressure from people around me? I probably would've never met Chris and known what a great person he was. That was a scary thought! Jenny had educated me; maybe it was my job to educate others.

"Chris doesn't deserve all of this, Mike." I felt the tears burning my eyes. "He graduated from the Air Force Academy. Most people will never achieve in their whole lives what he has already. They're only seeing his color, not him. What difference does it make?"

"You're right, Kathy." Mike wiped a tear from my face. "You always have been smarter than most. Give 'em some time. They're just afraid of what they don't know. That's all."

It felt good to know Mike was on my side. As much as he drove me crazy sometimes, I still cared about what he thought. "Everybody keeps saying that. I'm tired of people being so ignorant around here," I said. "Doesn't it make you want to go somewhere that isn't racist like it is here, Mike?"

"If I thought there was someplace perfect, I might wanna move there. But I reckon I'll have to wait until I die and go to Heaven for that."

Mike was right. That's what I hated about him. He was always so right!

Chapter 8

Jenny wasn't herself for the next few days, and all she talked about was leaving town. I felt a little sad that she had such a bad taste in her mouth about Possum Valley, but I understood and agreed with her. I was more hopeful than ever that my personal ad would pay off, and I could leave soon too. I was even considering applying to colleges and getting out that way; I just had to see this personal ad through first. I had received a couple more responses, but none were prospects. One was a mechanic from Knoxville who was in his thirties. And the other was a guy from Cairo, Georgia (is that really a place?) who sent a picture. I am glad he did, because I was able to rule him out at a glance. Rich or not, I have my standards.

My Jersey boy had written again to arrange a place to meet. Our rendezvous was to be a week from Friday, at Regas in Knoxville. This time the letter was typed, which seemed a little less personal, but truthfully, his handwriting was pretty bad, so I couldn't blame him. He told me to pick the nicest restaurant in Knoxville (which was a good sign), and Regas was the place I had always heard about. Obviously, I had never been to a restaurant like that, with white tablecloths and valet parking, so I was both excited and a little nervous. I had saved up money from my first several weeks at Seek & Find and had already bought my black dress, along with coordinating shoes, necklace, earrings, and purse. I'd started my tanning bed visits at Foxy Fannie's three times a week, and I had an appointment to get highlights in my hair today. I had never gotten highlights before, but Fannie, who had always cut my hair, suggested subtle highlights to frame my tan face.

"You will look sun-kissed, like you just got back from the beach," she explained.

"Say no more, Fannie," I held up by hand for her to stop. "You sold me at sun-kissed." She always did have a way with words.

I had to look perfect. I told my mystery man in my last letter that everyone says I look like Vanna White from Wheel of Fortune, so I knew his expectations would be high, and I had to make sure he wasn't disappointed when he saw me. First impressions were obviously critical, so Fannie was the only person in town I trusted to help me look my best.

Fannie Simpson owned Foxy Fannie's Hair and Tanning Salon near the post office. Her shop had the only tanning bed in town, and she probably got half her income from it alone in the spring and summer. Appointments had to be made weeks in advance just to get in. Fannie was in her early thirties, and she bought all the hair magazines so she could keep up with the latest styles. Her hair always looked up-to-date, which I thought was important for a hair stylist. She had black hair and had recently cut it like Joan Jett's. Some of the older women in Possum Valley said she looked like a prostitute because she always wore stilettos and lots of makeup and jewelry, but they obviously didn't understand fashion and how to look good. Most of the older ladies either pulled their hair back in tight buns or went to Fannie for a weekly super stiff hairdo that was held in place all week by an entire can of Aqua Net Hairspray. We called them the blue-hair ladies, but not to their faces, of course.

It began storming as soon as I arrived at Fannie's. Her salon was in a trailer, but she had decorated the interior with stylish black leather, neon, and lots of mirrors, which she said was all the rage in Atlanta and other big cities. I lived in a trailer, so I was used to the amusement park ride you felt in a trailer during a storm. I wasn't used to all the mirrors on the walls, though. They rattled and shook alarmingly while the wind and rain hammered against the frail structure.

"I don't know what I was thinking, with all these mirrors in a trailer." Fannie lit a cigarette as she adjusted a mirror.

"Well, I like the mirrors, Fannie." Janet Wilkerson yelled from underneath the hair dryer. "They make it look so big in here." I thought it was funny how the ladies under hair dryers always yelled, like we couldn't hear them. They were the ones that couldn't hear, not us. Janet was in her late forties, and came to get her hair done every Thursday. She lived in a nice doublewide trailer nearby, so she was used to the turbulence too. Her husband, Andy, worked in the post office and used to deliver our mail before George took over. Their daughter, Misty, was one year older than me. We were on the cheerleading squad together in high school. She had recently married her high school sweetheart, Danny Grimes, who was a popular football player. Misty loved science and had wanted to be a nurse, but she fell in love with Danny during her junior year and put all her focus and energy on him instead of her grades. All the cheerleaders (except me) were jealous of Misty because she had one of the best-looking, most popular guys in school. Mike was voted "Best Looking" in our class, and Danny was voted "Most Athletic," which were the two biggest honors a guy could achieve in our school—but this and his football achievements were the highlights of his life, so far. Fannie told me he didn't seem to enjoy working much, and had already lost two jobs for simply not showing up. He and Misty were living with Janet and Andy until they could afford a place, which according to Fannie, could be a long while. Fannie heard all the juicy gossip at the salon. She shared it with me when I came in for my tanning sessions, which made my visits even more rewarding.

"How's Misty doing?" I asked Janet as Fannie lifted the dryer from her head and checked her curlers.

"Misty's expecting a baby." She smiled, but her eyes told a different story. "She's trying to find a part-time job so they can save up for a trailer to put beside us. You may have heard Danny is helping Mike's dad in the construction business now. I'm hoping it's a good fit for him, but they're going to need more income now that a baby's on the way," she said in a tired voice.

Janet didn't seem interested in talking about her first grandchild. Instead, she seemed more concerned about how Misty and Danny were going to move out of her trailer and support their child. Having kids without money to take care of them was a vicious cycle that entrapped women in Possum Valley. Misty was just the latest casualty. It was sad that such a popular high school couple was now fantasizing about having their own mobile home, so they could move out of her parents' trailer. I wondered if the girls from our cheerleading squad were still envious of Misty. Sadly, they probably were. Marrying a good-looking guy and having babies were the stuff dreams were made of among my cheerleading peers. They couldn't see beyond Possum Valley, so it became their destiny. This is exactly the sort of thing I intended to avoid. I was not going to allow myself to fall for some local boy whose only claim to fame was being a star high school athlete.

"I heard about the cross burning in the Johnsons' yard." Janet walked by me in her purple curlers and black cape, and plopped down in Fannie's chair to get her hair done. "Whatever possessed Jenny to get mixed up with a *colored* boy?" she whispered, using the word *colored* as if it was polite terminology.

I could only think about Janet's daughter and barely-employed son-in-law living with her as I watched Fannie comb out her hair. Chris was an Air Force Academy graduate with a bright future. Couldn't she see the irony there? Although I was certain that Janet and her family had not been involved with the cross-burning, they, like most everyone in town, didn't seem to have a problem with it. To Jenny, they were all evil racists. I agreed with her that they were racists, but many of them, like Janet, didn't mean to be evil. It was difficult for me because I had grown up with these people, and I couldn't hate them. They were neighbors, friends, and classmates. But Jenny was my best friend, and I really liked and admired Kevin and Chris. Jenny was unwilling to give the people in town a chance, though, and they were unwilling to give her and Chris a chance. I felt stuck in the middle somehow.

"His name is Chris." I smiled sweetly at Janet, trying to be as respectful as possible. Mama would've told me to keep my thoughts to myself and respect my elders, but I just wanted to help Janet understand what a great person Chris was. "He is going to begin flight training to be an Air Force pilot soon," I added. "Jenny and I both enjoy hanging out with Chris because he is a nice person who loves his country, just like you."

I was hoping to appeal to her patriotism. I felt I needed a different approach, since I had failed miserably with Ted and Sandy. Janet and Andy were probably the most patriotic people in town. Andy's dad fought in World War II, and they had an enormous American flag on a flag pole taller than their trailer in the front yard that people used for a landmark when giving directions to visitors from out of town. And Andy dressed up like Uncle Sam every year in a costume that Janet made for Possum Valley's Memorial Day and Fourth of July Parades. He walked around on stilts in front of the high school band, throwing peppermint candy to the kids lining Main Street.

"He sounds like a nice boy, Kathy, but there are plenty of nice *white* boys for you and Jenny to hang around," Janet said.

"Janet, I think it's nice that Kathy has friends of different races. We could all learn a thing or two from her and Jenny." Fannie said. She looked at me in the mirror and smiled as she sprayed Janet's hair with Aqua Net.

Janet took the hand mirror from Fannie and looked at the back of her hair. "Well, live and let live, I guess," she said. I wasn't exactly sure what she meant by that, but I decided to assume she meant well. "Anyway," she looked in the mirror again, gently patting her hair on each side. "I'm all prettied up and ready for the weekend." She smiled at me and got up to pay.

"Now I'm off to buy groceries for my crew. Misty's eating for two now, and Danny eats like a horse, so it's hard to keep food in the house."

I kept my mouth closed. Mama would've been proud.

* * *

On my way home from Fannie's, I stopped by Jenny's house to show her my new highlights. I had spent a week's wages from Seek & Find on my hair and tan, but it was money well spent. I felt like I should be turning letters in an evening gown on *Wheel of Fortune* or guest-starring in an episode of *Magnum P.I.*, riding around in his red Ferrari, my golden hair blowing in the wind.

"Look at you." Jenny opened the door and hugged me. "You are gorgeous. I hope this mystery magazine man is worthy of you."

"I have a good feeling about him, Jenny." I was intoxicated with excitement. "I already feel a connection, just through our letters. It's as if I already know him."

"Let's just hope he's nothing like the losers around here." Her countenance changed, and I could tell she was thinking about Chris. I felt bad about being so blissful when my best friend was clearly miserable, but the moment I had spent most of my life preparing for had almost arrived, and I couldn't let anything spoil this opportunity for me. I tried to hide some of my enthusiasm and empathize with her the best I could.

We walked into the living room and sat down on the large, sectional sofa. It was too big to fit into our trailer and had large, plush, tan and brown pillows that coordinated perfectly with the rest of the room. The entire house was stylish and contemporary, but in a comfortable, lived-in way. "Have you talked to Chris?" I asked.

"I called him last night." She pulled a pillow from the sofa onto her lap and hugged it close to her. "He says he feels bad about what happened and doesn't want to cause my family any more trouble. Can you believe that? I told him that none of this was his fault, but he still thinks he should stop coming over here."

"It probably isn't safe for him, or for you and your parents, Jenny. I'm sorry." And I really was.

"It's so ridiculous! I am going to meet him in Knoxville on Friday. Do you want to come along? I'm sure Kevin would love seeing you, too."

"Actually, Kevin and I are supposed to go out this weekend, but he wants it to be just the two of us."

"Ooh! Sounds interesting," she smiled and raised her eyebrows. "What are you guys going to do?"

"Wouldn't you like to know?" I laughed. "I could ride with you to Knoxville and meet Kevin there to save him a trip out here." It sounded like a nice gesture, but my real motive was to prevent Kevin from seeing my home on wheels and from meeting the parents.

"Sure thing, Kathy. I hate making that long trip by myself anyway," she smiled warmly.

* * *

I could hardly believe my eyes when Jenny and I pulled into Kevin's aunt and uncle's driveway Friday afternoon. They lived in a subdivision on one of the famous Dogwood Trails in Knoxville. The Dogwood Trails were on streets lined with nice houses featuring manicured lawns lavishly landscaped with dogwood trees, other trees, and a profusion of flowers along their routes. Each spring, the streets were marked with pink arrows directing visitors through the trails as residents showed off their blooming trees and flower gardens bursting with color from tulips, daffodils, and azaleas. His aunt's house was a huge two-story on a cul-de-sac, with a giant water fountain in the center of the front lawn surrounded by rows of red and yellow tulips. The house reminded me of a smaller version of Graceland, stately with big white columns in the front. Mama would love it. All I could think of was how perfect it would be for an outdoor wedding. I was glad Jenny had driven her Mazda RX-7, because my truck would have looked out of place in this driveway. I smoothed my dress as I got out of the car, worried it would be wrinkled after the hour-long drive. I had decided to wear the floral sundress I'd bought for senior pictures last year. I had a pretty good base tan after lying in Fannie's tanning bed three times a week for the past month, so I thought the sundress would be a good choice for showing off my tan. My hair still looked good from the highlights, so I was confident that Kevin's aunt and uncle would approve of me. Of course, the tan and highlights were meant for my Jersey boy—but I was proud of myself for being able to "kill two birds with one stone," using them to impress two guys.

"Jenny, this place is a mansion," I whispered as we approached the front door.

Jenny rang the doorbell. "Maybe Kevin's family will be rich enough to suit your taste after all." She rolled her eyes.

Kevin answered the door in his bare feet, wearing a pair of khaki pants and a pale blue Oxford cloth shirt. He must have just gotten out of the shower; his hair was still wet, and he smelled strongly of his signature Dial soap. He was getting tan too, after being out on the lake in his aunt and uncle's boat the other day. He had asked me to go, but I was scheduled to work. The combination of the blue shirt on his bronze skin, the wet hair, and the Dial soap was intoxicating; try as I might, I couldn't hide my approval when my eyes met his. I smiled with my whole face. That's how Daddy has always described my smile when I was excited about something. "Everything lights up on that pretty little face," he would say. I could feel it happening. The eyebrows raised slightly, the eyes twinkled, the cheeks lifted so high I had to squint, and the teeth glistened. I must've looked like a five-year-old on Christmas morning.

"Good evening, ladies." Kevin kept his gaze on me and my Howdy Doody smile as he invited us in. "Come meet my aunt and uncle." We followed Kevin across a shiny marble floor into a beautiful room with an enormous stone fireplace. The interior of the house was just as impressive as the exterior. There was a large painting over the sofa with a light above it, like in an art gallery. No,

I'd never been in an art gallery, but I had seen them on television. The room must have been decorated by a professional because everything was perfect. The draperies were made of the same fabric as the sofa had been upholstered with, and the paintings, wall hangings, and carpeting coordinated with them perfectly. I had never been in a house so beautiful. I hoped my mouth wasn't gaping open as I tried to take it all in.

"Aunt Sue, Uncle Bill, this is Kathy Fillmore and Jenny Johnson." Kevin was the perfect gentleman, and his aunt and uncle were just as kind. His aunt was around Mama's age and looked very fit, like she was a member of a health club. His uncle was also in good shape, trim in his khaki pants and polo shirt. *Probably a golfer*, I thought. I couldn't imagine Daddy playing golf. I rarely saw him when he wasn't wearing a blood-stained shirt and holding a butcher knife. He and Bill were from two different worlds, even though they only lived about sixty miles apart.

As Chris and Jenny got ready to leave, Kevin told me he had to grab something upstairs. He came back down with a gift-wrapped box. My face started feeling hot. Was it for me? Why would he have a gift for me? Not that I would complain, of course.

"We'll meet you back here at ten thirty, so these pretty ladies can get back home before midnight." Kevin slapped Chris on the back as he walked past him, with the box still in his hand.

* * *

I was shocked when we pulled into the parking lot at Regas. He had told me he wanted to take me to dinner when we planned to go out, but he never mentioned where. How ironic that I had never been to the nicest restaurant in Knoxville before, and now I would be going twice in one week. I felt like a movie star when the valet came and took the keys to park Sue's car. I wanted the night to slow down so I could savor every moment. My old truck and Possum Valley seemed so far away, and my dream seemed within grasp, palpable. I was finally beginning to live the life I wanted.

We walked into the restaurant, and I noticed as Kevin opened the door for me that he had the gift in his left hand. He had made reservations, so we were seated immediately in a cozy, mahogany red booth with a white tablecloth and real cloth napkins. Luckily, the table setting wasn't a challenge for me, since I had studied all about which fork to use for what and the functions of all the silverware years ago, dreaming of the day I would use this valuable knowledge. I quickly placed the napkin on my lap before I forgot. We never even had napkins at home. We just used our sleeves or paper towels, when we had them.

The restaurant was dimly-lit with flickering candles in votives centered on each table. The white ceiling was low, rustic wooden beams running across it that matched the wooden floor, giving it a warm, romantic feeling. Kevin glowed scrumptiously in the pale candlelight as it danced across his face. He ordered prime rib, and I got the petite filet. Chicken was never an option for me after I had seen Daddy wring their necks and pluck them so many times. I had some dirty jobs, but I was grateful to Daddy for not giving me that one, at least. Somehow watching a cow or pig die didn't have the same effect on me as seeing a chicken run for its life before getting its neck broken.

We talked about Kevin's job, mostly. He had two more weeks before he reported for duty. "I wasn't planning to stay here the whole time. I had planned to go visit my dad, up in New Jersey. I usually spend a few weeks up there with him every year. But I didn't want to leave you. You aren't like the other girls I know. Something about you is so innocent and feminine."

Of course, he hadn't seen me shoveling manure.

"I want to get to know you better. You are genuine and smart, and the way you talk... It drives me crazy."

"The way I talk?" Oh, no. Here it comes. I tried so hard not to have a redneck accent, and he obviously detected it.

"You sound so sweet, and perfectly Southern."

OK, I could accept that. I didn't want to tell him how hard I had worked to have good grammar and pronunciation. I did, however, want to tell him he was gorgeous and like no one I had ever met. But the waiter arrived with our food, which was a blessing because I would have probably sounded like a desperate farm girl. OK, I *was* a desperate farm girl, but I wanted him to think of me as the Southern belle that he'd just so eloquently described.

I said a quick prayer in my head before we started eating. *Thank you, God. I feel like I have died and gone to Heaven. Thank you. Thank you.* Even though I knew

Daddy's cuts of steak were a little better, the steak at Regas tasted superior, somehow. I decided atmosphere and present company were huge factors.

After we finished eating, Kevin ordered a slice of the signature red velvet cake with two forks and pulled out the gift-wrapped box with the beautiful pink ribbon that I had seen before we left.

"I hope you like it." He smiled as he handed me the box.

This night was getting better and better. I loved gifts (even though mine were usually a disappointment). "May I open it now?" I tried to appear calm, but my heart was about to leap out of my chest.

"Of course. It's just a little something, but I think it is perfect for you."

I carefully removed the ribbon (I would keep it forever) and unwrapped the box. Inside lay the Japanese fan with cherry blossoms painted on it that we'd seen at the World's Fair.

"I wanted you to have this as a reminder of the time we first met."

I pinched my leg under the table just to make sure I wasn't dreaming. *Is this guy for real?* I couldn't speak. I just stared at the fan. "Sakura, right?" I finally asked, voice shaky. My heart was palpitating. *Am I having a heart attack? Oh, gosh. I can't breathe.*

"Right." He smiled, as if he was surprised I remembered. "I bought it the day we met because cherry blossoms are delicate and beautiful, just like you. You are my Sakura."

Delicate. It was the first time anyone had described me that way. Again, he hadn't seen me shoveling manure or feeding pigs in mud up to my ankles; with any luck, he never would. He was so romantic and sexy. *Why can't Mike be like this?* Why was I comparing him to Mike? Why was I even thinking about that idiot on such a perfect night?

"Thank you. This is the best gift I've ever received." My voice was still shaky, and I was suddenly sweating. Had I worn deodorant? I couldn't remember for sure. It really was the best gift I had ever gotten, considering I got a rifle for my eighteenth birthday instead of the dress I'd asked for. We shared the cake, and I had to admit he was stealing my heart.

* * *

"This has been the best night of my life, Jenny." I had planned to stifle my enthusiasm in case her night had not gone so well, but as soon as we got in Jenny's car that night, my feelings just gushed out like pouring pig slop from a bucket. "We went to Regas, and there was valet parking, and I'm in love! We had steak, and he ordered red velvet cake, and..."

"Slow down and catch your breath, Kathy." Jenny reached over and grabbed my arm as she drove out of Sue and Bill's subdivision.

"Sorry, Jenny. I'm just so excited. How was your evening?" I tried to calm down and compose myself.

"Forget about me for now. Obviously, you're excited; but I don't want to miss any of the juicy details. Start over, speak slowly, and don't leave out anything!"

Jenny was a true friend, and I knew she really wanted to hear my story. "It was just perfect, Jenny. Kevin took me to Regas, and that was amazing enough. But then he told me he was going to stay here until he had to report for duty because he wanted to get to know me better. He said I was delicate and feminine, and that he loved the way I talk. And he gave me this fan. He said it reminded him of me." I carefully pulled the fan out of my handbag and opened it. "They're cherry blossoms." I held it up and turned on the light so she could see it better.

"He is really into you, Kathy! How did he know you like cherry blossoms?"

"That's the really cool part." I folded the fan and put it back in my bag. "We saw the fan in the Japanese pavilion at the World's Fair, and I told him I liked them then. He bought the fan that day without my knowing it."

"Wow! That is *soo* romantic." Jenny turned to me and smiled.

"I know. I can't believe he bought it after we had just met."

"He obviously has good taste in women, and knows what he wants when he sees it. And you seem pretty into him too," she added.

"Well, it's hard not to be. He's gorgeous, smart, cool, romantic... I could go on and on."

"I totally agree. He is the whole package."

"Now, how did it go with Chris?" I turned to her, ostensibly assuring her she had my full attention.

"We had a nice talk," she said quietly. "He's leaving on Monday, though. He doesn't seem to be upset about what happened, but he said he doesn't want to cause problems for anyone. I tried to tell him we didn't care about what a few ignorant people thought. But he said he had planned to visit his parents in Philadelphia before he starts his job anyway.

"Enough about that. Your life is much more interesting right now," she reached over and patted my leg. "What about your mysterious personal ad guy? Are you going to cancel your meeting with him, now that you're getting hot and heavy with Kevin?"

Wow. I hadn't thought about him since I saw Kevin this evening. Even Mike had popped into my head, but not this guy. Well, it probably wasn't unusual, because I really didn't know him at all. And Kevin was just so...perfect. "I guess I'll still meet him, since he's already made plans," I said hesitantly. "And I wouldn't say I'm 'hot and heavy' with Kevin just yet."

"You don't sound too convincing right now," Jenny laughed. "And you just said you were in love a few minutes ago."

"Well, Kevin *is* great, but this guy could be too." I wasn't sure if I was trying to convince Jenny or myself. "I have to at least give it a chance, or I think I would always wonder what I'd missed."

"That makes sense," Jenny agreed. "Just remember that even if he is rich, that doesn't mean he will be right for you."

"Now you sound like Rita!" I snapped.

"Just sayin'."

Chapter 9

The next morning, while I was out feeding the pigs, I heard Mama yelling that Kevin was on the phone for me. I had gotten a late start since I didn't get back from Knoxville until around 12:30 a.m., after picking up my truck at Jenny's house. It was probably just about 8:30 in the morning, so I wasn't expecting to hear from him so early. My dismal morning was suddenly looking a lot brighter.

"Sorry I'm calling so early, but Chris is leaving on Monday. I thought we should get together one more time before he goes," Kevin said after we exchanged hellos. "I wanted to catch you early before you made other plans." I didn't want to tell him that my only other plans would have involved watching *Hee Haw* on our one and only small television, and eating microwave popcorn with the family. *Hee Haw* was daddy's favorite show, and he watched it religiously every Saturday night. Buck Owens was his idol, and although he loved all the *Hee Haw* honeys, Misty was his favorite. Mama, Rita, and I would roll our eyes at each other while Daddy's eyes were glued to the TV when "Misty's Bedtime Stories" came on.

"I'm still free." I tried to sound casual, even though I wanted to kiss his feet for rescuing me from another night of Buck, Roy, and the whole *Hee Haw* gang. "What did you have in mind?"

* * *

Kevin and Chris picked us up that afternoon at Jenny's house, and we drove to Pigeon Forge. We rode bumper boats, played mini-golf, and then had dinner at Krystal. (Turns out Chris and Kevin were big fans of the miniature burgers). We were having so much fun, I didn't want it to end. After dinner, Kevin said he and Chris had a surprise for us. I couldn't imagine what else they could have planned since this was more excitement than I normally had in a year's time. I was truly surprised at the irony, though, when we arrived at one of the many country music variety shows in Pigeon Forge. I had never been to one, but I knew enough to know they were similar to *Hee Haw,* with the country music and the corny humor. Even though the musicians and entertainers weren't famous like many of the stars on *Hee Haw,* I enjoyed this show much more than watching TV with the family. Maybe it was because this show was live, but I decided it was mostly the company that made it better. I was sitting beside Kevin, and he was holding my sweaty hand; that somehow made the corny jokes funny and the country songs music to my ears.

The drive back to Jenny's house was quiet. Meeting Chris had been such an eye-opening experience for me. Skin color might vary, but I knew down deep in my soul that below the surface, we were all the same. We all wanted acceptance, to love and to be loved. I thought about Ted, Sandy, and Janet. In so many other ways, they were decent people. But how could they hate someone they didn't even know? Daddy was right. That wasn't hate; that was ignorance and fear. Maybe hatred came from those things, though. If it did, how could we fix it? People in Possum Valley just needed to get to *know* Chris. But how could they, if they wouldn't allow him near them? I felt tears surfacing. We were missing out on so much by not allowing people who were different into our little corner of the world. Why did we all need to be the same? What if we only ate the same foods or listened to the same music or read the same books? How boring! Our differences were what made us interesting.

"Kathy? Are you listening?" Jenny interrupted my thoughts.

"I'm sorry. What did you say? I must have been daydreaming."

"That's something you should know about her, Kevin. She's a dreamer." Jenny turned around and winked at me.

"Well, she would definitely fit in out in California, then." Kevin put his free hand on my leg.

"I'm going to be in Berkeley this fall, Kevin's base is only an hour away from me, and Chris will be in Southern California, so we're trying to plan a weekend trip to San Francisco," Jenny said. "Do you think you could come out in late October?"

"That's sounds great. I'd love to." And I would, with all my heart, I would. But I had never flown in an airplane before. And how was I going to get the money? I would have to try to work overtime at Seek & Find and save every dime I could. I hated always having to worry about money. It had been that way my whole life. Money determined every decision we made. Did we have enough money for a road trip? Could we afford to go out to eat? Would we have enough extra for ice cream at the grocery store? I hated always having to consider the cost of every single thing I did. *Someday things will be different*, I reminded myself.

"It's a date, then!" Jenny grabbed Chris and kissed him on the cheek as we pulled into her driveway. "We'll work out the details and make it happen." Her voice cracked, and her eyes were as big as saucers as she fought back tears.

"I must really like you guys, to be willing to fly by myself for the first time." I attempted to lighten the mood a little.

"We are truly honored." Chris came over and hugged me. "We'll be sure to make the journey worth it for you, gorgeous."

I held onto him tightly. "You are so awesome, Chris. Good luck with your training. I know you'll make us proud." I wanted to say so much more, but I couldn't risk crying in front of Jenny and making it worse for her.

"Make your feisty little Yankee friend behave herself." He pulled away and turned to Jenny, who had tears streaming down her face now.

I was happy when they quickly got into the car and left before things got really ugly for Jenny.

As we watched them drive away, Jenny sat down on the front porch steps and wept. "I only knew him a few weeks, but I really liked him," she sobbed.

I sat down beside her and put my arm around her. "We'll see him again soon," I reminded her.

"It isn't just that. He shouldn't have to leave like this, feeling like he isn't welcome here." Her sadness began to turn to anger. "I want to find out who's responsible for the cross burning. We can't let that go. I *won't* let it go."

Chapter 10

It was Sunday, and I loved Sundays because my only chore was feeding the pigs. Even though Daddy didn't attend church regularly, he always wanted Rita and me to go with Mama, so he didn't make us do any extra chores. This Sunday was especially nice because I didn't have to work at Seek & Find, either. Of course, I needed the money if I was going to go to California this fall. But I couldn't even allow myself to think of how I would save enough money to fly to San Francisco—or how I was logistically going to arrange for a big trip like that, since I had never been out of the South and had never gone farther than Knoxville by myself. *Right now, I have to concentrate on making it to Friday*, I thought, which was only six days away.

Mama, Rita, and I were the first ones out the doors after church. Daddy liked to have lunch right at noon, so Mama always tried to hurry home to get it ready after church on Sundays. She always had something in the oven, so it only took her a few minutes to get it on the table.

Preacher Brown was at the door to greet us as we were leaving. "How's the man hunt going, Kathy?" he asked with a sly grin.

"I can tell you've been praying, Preacher Brown," I said as we walked past him.

When we got home, I quickly made a sandwich from the roast beef Mama had in the oven. I shoved it in a plastic sandwich bag and kissed Mama on the cheek as she transferred green beans into a serving dish. "I'm headed to Fannie's to lie in the tanning bed," I said as I passed by Daddy, who was watching TV on the sofa while Mama and Rita were putting lunch on the table.

"I don't know why you're wasting your money on any tannin' bed when you can get all the tan you want right here, working outside." Daddy shook his head in obvious disapproval.

Mama came to my defense. "Larry, she doesn't want an uneven *farmer's* tan. She wants to look like she's been lyin' in the sun instead of workin' on the farm."

"A tan's a tan, the way I see it. How in the world's anybody gonna tell a difference?" he argued.

"Tan lines, Daddy," I began, but decided it was pointless. "I'll be back." I rushed out the door and closed it before Daddy could say anything else.

Fannie was on the phone when I got there, but she waved me through since I had an appointment. As much as I liked Fannie, I was happy she was on the phone, so I could just go straight back to the Sun Spot, which was Fannie's name for the small room where the tanning bed was. She had hung a rustic wooden sign on the door with bright yellow letters that read *Sun Spot* in the center, with palm trees on either side. The o in the word *spot* had rays drawn around it like the sun, which was a nice touch. The sign looked like something you might see at the beach, and there was a blue and white striped canvas beach chair positioned beside the tanning bed where you could put your clothes and other personal belongings while you were tanning. To add to the beach ambiance in the room, Fannie had paintings of colorful beach scenes on the walls, a coconut air freshener that smelled like tanning lotion, and a cassette tape playing the Beach Boys, the Surfaris, or Jimmy Buffett. Fannie said she wanted her customers to enjoy the experience and feel relaxed, like they had been lying on the beach. It was a nice touch, and I generally did some of my best thinking in the tanning bed because it was so peaceful. I quickly turned on the bed, stripped down to my underwear, breathed in the coconut aroma, and got in. I lowered the lid, put on my protective eye goggles, and got comfortable. I was torn about meeting my want-ad guy now that things were going so well with Kevin. But I had to see it through, since the guy had planned to come all the way from New Jersey. And I had been looking forward to this moment for so long. I still felt like I was betraying Kevin somehow. We had only known each other for a few weeks, though, and it wasn't like we were going steady or anything. I was so touched that he had stayed here longer than he had planned so that he could get to know me better and had given me a cherry blossom fan. It wasn't expensive, but it was very romantic. He was so sweet and gorgeous. What was I going to say to him? I couldn't tell him. Why should I? We didn't have a commitment. We weren't a couple. I had to remember that. Yep. I always thought more clearly in the tanning bed.

I got dressed and looked in the full-length mirror. My tan was impressive, by anyone's standards. The goal was always the Bain de Soleil model, and I was almost there. Fannie was sitting on her neon pink sofa with her legs propped up when I walked out of the Sun Spot. She didn't do hair on Sundays, but she opened on Sunday afternoons during tanning season, spring through fall, for tanning bed customers. She had told me she didn't open the Sun Spot on Sundays for the money, but she felt it was her duty to make sure her customers got the tan they deserved. I loved Fannie.

"You are gorgeous, honey." Fannie stood up and inspected my highlights. "Was it hot in there? Can I get you some water?"

"I am a little parched," I said, as she ran her fingers through my hair.

"Your hair really took to those highlights. It looks like you've been at the beach all week." She walked over to the kitchen and filled a cup with water.

"That was exactly the look I was going for, Fannie." I took the cup of water from her. "You're an artist."

"Thanks, honey. And you're a beautiful canvas to work with, Kathy." She plopped back down on the sofa and patted the space beside her. "Sit down and let's chat a minute."

"What's up, Fannie?" I sat down beside her and put my water on the coffee table in front of us.

"I know you're all excited about meeting this new guy that's comin' into town, and I don't blame you one bit," she said. "It's slim pickin's around here, for sure. But I saw Mike the other day. He's lookin' mighty fine these days, and he's such a sweet boy." Her eyes searched my face for a reaction.

It was the same old song and dance. Everyone thought Mike and I would make the perfect couple. The only problem was that I had no interest in Mike. Nobody seemed to care about that. Sure, he was a great guy, but he was a redneck with no desire to get out of Possum Valley.

"Fannie, I really like Mike as a friend, but I don't see a future with him." I tried to be polite, because I knew she was only trying to help. "He is too complacent; he has no ambition," I explained.

"Well, sweetie, I'm not tryin' to meddle. You know me. I just know that sometimes we can search the world over for somethin', and it's right under our noses all the time. That's all."

Fannie's comment that she didn't like to meddle was like pigs saying they don't like mud. She lived to meddle, and she had plenty of opportunities as a hair stylist. But I had a feeling I knew why she felt the need to say something to me about Mike. I had asked Mama once why Fannie wasn't married, and she told me that Fannie had a boyfriend all through high school. She broke up with him right before graduation because she wanted to sow her wild oats. Meanwhile, he started dating another girl, and they ended up getting married and moving to Chattanooga after he got a job there. Mama said she had never gotten over him, and that's why she hadn't married. I appreciated Fannie's concern, but Mike was not my boyfriend. Frankly, I hoped he would fall in love with someone soon and get married, someone besides me. I loved Fannie for caring about me so much, but I could have done without her free advice.

"That's true, Fannie, but Mike is definitely wrong for me," I said firmly. "I have to see what else is out there. Possum Valley can't be all there is."

"I understand." She pulled a cigarette from the pack of Virginia Slims laying on the end table beside her. "I felt the same way at your age. I desperately wanted out of here, but now I realize I didn't know what I wanted until it was too late." She lit her cigarette and took a long drag before exhaling. Her eyes got watery, and she looked like she was going to cry. "You're not me though, Kathy. You're going to live your dream."

I didn't know what to say. I knew why she wasn't married, but it never occurred to me how unhappy she was. She always seemed to be listening to her customers about their problems. I wondered if she had anyone to listen to hers. "Thanks, Fannie. I hope so. It isn't too late for you, either. You're still young and beautiful. There's someone out there for you."

She took another drag on her cigarette. "Oh, sweetie. I've got my business. I don't have time for a man." She laughed, but the pain in her eyes lingered.

* * *

When I got back home, Rita and Clyde were in the living room with Daddy watching a rerun of *The Brady Bunch.* I almost felt a tinge of jealousy as I observed them from the kitchen. They looked so comfortable, sitting close on the sofa and just enjoying being together, even though Daddy was in the room. Trust me, it was never fun to have Daddy in the room when we were with boys. Daddy perched in his favorite chair and watched us like a hawk the whole time. We weren't allowed to be alone in the house with a boy, and he didn't allow any touching in his presence. Even though Daddy had known Clyde since he was born, he'd still get out his rifle every now and then when Clyde was around. "I don't want him getting too comfortable around here," he would say. Clyde and Daddy got along well otherwise, though. Clyde was a hard-working guy, and hard work was the best way to earn Daddy's respect. And Clyde knew not to sit in Daddy's chair—not that Clyde or anyone else was really dying to sit in his stained, twenty-year-old recliner with duct tape covering the spots where it had ripped from wear and tear over the years. Mama had initially used the matching cloth from the arm rest covers to patch the torn areas on the chair, but she finally ran out of fabric. The cloth on the arms was completely worn off now, and Mama said it wasn't fit for the garbage dump. But that chair was like a throne to Daddy, and nobody sat on the throne except the king of our doublewide.

I thought about Fannie as I watched Rita and Clyde laughing together. She and her boyfriend were probably close like Rita and Clyde, and she gave that up for a dream that never materialized. Would I regret leaving Possum Valley and not pursuing a relationship with Mike like everyone thought I should? No; Fannie was right about one thing. I wasn't her. I wasn't Rita either. Everyone seemed to want to complicate my life lately, but I owed it to myself to follow my dream. I wouldn't be able to live with myself if I didn't try.

"Hey, Kathy." Rita looked up when an advertisement for Rice Krispies came on. "Come watch TV with us."

"Thanks, but I'm going to go look at some catalogs for college," I said. Jenny had given me some catalogs from universities in California, and I promised her I would look through them. I was going to leave Possum Valley one way or another; if I couldn't find a guy to get me out, college might be my Plan B.

"You missed the excitement earlier." Rita followed me as I started toward my bedroom. "The sheriff was at Heath and Henry's."

Sheriff Turner had been to their house before, for domestic violence. We had called him a couple of times ourselves, as well as the other neighbors. The brothers had called the sheriff on each other, too. "What else is new?" I wasn't trying to be rude, but I had no idea why she was telling me about something that happened pretty regularly and certainly wasn't big news. The sheriff would come out and give them a warning, but that was it.

"Well, Heath and Henry weren't making any commotion that we know of, but Sheriff Turner arrested them this time," Rita said. "We have no idea why."

"I hope he keeps them." I shrugged. "They need to be locked up anyway."

"Don't you feel a little bad for them, though?" Rita looked at me with big, sad eyes. She was always more forgiving than I was.

"No, Rita," I said in a more hateful tone than I intended. "I really don't," I continued, softening my voice a bit. "They have tried to kill us before, you know."

"But they only do that when they're drinking. They're OK most of the time."

"Oh, *sure* they are." I was getting annoyed with Rita's naivety. "We can both name women around here whose husbands *only* hit them when they're drunk. Does that make it OK?"

It was true. Although there were plenty of good people in Possum Valley, it had its share of wife and child beaters. People wanted to blame their bad behavior on stress and poverty, but Daddy always said being really poor or really rich didn't make you a better person, it just made you more of who you *really* were. "People say if they were only rich, they'd be more generous, but if you're a stingy, good-for-nothing person to begin with, you'd be just the same if you won the lottery," he'd say.

"OK, Kathy." Rita looked a bit annoyed with me, too. "I guess you're right, but a little compassion wouldn't kill you."

"Compassion won't kill me." I was on a sarcastic roll and couldn't stop. "But Heath and Henry might, one of these days." I gave her a big smile, and she couldn't help smiling back as she shook her head. "You're impossible," she said. The nice thing about Rita being so merciful was that she always forgave me, too.

* * *

I had just gotten comfortable on the bed and started looking through majors offered at Berkeley when the phone rang. I picked it up on the first ring, because I was already bored just thinking about college. It was Kevin. He wanted to know if he could come by the next day, since he still didn't know where I lived. Lucky me. Fine, *lucky* is not the right word here. As "luck" would have it, let's say, the next day was manure Monday, which took up most of my day. Then I had to work at Seek & Find all evening. I hadn't planned to invite Kevin to the farm or introduce him to Mama and Daddy at all, since I'd assumed I would never see him again after he left. But we were supposed to meet in California in October, and we seemed to be hitting it off so well. I wondered if I should let him see how I lived; I would run the risk of scaring him away, of course, but that was going to be the real test for any guy I dated from outside Possum Valley. Could he handle Daddy and the pig farm? I couldn't hide them forever, and I knew it was wrong to try.

"I have to work on the farm and at Seek & find tomorrow, but maybe you could come another day this week." I swallowed hard, not fully believing I had just invited Kevin to come here. How could I possibly have the farm looking decent this week? I'd be lucky if he didn't get a cow's head stuck under his car on the way up the driveway. *No.* I had to make sure that didn't happen. And I'd have to make sure Daddy wasn't killing a cow the day Kevin came. I had to make sure things were as normal as possible.

"Let me get back to you about the day," I said. "I'll need to check my work schedule." That was a lie. I got my work schedule every Saturday, so I knew exactly when I was working. I just needed time to clean up some, and try to find a day that Daddy wouldn't be covered in blood from head to toe.

"Sounds great, Kathy," he replied. "I am available any day except Friday."

"Perfect." I couldn't believe my luck. I needed an excuse not to see Kevin on Friday because of my date with the want-ad guy, and he wasn't available. At least that was settled. Now I just had to worry about Kevin coming here to the farm the rest of the week.

When we hung up, I walked back into the living room, hoping to talk to Daddy about his slaughter plans for the week. But Daddy's chair was reclined, and he was snoring. Sunday was the only day Daddy got a chance to rest, so I quietly opened the sliding glass door and went out on the deck, where Rita and Clyde were sitting on folding chairs. A couple of years before, Daddy had promised to get Mama a picnic table with some benches for the deck. We still had the same blue and white, woven nylon strap folding chairs that we'd had for years at that time. The nylon was torn and frayed on most of them, so they could be a little painful when you sat on them in shorts. Daddy got Mama a gas grill for her last birthday, so he had sufficiently appeased her for a while. "As soon as I get the money, I'm gonna get you that picnic table, honey," he would tell Mama. I knew he meant it at the time, but when he did get the money, we always needed it for something else.

"Guess you didn't wanna listen to Daddy snoring either," Rita said. "He just gets louder and louder until it's impossible to watch TV in there."

"I'm just waiting for him to wake up so I can find out when he's killing cows this week." I sat down on one of the torn chairs, since Rita and Clyde had the only two good ones. "Kevin wants to come here and meet everybody this week, and I don't want cow guts and pieces laying around if I can avoid it."

"I wouldn't worry about it," Clyde said as he slipped his arm around Rita. He was much bolder when Daddy was asleep. "If he really likes you, guts won't make a difference." Naturally, guts didn't make a difference to Clyde. He grew up on a farm, and besides, he was lucky to get a girl like Rita, as far as I was concerned.

"Wow. We finally get to meet a guy that meets Kathy's approval." Rita moved around in her chair, pushing Clyde's arm away with her shoulder. "Maybe she'll fix me up with one of his friends." Rita liked to tease Clyde and even make him a little jealous on occasion, but I knew how much she cared about him. She wouldn't have traded him for all the money in the world. I often wondered how we could be sisters raised by the same parents and be so different. Sure, Clyde was crazy about her and treated her like a princess, but like Mama's friend Jolene always said, love won't pay the bills.

* * *

A loud knock on the front door diverted our attention and made Daddy suddenly jump up from his chair, mid-snore. Rita opened the sliding glass door and told Daddy to stay seated, she would see who it was. He sat back down in his chair, still disoriented from just waking up. Clyde and I waited on the deck for Rita, who returned with Jenny walking behind her.

"Look who I found." Rita said, as she opened the door and ushered Jenny out onto the deck.

"Sorry to just barge in without calling, but you guys will never believe this." Jenny was talking even faster than she normally did, with her Boston roots more evident in her accent than usual. "Sheriff Turner has arrested suspects for the cross burning in our yard."

"Suspects?" I asked. "How many are there? Do we know them?"

"Oh, you definitely know them," Jenny said. "They're your psychotic neighbors."

"Heath and Henry?" I couldn't believe what I was hearing. Of course, I'd always thought they were insane, chasing each other around and threatening people, but I didn't think they knew about Chris. They rarely interacted with other people.

"Yes," Jenny replied. "Heath and Henry. I guess you didn't see the police cars."

I looked at Rita and wondered if she still thought I should be more compassionate. I held my tongue, but she knew what I was thinking.

"I told Kathy that Heath and Henry had been taken by the police while she was at Fannie's," Rita interjected. "But we thought the police had finally gotten tired of coming out here for domestic disturbances."

"Why do they suspect Heath and Henry?" I asked.

"They've been bragging about it at the Valley Barn Dance Hall," Jenny said. "I heard they got drunk and started talking about how they sent a clear message to the Yankee family about hanging around with the 'wrong people.' What a joke! As if we'd be better off hanging around with people like *them*."

"Can't argue with that, Jenny," Clyde finally spoke up. "Heath and Henry aren't exactly good role models in the community."

Somehow, I felt good about Heath and Henry being the cross burners. I guess I was just glad it wasn't anyone that I associated with voluntarily. I had been worried it might be Jenny's neighbor, Johnny Parsons, or even Ted, our other neighbor. I already felt bad enough that something like this happened while Kevin and Chris were around, but I didn't think I could've ever forgiven a friend or neighbor for doing something so horrible. It seemed a little less terrible that the people who did it were the town drunks, widely considered crazy.

"We've got to let Kevin and Chris know that the guys who did this are a couple of crazy drunks," I said.

"That doesn't make it OK, though." Jenny seemed irritated by my enthusiasm.

"I know, I just think it's good to know that it wasn't a respected person in the community...or someone we associate with," I explained.

"I guess so," Jenny agreed. "I'm planning on calling Chris tonight. I'm sure he will be relieved to know the sheriff caught the people who did it. He actually felt badly and was worried about my safety."

* * *

After Jenny left, I went to my room, closed the door, and flopped down on my bed. As I gazed up at the fly strips hanging from the ceiling, I thought about Chris and everything that had happened since Jenny and I had met him and Kevin. In some ways, they had complicated our lives, but they had also made life more interesting. I had been so happy since meeting Kevin, and I wanted him to remain a part of my life. I didn't even care if the personal-ad guy didn't show up on Friday. Kevin could give me a better life than I had, by far. Maybe I wouldn't be filthy rich, like I'd always wanted, but I wouldn't be filthy poor like I'd always been, either. I reached over, took a deep breath, and picked up the phone. It was time for Kevin to come over and meet the family. I was confident that if he liked me as much as I liked him, he wouldn't care where I lived. But I still crossed my fingers for good luck.

Chapter 11

I woke up at five a.m. on Wednesday. I didn't need to be awake until six, but I couldn't sleep. *Why, oh why did I invite Kevin to come over here today?* I must have been insane. It was such an impulsive thing to do, and I hadn't even asked Daddy if he was slaughtering. I had to know, so I got up and got dressed as soon as I heard him and Mama stirring in the kitchen.

"You're up early." Mama was mixing some pancake batter. "Want some pancakes? I have chocolate chips." Chocolate chip pancakes were my favorite and always a treat at our house, since Daddy preferred bacon and eggs. "Sounds great," I said. "I'll help you."

Daddy was waiting for the weather forecast on the radio, as he did every morning. The weather report was broadcast every thirty minutes; it was almost time for the 5:30 update.

"Today would be a great day to play hooky from work," the weather guy joked. "We're expecting sunny skies with low humidity and highs around eighty-four degrees."

Daddy turned off the radio. "Today would've been a good day to get some rain. I don't have any slaughterin' to do. I guess I'll have to start loading up some of the dried manure and do some fertilizin'."

Question answered. Problem solved. I could live with his fertilizing the vegetable garden. I had tried to clean up the yard as much as I could the day before. I couldn't do anything about Daddy's old truck parts, but at least there were no animal parts laying around.

I put a handful of chocolate chips in the pancake on the griddle. "My friend

Kevin is coming by after lunch today," I said nervously. Daddy didn't like meeting new boys, almost as much as I didn't like his meeting them. I was bracing myself for what I knew he would say in response.

"Well, that's just fine." He took a deep breath and exhaled loudly through his wide-open mouth. "I need to clean my rifles anyway." Of course, he wasn't joking like other fathers joked about cleaning their rifles when their daughters brought a boy home. He had done it to me before, on the few occasions that I had invited a boy over, and had done it to Rita countless times. To say he enjoyed humiliating us and terrorizing boys would be an understatement.

"Do you have to, Daddy?" I pleaded. "I really like this guy."

"All the more reason he needs to know your daddy's armed and ready." He winked at me as he opened the closet and pulled out a couple of rifles and a shotgun. He had a rifle or some kind of gun in every room of the house, just in case a thief was ever desperate enough to break into our trailer. The most valuable items we had were the guns, so at least he had plenty of guns to protect his guns. I rolled my eyes as he turned and carried the guns to the living room and leaned them against the side of the entertainment center. I didn't say any more about it, I just put my pancakes on a plate and sat down at the table. I drowned my pancakes in syrup, still grateful that he wasn't slaughtering an animal today. *You can't have it all*, I told myself, stuffing my mouth with pancake.

When I finished eating, I helped clean up the kitchen and went to feed the pigs. I wanted to get my chores done early so I would have time to clean up, rush over to the tanning bed, and get back before Kevin arrived. I didn't have an appointment for today, but Fannie never minded if I dropped in. Unfortunately, I wasn't the only person who had decided to drop in that day. Susie French was waiting for the tanning bed when I got there. Susie was a junior in high school and had just joined the cheerleading squad my senior year. Since school was out, the high school girls came in to work on their tan a lot during the week. Some of them were lucky enough to be preparing for beach trips, and others were trying to get a base tan for the lake or pool. The rest, like me, were just trying to look like they'd been to the beach or the pool.

"Kathy, you sure are a sight for sore eyes," Susie ran up and hugged me enthusiastically. You would've thought we were best friends, by the way she was acting. In reality, she talked about me behind my back all the time, saying things like, "I don't know *how* Kathy got elected cheerleading captain every single year since she was a freshman," and "Mike should give up on her because he could do way better anyway." Everyone knew Susie had a crush on Mike, but she couldn't seem to understand that as long as she gossiped about me, Mike would never be interested in her. He had been devoted to me since we were little kids. He had gotten into a fight with Jeff Amos in fifth grade because Jeff said I was stuck up—and he was still there to protect me, whether I wanted him to or not.

"How nice to see you, Susie," I lied. Jenny would be very disappointed in me. No, not for lying, but for being a pretentious Southern belle. She would tell me that I was just as bad as Susie. Perhaps I was, but it was just the way things were done in the South, something Jenny couldn't comprehend. Southern girls were taught to never express their true feelings, at least not to someone's face. You "politely" did that later, behind the person's back.

"You look amazing!" Susie grabbed my arm and pulled me over to Fannie's couch. "How's Mike doing? Have you seen him lately?" And there it was. I knew it wouldn't take her long to steer the conversation toward Mike.

"Oh, thanks." I flashed my sweetest smile at her, tilting my head toward my right shoulder. I knew how to turn on the charm when I needed to. "I see Mike all the time," I said. "In fact, he brought me the most beautiful yellow roses for my birthday." Sure, I could have just said I see him at work a lot, but mentioning the roses and watching the envy erode her sparkling smile gave me much more satisfaction. This was the part of being Southern that I liked best: being able to crush someone without ever saying an unkind word. Bless her heart.

"All clear." Fannie emerged from the Sun Spot. "You're next, Susie."

Fannie always wiped down the tanning bed and made sure there was no trash in the room after each customer left. I appreciated her cleanliness and attention to detail.

"Thanks, Fannie." Susie got up from the couch and turned to me. "Good talking to you. I'll see you again in a few minutes," she flashed me another fake smile, as she walked in the Sun Spot and closed the door.

"Hey, Kathy." Fannie smiled at me. "This is a nice surprise."

"I just can't stay away, Fannie," I said. "I don't know which I like better, hanging out with you, or lying in the tanning bed."

"Oh, people only come here to see me, of course," she laughed.

Fannie sat down beside me on the couch, turning to face me as we heard the familiar hum of the tanning bed in the other room. "That girl's after Mike, isn't she?" Fannie whispered.

"I guess so, Fannie, but I don't really care," I shrugged.

"I could hear you two talking from the other room." She stared at me intently. "You didn't sound like a girl who doesn't care."

I rolled my eyes and sighed heavily. "You never give up, do you?"

"That's all I'm gonna say." She held up her hands in surrender.

"Wooo hooo, witchy woman; see how high she fli-i-ies." I sang the Eagles' tune loudly with the radio as I drove back home from Fannie's. Yes, I was thinking about Susie as I sang. Mama always told me if I couldn't say anything nice about someone, don't say anything at all. She never mentioned singing, though. I didn't like Susie. Not because she was chasing after Mike, like Fannie thought. *Oh, well, none of that matters,* I thought. I had to focus on getting home and preparing for Kevin to arrive. I was in a good mood. *Why shouldn't I be?* I thought, as I pulled into the driveway. I looked amazing with my tanned skin and big, blonde hair, hopefully so amazing that maybe Kevin wouldn't even care about where or how we lived. He would see me and...

Oh, no. Not Granny.

Her two-toned green station wagon was parked in front of the trailer when I pulled up. My heart sank, and I started to feel sick to my stomach. *Why? Why did she have to visit today, of all days?* Perhaps it wouldn't have been so bad, if my granny were like normal grandmothers. But Granny was anything and everything but normal. First, she always had a dip of Bruton snuff tucked behind her lower lip, making her look like she'd just had a root canal. She carried two cans with her at all times: a can of Bruton and an empty can to spit it in. I remember when I was little, I had always been curious about Granny's snuff. One day, when no one was around, I saw her can of Bruton on the floor and decided to take a sniff before tasting a little. Just smelling it brought tears to my eyes, it was so strong. I decided against tasting it. Good call, I'd say.

Secondly, Granny was dying. She had been dying for as long as I could remember. This used to really concern me, before Mama explained to Rita and me that Granny just liked the attention and was actually as healthy as a horse. In fact, the women on Mama's side of the family were known for their longevity.

My great grandma, Margie, was in her eighties and lived just down the street from Granny. We mostly saw her on holidays. She still mowed her own yard and kept a garden, which she said kept her young. Grandma Margie's mother, Mamaw Perkins, lived to be 101—and she might have lived even longer, but she tripped over a mop bucket she'd left in the kitchen (yes, she still cleaned her own house) and broke her hip. She never made it back from the hospital. That was about two years ago, and since then, Granny vowed she'd never go to the hospital because she said they just let old people die in there. It didn't seem to matter to Granny that Mamaw Perkins was 101 and had a broken hip when she went in the hospital. Granny seemed to love to complain, and Daddy always joked that people needed to have an extra half hour if they asked Granny how she was doing. "Lord, have mercy," she would say, as a little brown trickle of snuff slid down one side of her mouth. "I'm barely makin' it. I'm so weak I can barely go." From there, she would go into a long dissertation about her multiple aches and pains, her voice fading more and more into a feeble whisper the longer she talked about her ailments. She always sounded frail, like she was on her deathbed, except when she talked about her soap operas. Then her face would light up, her voice became robust, and she would stare past us as if she could see the events unfolding in her "stories," as she referred to them. But they were much more than just stories to her. They were Granny's reality, and she planned her entire life around them. Doctors' appointments, grocery shopping, friends, family, everything was secondary when her soaps were on. She went to bed worrying about what Nikki on *Young and the Restless* was going to do when she found out that Victor had been secretly dating her best friend. "Poor Nikki needs to find a husband and a friend she can trust," Granny would say, shaking her head from side to side. "But she's no saint herself, of course. Did you hear what she did last week?" We all just went along with her, because the people in her stories were as much a part of her life as we were, maybe more.

Granny was sitting on the living room sofa with her spit can on the floor beside her left foot when I walked in. "Lordy, Lordy, there's Kathy," she said. "Come here, child, and give your poor, old granny a hug. I wasn't sure if I'd ever see you again, honey. I've been so sick, I'm past going." She looked at me and then lowered her head and shoulders, as if the weight of them was too much to bear. I walked over to hug her. Granny always smelled like a mixture of snuff and cheap, old-lady perfume. She stretched out her arms, the flabby flesh hanging down several inches. *Was that genetic? I really need to research that,* I thought, worried.

"You're looking good, Granny." I tried using the power of positive thinking that I had read about in a magazine at Fannie's. *Be positive and smile. Your cheerful attitude will be contagious,*" the article had said. Daddy wasn't exaggerating about the half hour, so I hoped that saying something positive before she had a chance to be negative would make her less likely to complain. Not to mention the smell of Bruton mixed with cheap perfume made me want to make a quick getaway.

"Well, it's probably the lighting in here." She was determined to keep her pessimism intact. "It's so dark, you can barely see, so I reckon a corpse would look good in here. You look as pretty as a picture, though, Kathy. I can see that much."

"Granny!" I decided to try humor. "I don't know if that's a compliment, since you just said a corpse would look good in here." It worked. She laughed so hard, she had to spit out her entire clump of snuff.

"Sit down and talk to your poor, sick granny," she patted the spot beside her on the sofa with her gnarled, pasty hand. Granny was only in her early sixties, but her hands looked like they were at least eighty. Mama said it was a family trait, and her hands did look much older than she was. I was certain that I had inherited the old hands also, since I already had the signature oversized knuckles and the beginnings of rope-like veins that snaked around prominent bones.

"Oh, Granny, I'd love to, but I have to get ready for my friend who is coming over in a few minutes," I said. "Maybe we can talk later, if you don't have to go watch your stories." *Please, Lord, please, please let her go home and watch her stories.*

"I'm not goin' anywhere, honey." She grinned, as she secured another wad of snuff behind her lip. "I can watch my stories right here."

"That's right." Mama walked into the living room from the kitchen. Granny's going to stay for dinner, so with you, Kevin, Rita, and Clyde, we'll have a full house."

Mama enjoyed cooking for a crowd, even though she barely had enough money for groceries some weeks. It was like a challenge for her to make a meal go further by making a casserole out of what she had. Mama's food was always good, but it wasn't the food I was worried about.

"Perfect," I tried to sound sincere, but it came out more sarcastic.

I walked to the bathroom and sprayed another layer of Aqua Net on my hair. I still looked good, but unfortunately, even Christie Brinkley wasn't pretty enough to distract a guy sitting in a dilapidated doublewide watching her daddy clean his guns and her granny provide commentary on her stories and multiple illnesses while spitting snuff into a green bean can.

* * *

Rita and I were in the kitchen helping Mama chop onions when Kevin knocked on the door. Granny's stories were just going off, so it was about four p.m. Kevin was right on time, as usual. Mama was cooking chicken casserole for dinner; Rita and I had made some blackberry cobbler for dessert, using the wild blackberries Rita had picked back in the woods the day before. My heart was pounding in my chest and my hands were sweating when I opened the door. He looked too good. Too good for our mobile home with the fly strips hanging from the ceiling. I should have taken those down. You know how you see something so much, you get used to it and forget it's even there? You see it every day, but you don't really *see* it. *It's too late now, though,* I sighed. *They're up there, dead flies dotting them like chocolate chips on a cookie.*

"Howdy, there." Daddy walked over with a shotgun in hand, his face hard and unfriendly. I'm Kathy's daddy, Larry."

Painfully reminded of why I didn't remember the fly strips, I realized I was more concerned about Daddy. And Granny, and Clyde and... *Oh, dear Lord, what have I done?*

"Nice to meet you, sir." Kevin sounded so respectful and professional, as if he were talking to a superior officer. Daddy wasn't used to that. But I could tell from the look on his face that he liked it. "That's a nice twelve-gauge you have there." Kevin didn't seem to be intimidated by the shotgun. Most guys started shaking and couldn't speak without a stutter when Daddy greeted them with a gun. I could tell he already liked Kevin. Next thing I knew, Daddy had stolen Kevin and was showing him all his guns, but not in an intimidating, keep your hands off my daughter kind of way. He and Kevin were actually discussing guns. "I'd love to have a gun like that someday," I heard Daddy say from his bedroom, where he had taken Kevin to see the rest of his collection. Daddy had never even shown Clyde his special collection, which he kept back in the bedroom.

The rest of the afternoon went this way. Kevin easily won Mama's heart by taking an interest in her Elvis collection. He seemed genuinely impressed that Mama had every album Elvis had ever made. Granny actually became animated when talking to Kevin about how Papaw was a Marine during World War II, and how handsome he looked in his uniform. She told him how he had taken a lot of the horrible events that occurred during the Battle of Iwo Jima to his grave, never discussing them, even with her. "He was a good man," she said, her eyes tearing up. "He loved his country, his God, and his family. He provided for us until the day he died."

Kevin put his hand on Granny's shoulder. "I wish I could have met him," he said in a very sincere voice. "We owe so much to his generation." Granny started to blush as she shyly looked at Kevin and smiled bigger than I had seen her smile maybe ever, liquid-y snuff flowing freely down her chin.

Kevin seemed to know just the right thing to say to everyone in the family. He talked knowledgably about chickens and farming with Rita and Clyde, and went on and on about Mama's home-cooked dinner. Everyone was gushing over him by the time he left, especially me. Was this guy for real? I hoped so.

But that night I couldn't help but wonder how *he* truly felt about *us*. He was so charming and seemed very interested in all of us and our lives, but could he really be OK with our doublewide, which was a far cry from his aunt and uncle's mansion in Knoxville, and the fly strips, and Daddy, with his junk laying all over the yard, and Granny, with snuff running down her chin? How could a guy like him be interested in a girl like me? I began feeling very inadequate, wondering if he would ever call me again.

But he did. The next day.

"You have a great family," he said, when I asked if he enjoyed his visit. "People from the country are so down to earth, and just...*real*. It's refreshing." He paused for a moment. I wanted to say something, but I didn't know what to say. People from the country? I lost him after that. Did he think we were too different? There was an uncomfortable silence that we'd never experienced since we met. "Kathy," he finally spoke, "You aren't like the other girls I know."

Here we go. I knew it. He is going to tell me it's been real, but he can't date an unsophisticated country girl like me. I was kidding myself to think that I could keep a guy like him interested, when he saw my background and who I really was.

"I...I know this sounds crazy," he continued, "but we have something special. I think we owe it to ourselves to see where this goes."

I still couldn't speak. *He still likes me! Me, with my family, the trailer, and the pig farm*. I wanted to hang up right then and call Jenny. She was always the first one with whom I wanted to share good news. It seemed too good to be true. *He* seemed too good to be true. Daddy always told me when something seemed too good to be true, it usually was. Could Kevin really be this perfect, or was Daddy right? That was silly. I had no reason to believe that he wasn't just as great as he appeared. "You always have such a hard time just enjoying the moment," Jenny had told me many times. She was right. I needed to stop second-guessing everything and simply embrace my good fortune. I was so enamored with Kevin I didn't even want to meet the personal ad guy. I had a great guy right here under my nose. But I couldn't let him down at this point. Plus, OK, I *was* curious.

Chapter 12

Well, look at you." Mama said when I walked into the living room. "Pretty as a picture. You'll have boys around you like chickens around a June bug in that outfit. I'm glad Rita and Clyde are going to be with you." She didn't like it, but she had agreed not to tell Daddy about my blind date, since she knew it meant so much to me. "I reckon you're an adult," she had said when I told her about my plan. "Your daddy can't treat you and Rita like his baby girls forever." But I was pretty sure he intended to try.

"I'm a little nervous in these heels, Mama," I said as I practiced walking across the living room.

"Just stand up straight, and be the confident, beautiful girl God made you, Kathy," Mama smiled. You'll be just fine." I loved Mama, and silently swore again that someday I would buy her a house near Graceland.

My hair started drooping the moment we walked out to get in Clyde's car. I had worked on it for over an hour, using a blow dryer and styling brush to get extra volume before using my hot curlers. I sprayed hairspray on it until every hair was in place, but the summer heat and humidity had arrived in East Tennessee. No amount of hairspray could prevent limp hair in those conditions. I was already nervous, and this latest hair development made it even worse. I still didn't like the idea of Rita and Clyde coming, but Rita insisted on it; she said she would tell Daddy herself if I didn't agree. I certainly didn't want to get Daddy—who would probably show up with his shotgun—involved, so I unwillingly consented. Mama only knew about it because she had asked questions about the new dress and shoes, and I didn't want to lie to her. Mama and

I were very different, but she loved Rita and me and we could always depend on her for support. She had made sure Daddy was gone to get gas for the lawn mower so he wouldn't be around when I left in my new outfit.

I tried to remember Mama's words as we made the hour-long drive to Knoxville. I was sweating, even though Clyde had turned the air conditioning on high. My hair was already a mess, and I felt like my make-up was sliding down my face. I wanted to go back home and call Kevin. What was I doing, anyway? I had a perfectly great guy with the potential to make very good money. But what if we didn't work out? This other guy could be insurance. I needed a back-up plan, right? It's always good to have a back-up plan. Daddy would agree. My heart was racing by the time we pulled into the parking lot at Regas. I suddenly felt like I was going to be sick.

"Are you OK?" Rita asked. "You look a little pale."

"I feel like I'm going to throw up, Rita. I don't know if I can do this."

"Of course you can, Kathy." She turned around and wet her middle finger with her tongue and wiped under my left eye. "Just getting a little mascara smudge there, honey. You've been looking forward to this moment forever. We just need to breathe. Scoot over, and I'll come back there."

Rita climbed into the back seat and grabbed my hands. She squeezed my fingers tightly, and we both inhaled deeply. We slowly let the air seep out of our mouths simultaneously, performing a ritual that we often did together in moments of crisis. I could feel her cool breath on my face, just as I did when we were in middle school and Rex Reynolds had just broken up with her. I had found her crying in her room after school, and I taught her to breathe just like we were doing now. I had learned the technique from Jolene, who said she'd learned it back in the '70s, when she used to do yoga. Nobody did yoga anymore, since it was considered a pointless exercise for hippies, but I often wondered if it would be more useful than all the bouncing around in aerobics classes. All I knew was that it always seemed to calm me down.

"Thanks, Rita." I hugged her very carefully, trying to avoid messing up my hair any more than it already was from the humidity. Rita was a good sister, always had been. I wondered if I took her for granted too often. Probably so. We got out of the car, and Clyde gave his keys to the valet. I smiled, thinking about how absurd it was for Clyde's old rusty truck to be valet parked. I suddenly felt a lot better.

Well, at least until I tripped on the rug in front of the door.

My heel caught on the edge as I was confidently gliding along like I was on the red carpet in Hollywood, feeling eyes on me as the doors to Regas swung open.

I was down. On the ground. And if eyes weren't on me before, they most certainly were now.

"Are you all right, ma'am?" I heard someone say.

"Kathy, do you think you can get up?" Clyde kneeled over me with a compassionate look on his face. "Have you twisted your ankle?"

"Kathy, honey, take my hands. We'll breathe again." Rita said, the sympathy obvious in her voice.

No amount of breathing was going to fix this. I wanted to hide, crawl in a hole and die, anything to make me invisible.

"Talk to me, Kathy." Rita's voice was shaking now. "Are you hurt?"

"My pride is mortally wounded," I managed to say. "I'm not hurt, though."

I started to get up, and Clyde took my hand and helped pull me to my feet. When I regained my balance, Kevin was looking straight at me, his head towering above the restaurant employees that had surrounded me. What was he *doing* here? What was Kevin doing here?

I looked around for a girl or his aunt and uncle, but I didn't see anyone. Whoever was with him could be in the restroom though, or maybe he was meeting someone here. He wouldn't come to Regas alone, or with another guy; *surely* he wouldn't have the audacity to take another *girl* to Regas.

"Rita." I grabbed her arm and pulled her to me. "Don't look now, but Kevin is here."

"Your Kevin?" she gasped.

"Yes. My Kevin. Why would my Kevin be here?" I said, as he started walking toward us. "He must have seen me fall, Rita. I want to die. I wish I was dead."

"Hi, Kathy." There was a look of concern on his gorgeous face. "Are you OK?"

He did see me fall. Great. This night was getting better and better. "Oh, I'm fine." I lied. "I was just getting a closer look at the rug. It's authentic Persian, in case you were wondering."

I'm an idiot. Why did I say that? What kind of moron would say that? Breathe, Kathy, breathe.

He laughed. Probably just a polite laugh. He was probably the politest person, male or female, that I knew.

"So, did you come to Regas just to see my performance, or what are you doing here?" I asked, feeling a little braver and trying to change the subject. And, of course, I *was* very curious.

"Well, I'm supposed to meet someone here for the first time, but so far, she's a no-show, he said nervously, moving his head from side to side scanning the room. "How about you? Are you guys celebrating something tonight?"

"Um, we're...I'm..." My voice drifted. Did he say he was meeting a *girl* for the first time? *She* hadn't shown up? Why is he meeting another girl? *No way.* No way he could be my man of mystery. Could he? No. He's not from New Jersey. He's from San Francisco. But still, he's seeing *another* girl? I was suddenly furious.

"We're supposed to meet someone here too," I said, my voice sounding strange.

"Kathy, come to the restroom with me," Rita gave me a stern look. "My contact is bothering me."

Rita had just gotten contacts last year. She had worn glasses since she was in sixth grade. I was always secretly glad it was her and not me. My eyes were perfect.

"OK, Rita, but what if..."

Rita read my mind. "Clyde is here. He'll watch for our guest, won't you, babe?"

"Yeah, sure," Clyde looked confused, but then again, he usually did. "I'll be here."

We got a few feet away from Clyde and Kevin, who had started talking about some football team, when Rita grabbed my arm. "Oh, my gosh!" She half whispered, half yelled. "I think Kevin is your blind date, Kathy!"

I turned and faced her. "I thought that for a split second too, Rita," I said in a calm voice. "But Kevin is from San Francisco, and my date is from New Jersey."

"This is too much of a coincidence though," Rita continued, as she followed me into the ladies' room. "There's no way both of you would be at the *same* restaurant to meet a blind date on the *same* night. Come on, Kathy. And both dates are *late?*"

My heart started racing. I had just remembered that Kevin's dad lived in New Jersey, and Kevin went to visit him every spring. *What if... No, couldn't be.* That couldn't be possible.

"Rita," I hesitated. I really didn't want to say anything to Rita about Kevin's dad because I knew she would jump to immediate conclusions, but she was right about it being too much of a coincidence. "Kevin's dad lives in New Jersey, and he usually visits him in the spring. Do you think..."

"I'm sure of it, Kathy," Rita interrupted. She interrupted me all the time, and I hated it. Tonight was certainly no exception. "What are you going to do?"

"Well, either way, we know he's meeting a girl, so I am furious! Who does he think he is? He's supposed to be dating me. He stayed here to get to know me better. Why would he be on some random, blind date?" I fumed.

"I could ask you the same question, sis." Rita glared at me, raising her eyebrows. "Why are you any different?"

"It's completely different for me, Rita, and you know it. I have been waiting for this moment for years!"

I wanted to cry.

Rita could tell that I was upset, and her voice softened. "I know, honey, but you can't expect Kevin to date you exclusively if you are dating other people."

"But I'm not dating other people." I tried to hold back tears by looking up and holding my breath, but one cascaded down my cheek and then another. "I had planned this. I'm here because I had already planned it."

Rita went into a stall and got some toilet paper and handed it to me. "Maybe Kevin was just going through with it for the same reason you were. You really can't be angry with him."

"Whatever, Rita." I patted under my eyes with the toilet paper. "I can't deal with this. Could you just go find out if he's here to meet me and come back? I'm not leaving this bathroom until I know what's going on."

"Come on." Rita smiled sympathetically. "You don't want to stay in here. Let's just go out and enjoy a nice dinner at Regas no matter what. We got all dressed up and everything." Rita grabbed some more toilet paper and blotted my face. "You still look fantastic."

I looked at myself in the mirror. My hair was a little flat, but I did still look pretty good, and I did get all dressed up. Why should I go home just because Kevin was an idiot? "All right." I stood up tall and pushed my shoulders back. I learned this technique from a magazine article about good posture. It said that having good posture exudes confidence. I needed to stay confident and let him know this didn't bother me, even though it really, really did. I lifted my chin. "Let's go." This guy obviously didn't know who he was dealing with.

Kevin and Clyde were sitting on a sofa by the fireplace when we walked back in. "The hostess just came over and told me our table is almost ready," Clyde said.

"They've already called my table, so I guess I'd better go." Kevin looked around like he had lost something.

"Has your date arrived?" Rita sounded surprised.

"No, but hopefully she'll be here soon. I just asked the hostess, and there were no messages for me. Maybe she stood me up." He shrugged his shoulders as if he didn't care if she had or not. This whole thing meant so much to me, and it was just another date to him. He probably dated a new girl everywhere he went. I felt the tears coming again. I hated him.

"Clyde, party of four," the hostess stood by the wall with four menus.

"That's us." Clyde got up. "Hey, Kevin, why don't you join us for a while? Kathy's date isn't here yet either."

I had always thought Rita could do better, but I had never hated Clyde like I did at that moment. I looked at Rita. She was trying to avoid eye contact with me, but I kept my eyes on her until she did.

"Oh, I'm sure Kevin wants to make sure they don't give his table away, Clyde," Rita said.

"So, Kathy, you have a date tonight?" Kevin legitimately seemed surprised. Had he not realized that I *was* his date?

Rita nudged me. "Just tell him, Kathy. This is ridiculous."

She was right. I felt so stupid, and I just wanted to get it over with. "I'm pretty sure that you are actually my date, Kevin."

"What?" Kevin looked at me and grinned. "Oh, I knew that, of course." He tried to play it cool, but he obviously had no idea.

"Well, I guess we would've figured it out sooner if we had gotten each other's name instead of being mysterious," I said in a strained voice. "But I just received a letter recently. How did you..."

"I just sent it to my dad in New Jersey and had him mail it for me...so you wouldn't suspect anything." He laughed nervously. I had never seen him nervous before, and it wasn't attractive. "It was more fun this way." He smiled as if nothing was wrong. His smile was so perfect, but I wasn't going to let him off the hook. No way.

"OK. It's settled then. Let's go sit down," Clyde said, as he nodded to the waitress. "I'm starvin'."

Chapter 13

I didn't want to get up the next morning. But like daddy always said, those pigs won't feed themselves. Actually, they would if they had access to the food, but Daddy monitored the diet of all our livestock to ensure they would be "prime eating" (as he called it) when the time came. I got up, turned on the radio, and started getting dressed. "Escape," by Rupert Holmes came on, and I couldn't help but think of the irony: the song was about a couple that had each written to a personal ad column to find a new lover, only to end up learning they had answered each other's ad, not realizing how much they had in common. I had always liked the song because I thought it was a great example of how when two people are meant to be together it just works out, against all odds. I had allowed Kevin to drive me home from Regas, because he said he really needed to talk to me. My curiosity got the best of me, so I let him. He finally admitted that he had no idea I was the girl he was meeting. He said that he'd arranged the date before he got to know me, and wouldn't have done it otherwise. I wanted to stay upset with him, especially since he was so quick to try to weasel his way out of the whole thing at the restaurant, pretending he knew he was meeting me. But the reality was that I had done the same thing. He didn't want to stand up the girl, he'd said, which I had to admit was noble. And what were the chances that we would end up meeting each other *again*, through a personal ad? It had to mean something, that we would choose each other whether we met in person or in a personal column. Just like the song, we had chosen each other twice. The more I thought about it, the more romantic it became. Kevin had met my parents, and even seemed to like them. He wasn't exactly rich yet, but he was going to be a lawyer in the Air Force, and lawyers did have the potential for wealth. If he and I were meant to be together, he would definitely have money one day, because one thing I knew for sure was that I was meant to be rich. I felt elated as I began pouring slop into the trough for the pigs. The pigs gathered around me, snorting and eating greedily. With any luck, this pig farm would be in my rear-view mirror before long.

I locked the gate to the pig pen and headed straight to my bedroom when I got back inside the trailer. I opened the top drawer of my dresser and pulled out the college catalogs that Jenny had given me. If Kevin was going to be in California and he was to be my soul mate, I decided I had to find a way to be there with him and convince him of that. I had zero desire for a career, but I did need a reason to be in California; going to school was the only valid reason I could think of.

English?

I had a great vocabulary, and I was good at grammar, spelling, and reading comprehension. English was a definite maybe. I had zero interest in science, and detested math. I hated the thought of being in the medical field because if I ever did have to work (God forbid), I would hate being around all those sick people. So, English seemed the most doable, out of all the choices. I could be an English major! This could work. I could go to *college* to get a husband! I had to talk to Jenny. She would be thrilled about my going to college. I picked up the phone. I had so much to tell her. I hadn't even had a chance to let her know about my "mystery date" last night. I knew she would think the whole thing was hopelessly romantic, and it was. I finally had my ticket out of Possum Valley.

* * *

Jenny cried when I told her I wanted to go to college in California. I had decided to drive over to her house, so she could help me fill out the application and financial aid forms for UC Berkeley. She told me she was excited that I might be with her, but she was even more excited that I was getting a degree instead of wasting my future on some crazy dream of marrying a rich man. She was so happy, in fact, that I didn't have the heart to tell her that my going to college in California was all part of my master plan to get married. What she didn't know wouldn't hurt her, I reasoned.

I told her all about my "blind date" with the guy from New Jersey, and how it ended up being Kevin. She didn't believe me at first, but when she realized I was serious and I reminded her of the Piña Colada song, I thought she was going to cry again. She agreed that we were meant for each other since we had so much in common. And since if I got accepted to UC Berkeley, I would still be able to date him. She called it destiny. Obviously, I was facilitating destiny a wee bit, but if something is meant to be anyway, why not nudge it along?

"Oh, Kathy," she hugged me tightly as we sat on the corner of her bed. "I'm so happy for you, and I'm really glad you are finally letting go of your plans to marry for money." I loved Jenny. She was a little naïve at times, but a great friend, nonetheless.

After Jenny and I filled out the application and financial aid forms, I had to write an essay about my future goals. I knew I couldn't write about my real goals, so I made up a story about wanting to be the first one in my family to go to college and have a career, instead of staying on the farm where I had no opportunity to fulfill my dreams. The essay turned out so well, I almost believed it myself. I definitely wanted to leave the farm, so it was partially true, anyway. I felt a little bad for not being completely honest with Jenny, though. When she asked me why I had changed my mind about going to college, I told her that she had inspired me to pursue a career because I loved her independent spirit. That part was true. I did admire Jenny for pursuing her dreams, and for not needing anyone's approval. Jenny had always been an inspiration to me, since most girls in Possum Valley never aspired to do anything other than stay right there and repeat the same lives their parents had. I wondered if most of them even knew there were other options. I loved Mama and Daddy, but I didn't want to live their story. I wanted to write my own.

* * *

"College? Kathy, why on earth would you want to go to college, even if you did get a scholarship?" Daddy wasn't as thrilled about the possibility of my going to college as Jenny was when I brought it up after dinner that evening. "You belong here in Possum Valley, where you grew up, where all your family is.

They're all just a bunch of hippies out there in California."

"But Daddy, I could get a degree and have a career making good money," I argued, realizing it wasn't a bad idea, really.

"What kind of career would you have? You never said anything about a career," Daddy said.

"Kathy could do just about anything she set her mind to, Larry." Mama smiled and winked at me. "But, there's no need for you to go all the way out to California, honey. The University of Tennessee is just about an hour away. You could even commute from home," she continued.

Would they *ever* understand that I didn't want to be at home? I was desperately trying to escape from home. "Jenny is going to school out there, and UC Berkeley is a really good school," I said. "If I get accepted there with a scholarship, I will have lots of opportunities." I was just parroting what Jenny had told me, but it sounded good, so I went with it.

"You still haven't told us what kind of career you think you're going to have," Daddy said. I was getting frustrated. Didn't he want me to better myself?

"Well, I might want to be a writer for a newspaper or a magazine. That sounds like fun," I said. The idea of being a writer just came to me. I had never even thought of doing that, but it did sound like it could almost be fun.

"She'd make a good writer, Larry," Mama looked at me and smiled. "She's always been so good with words." I never thought of it before, but Mama seemed to want me to have a better life than hers. She never complained, but maybe she wanted more for Rita and me.

"I still say she'd be better off here on the farm where she belongs, instead of traipsing across the country." Daddy was slowly beginning to cave in, just a little. I could always tell by the tone of his voice. Now, a scholarship to Berkeley was all that stood between me and success, but I had a good feeling about it.

* * *

I decided not to tell Kevin about my decision to apply to UC Berkeley, because I didn't want to be embarrassed if I didn't get in. He was obviously very smart and had gone to the Air Force Academy, and I didn't want him to think of me as some redneck loser from Possum Valley. I was almost excited about the idea of going to college at this point. It had never occurred to me before that I would probably be more interesting to a rich guy (and to Kevin, of course) if I had a college degree. I knew that I was the intellectual equal of Kevin or just about any other guy I might meet, but *they* might not be aware of that. Honestly, I wasn't sure that being smart really mattered much to guys if a girl was pretty enough, but maybe it would give me an edge over the other pretty girls. After all, Kevin was going to be in California; I'd always heard there were lots of pretty girls with blonde hair and dark tans out there, so I might need more than just my looks to be competitive. Sure, Kevin liked me, but let's face it, I didn't have a ring on my finger...yet.

* * *

Kevin only had two days left in Possum Valley before he had to leave for California, and we had planned to spend our last night together (for now, anyway) having dinner at Ye Olde Steak House, a very popular restaurant in Knoxville that had been around since the '60s, and was known for having the best steak in town. After that, we were going to see the movie *E.T.* He had let me choose the movie, and I chose *E.T.* because I thought it would be something we would both enjoy. The time we had spent together went by quickly, but I felt like I had known Kevin for a long time. So much had happened since he arrived, and I felt like my life had become so much more interesting. I had met two great Air Force guys, and I became friends with the first black person I had ever met. I had been hiking in the mountains and had gone to the World's Fair. I had been to Regas, the nicest restaurant in Knoxville, twice, and I had possibly fallen in love. I wasn't sure how to tell if I was really in love, but all I knew was that I was truly going to miss Kevin, and I couldn't think about anything else besides going to California to be with him.

I had also seen how wrong and horrible racism was. Chris was a wonderful guy with a bright future. I couldn't help but wonder how often guys like Chris had to endure hatred due to the type of ignorance that had caused Heath and Henry to burn a cross in Jenny's yard. Heath and Henry were not charged for the cross burning, because there was supposedly no proof that they intended to intimidate or harm anyone. But justice was still served, since Henry had been found dead on Main Street after being struck by a car shortly after the brothers had been bailed out of jail by their sister Jean, who lived somewhere in Georgia. According to the police report, Henry had lain down in the middle of the street during one of his drinking binges. Most people in town didn't expect Heath to survive long without Henry; they had always been inseparable, in a twisted sort of way. At any rate, when Jean came up for Henry's funeral, she took Heath back to live with her. Everyone in town seemed to be happy he was gone, but we couldn't help from feeling a little sorry for Jean, who seemed like a decent person. Anyway, I was looking forward to seeing Chris again soon, if I was accepted to UC Berkeley. I wanted to tell him about how Heath and Henry had been punished for what they had done, even though they hadn't been charged with a crime by the law. I didn't know if it would make him feel any better, but it would make me feel a lot better. Obviously, I wasn't responsible for what Heath and Henry did, but I still felt bad because they were my neighbors.

* * *

Kevin arrived at my house for our last date before he had to leave with a dozen red roses. He obviously didn't know that yellow was my favorite color, as Mike did, but they were beautiful anyway. But the most impressive part about the roses was the vase. He had bought a black vase that had beautiful cherry blossoms hand-painted on it, at a shop near his aunt and uncle's house, he said. I was so happy I wanted to cry, not just because he was so thoughtful, but also because I would still have this beautiful vase after the flowers died. I had only gotten flowers once from Mike, so I felt a little sad when I had to throw out the wilted blooms that were once so beautiful. For some reason, it reminded me of a beautiful young girl growing old, her beauty fading as her skin wrinkled and her hair greyed, until she finally died. It seemed like such a waste. But having this vase to remind me of the flowers when they were beautiful and of Kevin bringing them to me was the perfect way to cheer me up. To think, I had actually considered never speaking to Kevin after the personal ad confusion. I was so glad that I had realized how perfect he was for me. I just wish Rita agreed. I had told Rita last night about my plans to go to UC Berkeley to be close to Kevin. She was the only person I had been completely honest with about the whole thing. On one hand, I didn't really want to tell her, but I couldn't help wanting an objective opinion about my plans. I knew Rita would be objective, because she always had been with me. And this time was no exception.

"You can't assume Kevin is your soul mate just because you and he both decided to go on a date with other people, and the other people ended up being the two of you," Rita said. "You're crazy to go to college, which doesn't even interest you, in *California*, which is on the other side of the nation, for a boy you barely even know."

I regretted telling Rita. She didn't understand anything. Her opinion wasn't objective this time. In fact, she was very biased, and obviously wanted me to be stuck in Possum Valley for the rest of my miserable existence just like her, I told her. She and I ended up having a big argument, and I honestly didn't care if I ever spoke to her again.

I wished I knew if I had been accepted to UC Berkeley so I could surprise Kevin with the news, but that would have to wait. I promised him that I would try to visit him in California as we had planned, and he seemed happy about that. Little did he know, if I had it my way, he would be seeing much more of me. We had a very nice meal at Ye Olde Steak House. The steaks there were as big as any cuts Daddy did for his customers, and the quality was almost as good. I had to admit, as much as I disliked farm life, Daddy had the best steaks anywhere. The movie made me cry, which wasn't what I was hoping for, since it messed up my mascara, but I loved it anyway. I wasn't sure if it was the movie or being with Kevin, but I thought it might have been the best movie I'd ever seen.

Kevin and I stood outside the car when we got back to the farm. The summer air was still sticky and hot, even though it was nearly midnight. It was a clear night, with a blanket of stars lighting up the black sky, and it would have been the perfect backdrop for a romantic finish to a perfect evening—except for the mosquitos. Mosquitos were always bad around the farm in the summer because of the pond in the back. *Just my luck, they are out in force tonight.* I had worn a white sleeveless top with some khaki shorts, so they had plenty of flesh to ravish.

Mosquitos had always seemed to have a special affinity for me, and I was having trouble standing still as they feasted on my bare skin. I'd recently read somewhere that mosquitos urinated on their victims after biting them, and I was trying hard not to think about that as I attempted to casually knock them off me. I usually avoided being outside on the farm at night in the summers, but I didn't want to go inside and risk waking Daddy. I usually worried about him appearing with his shotgun when I brought a boy in late at night, but with Kevin, I worried more that he would want to strike up a conversation about ammunition or some past war, since he liked Kevin so much. Daddy was very patriotic, and I think he really admired that Kevin was in the Air Force. The fact that Daddy liked the guy I was interested in made me feel a sense of pride, for some reason.

"Are you OK, Kathy?" Kevin asked in a sympathetic tone. "You seem fidgety this evening."

I didn't want to tell him that the mosquitos were eating me alive, because I desperately wanted to stay out there under the stars with him and talk. I was determined to not allow the blood-sucking vermin to spoil the moment.

"I'm fine," I lied. "I'm just thinking about how much I will miss you when you're gone." That part was true.

He pulled me close to him and gently kissed me. "We're together right now, so let's take advantage of that." He kissed me again, harder this time until we were both consumed with desire much fiercer than I had ever felt before. We couldn't get enough of each other as he pushed me up against his car and reached for my shorts.

"We can't, Kevin." I pleaded. "There's just a thin layer of fiberglass between us and Daddy, and he would kill us both, literally."

"Let's go somewhere, then." He kissed me passionately again.

"I'm sorry, but I can't. I'm just not that kind of girl." It sounded so trite and stupid, but I didn't know any other way to tell him that I was worth more than a quick moment in a car somewhere.

"I know you aren't," he pressed. "You really mean something to me, Kathy."

"In that case, you won't mind waiting," I said. I tried my best to sound confident, but I was terrified he was going to hate me now. But Daddy had always told Rita and me that his girls deserved a boy that was willing to wait until marriage, and if we gave out free milk, nobody would want the cow. Of course his analogy was farm-related, but it did make sense.

He looked deeply into my eyes as if he was carefully considering whether

I was serious or not. I stared back at him boldly, making sure he knew I was indeed serious. "You sure have a mind of your own, Sakura. I like that about you."

He smiled and put his hands on my shoulders, keeping me at arm's length. "You are beautiful, you know. And you're one hundred percent worth the wait. I just hope you won't keep me waiting too long."

Whew! That was close. Guys had hit on me before, naturally, but this was the only time I was tempted. It was hard to say no because I didn't want to disappoint him—but also because I didn't *want* to say no. Maybe this was what love felt like.

Chapter 14

THREE MONTHS LATER

Hurry, Kathy!" Mama called from the kitchen. "You're going to miss your flight."

I could tell she had been crying all night when I walked into the room carrying my last piece of luggage. She and Daddy had bought a set of Samsonite luggage for me as a gift for getting a scholarship to UC Berkeley. I had actually won a couple of scholarships, enough to pay for the tuition, room, and board. One of them was a hardship scholarship that took into consideration my parents' income, as well as my grades. Daddy didn't like the idea of a "handout" as he called it, but I explained to him that I wouldn't have gotten it if I hadn't been at the top of my class academically. I was the salutatorian, right behind Jenny, who was our valedictorian. I owed a lot to Jenny: not only did she push me to attend college, she had pushed me in school because she believed I could do it. I was behind her by less than a point. Perhaps I could have even surpassed her, if I had really tried, but I knew how much being valedictorian meant to her. I didn't even plan to go to college at the time, so I didn't try quite as hard as I could have. Of course, I would never tell Jenny that I could have probably surpassed her. Things were perfect just as they were, and I had no reason to compete with my best friend.

"Mama, you've been crying." I put my suitcase down and put on my shoes. "You said you weren't going to do that."

The sun was beaming through the kitchen window, exposing a dirty film on the glass as I looked out into the back yard, avoiding Mama's tear-streaked face. The maple tree outside was a brilliant yellow, almost blinding, as the sun glistened down on it. Autumn was always beautiful in East Tennessee. It was my favorite time of year, at least until spring rolled around, and then spring was my favorite. They were both so spectacular with the colorful trees and flowers, it was too hard to choose one and stick with it. Fall had come a little early this year because of the cool temperatures. The trees in the back yard were already adorned with shades of yellow, red, and orange, and fallen leaves were scattered all around them, making the perfect autumn scene. I thought about raking leaves with Rita when we were younger, making big piles and then jumping in them. We had to rake them several times because we kept scattering them each time we jumped. We were always so happy, just playing outside under the trees in the crisp, autumn air. We had no idea we were poor back then. We had everything we needed, and entertainment was as simple as a pile of leaves.

I reluctantly turned back toward Mama as she walked toward me. "I-I know, Kathy, but what am I gonna do without you?" She buried her face in my shoulder, getting my new red sweater wet. I didn't wear red much, because it wasn't one of the colors listed on the color wheel for my skin tone, but I wanted to wear something bold to begin my brave, new odyssey.

"Mama, you know I'll be back to visit. Besides, you said yourself this is a great opportunity for me," I said, gently lifting her head off my shoulder. I didn't want to be rude, but the sweater was dry clean only.

"You're right. I want you to be happy. And Kathy, I want you to know I'm proud of you. I could never do what you're doing. You're so fearless." She lifted her head up and straightened her shoulders, drying her eyes with her nicotine-stained hands. "I will miss you, but I know you're ready for this."

"Thanks, Mama." A part of me felt like maybe I was doing this for her too, her and all the women here in the valley. Maybe my leaving would pave the way for others in the future. "Where's Daddy?" I suddenly realized I hadn't seen him all morning. "He's coming to the airport with me, right?"

"Daddy went to the Co-op to get some feed," she said hesitantly. "He didn't need any, but Kathy, he's not handling your move well, honey. He's always been so crazy about you, you know. He just couldn't stay around without gettin' all choked up, and your daddy's not one to cry."

It was true. I had never seen Daddy cry once. Not even when his daddy passed away. On the surface, it didn't seem that Daddy cared much for me at all, always buying me things I didn't want like guns and trucks... But I knew how much he loved me. He was big and smelly and annoying, but he was my daddy, and I loved him too. And on some strange level that I couldn't explain, I was even proud of him. He had the best cuts of meat around, he worked harder than anybody I knew, and he took pride in what he did. He was living his dream, and deep down, I admired him for it, even though I didn't understand it.

"Jenny and her parents will be here soon. I wanted to tell him bye." My voice cracked. I hadn't expected to cry. I had been wanting to leave for years, but the tears were suddenly streaming down my face like a waterfall. How could I leave without telling Daddy goodbye?

"He left you a note." Mama handed me a sheet of notebook paper folded over once. I opened it, trying to wipe the tears away so I could see to read it.

Dear Kathy,

I know you need to do this, and I won't try to stop you, as much as I'd like to. I've worked you hard over the years, but it's because I knew you could handle it. You've made me proud. I know you'll succeed at whatever you try to do, but if you ever want to come back home, there will always be a place for you here.

Love,

Daddy

It was a simple note, but I knew it was hard for him to write. All these years, I thought he was disappointed that he didn't have a boy to help him with the farm, so it meant a lot to me to know that he valued me and believed in me. Daddy never expressed his feelings for us well. His generation just didn't do that. I longed to hug him and tell him how much I loved him, but some things you feel so much, you don't have to say them.

A car pulled up just as I folded the paper and stuck it in the outside pocket of my suitcase. "Mama, Jenny's here," I said somberly.

Rita appeared from her room and ran over to hug me. "You know I'm going to inherit your manure hauling and pig feeding duties." Tears were streaming down her face as she grabbed me and hugged me tightly. "I'm going to miss you."

"Of course you'll miss me; you'll be doing my chores," I joked, trying to lighten the mood.

Mama came over and put her arms around both of us. "We're all going to miss you, baby."

I had wanted to leave Possum Valley for as long as I could remember, so the fact that I was nearly hyperventilating was surprising. Leaving was harder than I ever imagined. I wasn't giving up anything...well, nothing except everything I'd ever known. There was a knock on the door, and I immediately pulled away from Rita and Mama, dried my eyes, and went to answer it. *Jenny's timing is perfect*, I thought, as I walked toward the door. All the crying was ruining my makeup.

"Jenny, you're right on time," I said as I opened the door. But it wasn't Jenny. It was Mike.

"People tell me I look like Jenny, but I don't think I'm as purty," Mike joked as he stepped inside.

"Sorry, Mike," I said. "I wasn't expecting you."

I really wasn't expecting Mike, and didn't want to see him. I didn't want to think about him, or the fact that I was going to miss him, too. I had known Mike all my life, and we'd been close growing up, but I didn't want all this drama. Where was Jenny, anyway?

"Kathy, I couldn't let you leave without sayin' goodbye," he said.

"Oh, Mike, I wanted to get together," I lied. "But I've just been so busy with everything."

"I know," he said, but I could see the hurt in his eyes. "I brought you somethin' that I hope you'll like." He handed me a small box wrapped in purple paper with a big, yellow ribbon on top. "Go ahead and open it," he said.

I took off the ribbon, being careful to save it. We had always reused ribbons at my house, but I thought I might just save this one and not use it again; it was so pretty. I tore open the paper, and there was a cassette tape inside. I was surprised, because I didn't expect him to give me music. He knew I already had all the Eagles and Fleetwood Mac cassette tapes, and I didn't really like any other bands enough to buy their music. I was even more surprised, though, when I looked at the label. It was Mike. He was standing in front of a corn field with a cowboy hat on. *Mike Ledbetter* was printed in big letters at the top of the cover, with *Love Left Me Scarred* at the bottom.

"Mike!" I couldn't contain my excitement, and I grabbed him and squeezed him hard before I realized what I was doing. "You've got an album! How did this happen? And why didn't we know about it?" The tears were coming fast and hard again. I was so happy for Mike. He had achieved his dream. I knew he had the talent, but never believed he had the initiative to actually make an album.

"It's a surprise." He grinned sheepishly, showing his dimples. I could see why all the girls liked him. He was so talented and good looking, but didn't even seem to know it. "I recorded the music and sent it to some record labels in Nashville a while back, and now I've signed a contract." He shrugged as if it wasn't a big deal.

"Do you mean I may be hearing your music on the radio out in California?" I asked, my heart nearly leaping from my chest.

"With any luck you will, but I'm giving you the cassette tape just in case," he said, then winked.

"Oh, I have a strong feeling we'll all be hearing you on the radio soon," Mama walked over and hugged Mike. "We're so proud of you. I always knew you'd be a big star someday."

"Very proud of you," Rita agreed, looking at me. "Do you know what this means? You're gonna have to fight the girls off with a stick, as if you don't already."

"I guess I'll just have to manage somehow," Mike smiled. Dimples again. I never realized until now how much I liked those dimples.

Jenny knocked on the door just as I was trying to regain my composure. I had so many emotions, my head was swimming and my heart was pounding. I wanted to leave Possum Valley, but was I really doing the right thing? I loved my family, and Mike was so...so what? I felt so confused. But he was pursuing his dream, and I had to do the same. Maybe that's why I was confused about my feelings. I was so proud of Mike for trying to better himself, and not limit himself to Possum Valley when he had so much more to offer. And I'd never been away from Mama, Daddy, and Rita. I was sure it was normal to feel this way.

"Jenny, come in, honey. We're all just standing around crying because Kathy's leaving, and celebrating because Mike has recorded his first album," Mama said, as she opened the door.

I was never happier to see Jenny than I was then. She would put everything back into perspective for me. I was going to be a college student at Berkeley, and I was going to marry the guy of my dreams. I just had to stay focused on my goals, that was all.

"An album? Are you serious? That's amazing, Mike!" Jenny exclaimed, looking at me as if she was trying to determine how this news was affecting me. Why did both Rita and Jenny look at *me* when they congratulated Mike about his album? Had they been talking to Fannie?

Jenny walked over and put her arm around me. "You're not going to back out, are you, Kathy?"

"Why would I back out?" I said a bit too defiantly. "I'm ready to go right now."

I felt the tears stinging my eyes again, as I desperately tried to hold them back. I needed to get out of here. I couldn't breathe. Why did Mike have to come over and tell us this right as I was leaving, anyway? He could've done it yesterday, or last week. *Why now*? This was too much to deal with. I didn't even really care, though. Why would I care about his album? Of course, I was happy for him, but that was it. It didn't affect my life in any way.

So, why couldn't I stop thinking about those dimples?

* * *

Don and Peggy left us at McGee Tyson Airport in Knoxville after tearful goodbyes. I was both terrified and excited to embark upon my new life, knowing I was leaving everything I knew behind me with no idea of what might lie ahead. But as I looked around at all the other people on the plane who seemed to be going places and living a life so foreign to mine so far, I was certain that I had made the right decision. I could never live the life I wanted if I stayed in Possum Valley. There was so much to do and see, and I wanted so much more out of life than a pig farm. This was my big chance, and nothing was going to stop me.

"Are you OK?" Jenny asked as we took off.

"I feel great, Jenny," I said, my heart turning flips. "My whole life is out there waiting for me." I sort of believed what I said, but I felt more scared than

I ever had in my life. Leaving everything behind was much harder than I had imagined.

"I know you're afraid, Kathy," Jenny put her hand on my arm as the plane took off. "It's OK, though. I'm scared too, but if we never do anything that scares us, we're never going to do anything."

I was so glad Jenny was with me. She always knew what to say.

As the plane approached San Francisco, the pilot got on the intercom and told us we should be able to see the Golden Gate Bridge from the left side of the plane. Jenny had let me have the window seat since I had never flown before, so I looked out my window, and there it was. It was so much bigger and more beautiful than I remembered from pictures and television, stretching out over the bay against the brilliant, blue sky. I was sure I'd never seen a sky so blue. As we continued descending, I saw the tall buildings of the city, surrounded by water. It was the most beautiful thing I'd ever seen.

Chapter 15

Jenny had arranged for a taxi to pick us up at the airport and take us into the city for dinner before we headed to Berkeley. I couldn't believe it when I saw all the yellow taxis lined up outside along the street, just like in a movie. I felt like a new puppy experiencing the world for the first time, staggering around and trying to take in all the sights and sounds. Nothing I had ever seen in Knoxville or anywhere else had prepared me for this place. As we drove into the city, I was mesmerized by all the tall buildings and the picturesque Victorian houses. And all the *people*. There were droves of people everywhere I looked. I couldn't believe people really lived this way, so close to the gorgeous bay and the magnificent Golden Gate Bridge. Jenny had the taxi driver take us by the Painted Ladies, the colorful Victorian homes across from Alamo Square Park. I asked him to stop at the park so I could take some pictures. "It will only take me a minute to find my camera in my luggage," I assured the driver, as he opened the trunk for me to retrieve my suitcase.

"Kathy, we'll be back here plenty of times." Jenny laughed at my childish excitement, as I frantically looked for my camera. "Berkeley isn't far from here, you know." I had to have the photos right then, though. I wanted to send them to Rita and to Mike. Mike's parents would love the architecture here, since their home was modeled after a less impressive version of a Victorian home.

After I got my pictures and tried unsuccessfully to really soak up all the beauty being thrust at me, Jenny asked the taxi driver to take us down Lombard Street. I had never heard of it, but it didn't disappoint. More beautiful homes and landscaping lined the amazingly crooked street. I took pictures of everything as we drove along. "Jenny, we have to come back soon." I grabbed her leg and squeezed hard. "I am so excited! Oh, and I have to ride on one of the cable cars, and go to China Town." I felt alive for the first time, and I never wanted to leave this amazing city.

"I promise we'll be back, Kathy," Jenny assured me. "This is one of my favorite cities. I'll enjoy showing you around."

Our last stop for the evening was a seafood restaurant on Fisherman's Wharf. I had never seen so many people. There were street performers, tourists, and homeless people everywhere, and I couldn't believe I was really there, right in the middle of it all.

* * *

I was in Berkeley for a whole month before I saw Kevin again. He was busy with his new job at Travis Air Force Base, which was about forty miles northeast of Berkeley, and I had been busy getting used to life as a college student. Kevin seemed excited when I told him I was coming to California to attend UC Berkeley and would be less than an hour away from him, but there was something strange in his voice that I couldn't discern. Maybe it was just that it was such a shock. I could still barely comprehend it myself. Everything about my life was different, and I still couldn't believe I was really in California. It was nothing like I had imagined. My only knowledge of California came from television shows, like *The Beverley Hillbillies*. Central California, where we were, was very different from the landscape of Los Angeles that I had seen on TV. Outside San Francisco, there was so much natural beauty to see, from massive redwood trees to breathtaking mountains, and rugged cliffs hanging over the Pacific Ocean like giant claws reaching down into the wild blue depths.

Berkeley was a quaint, artsy town with plenty of nice shops and restaurants. Jenny and I rented an old house off campus that was used for student housing. The people here were very different from anyone I had ever known. In some ways they were strange, but mostly I thought they were cool. Many were creative and eccentric like Mama's friend Jolene and her sister, Candy, but they were also very politically active and fought for causes that were important to them, like abortion and nuclear war. I admired their enthusiasm and passion, even if

I didn't always agree with them. The only time I had ever seen anything similar to a protest was when a landfill was scheduled to be placed on the outskirts of town in Possum Valley. The mayor and most of our citizens had a rally at the proposed dump site, equipped with a microphone and podium, a local bluegrass band, and plenty of signs with the pictures of animated grinning possums with fists raised in the air like the one that adorned our welcome sign, only these possums were in the midst of a trash pile. Tire tracks ran across them, with a caption that read *Don't tread on me.* Sherriff Turner was there to keep the peace, because most people had guns in their trucks and weren't afraid to use them. Fortunately, the opposition didn't show up. But the local newspaper reporter, Jim Jenkins, was there to get the story. The dump still went in a year or so later, but not without a battle. Daddy said, "You may not be able to fight the system and win, but you can sure give 'em a fight they won't forget."

I had to admit I even enjoyed being a student, even though I wasn't sure how algebra would ever benefit my life, since I never used what I had learned in high school. The only math I really used other than basic addition and subtraction was percentages, so that I could figure up how much a dress or a pair of shoes would cost if the price was marked down a certain percentage. But even algebra might be more beneficial than the philosophy class I was taking. Did a falling tree make a sound, if no one was around to hear it? Well, of course it did, but I wasn't sure why I needed to know that. My classes were interesting though, and the more I learned, the more I realized there was a lot I didn't know. I still had my objective of getting married, but I was glad I had chosen to go to college. Our professors told us there was nothing we couldn't do if we had the desire, and they treated us like we were the future and the hope of America. And I was beginning to believe it.

Back in Possum Valley, our teachers' expectations for us were very low in comparison, and I thought that was part of the reason people there didn't achieve anything. They had no one to believe in them and their abilities. I had no plans to ever go back to Possum Valley, now that I knew how much I had been missing. I felt sorry for Mama, Daddy, and Rita, wasting away on that old farm. The most exciting thing that ever happened around there was a cow getting out of the fence or a funeral fight. Well, maybe I sort of missed the quiet nights there, where all I heard were crickets, and all I saw were stars in the still, dark sky. Here, there were cars and people making noise all hours of the night, it seemed. And the people. The people in Possum Valley might not have been as educated and cultured (OK, not even close), but they were mostly good people with morals and convictions. They didn't go around demonstrating and protesting on a regular basis like they did at Berkeley, but when you weren't sure if you were going to have money for food or electricity the following week, most everything else (like protesting the removal of a tree) seemed trivial. I had learned in one of my classes that according to some guy named Abraham Maslow, basic human needs such as food, clothing, and shelter had to be met before an individual would desire secondary or higher-level needs like self-esteem and reaching his potential. I felt I could understand this theory better than most, because people here couldn't comprehend the kind of poverty that existed in Possum Valley. In fact, I felt so far removed from it now, it was hard for me to believe it myself sometimes. Poor country people didn't think they had the power to change things, so they often didn't try. It seemed like I had to come all the way to California to understand the people that I grew up with in Tennessee. Sometimes when I lay in bed thinking about all the people back in Possum Valley, my people, I wondered if it was my duty to go back and try to make a difference. But I decided it wasn't my problem. I cared, but not enough to go back there.

* * *

I had some free time that weekend, so Jenny and I were driving up on Sunday to surprise Kevin. I had told him I would be studying all weekend, so he wouldn't be expecting me. I knew he would be in town though, because he said he was just going to hang around the new apartment that he had rented off base, and watch football all weekend. I was so excited to see him again. As much as I loved California and had plenty to keep me busy, I had to stay focused on my marriage goal. I needed to keep up my grades to maintain my scholarships, so I was trying my best, but I was ready to work on my primary mission: a husband. We had driven down Highway 1 to Big Sur along the coast last weekend, and Jenny had to stop multiple times so I could take pictures. I used up three rolls of film. I had never seen anything so beautiful as the brilliantly blue, white-capped waves from the Pacific Ocean, crashing against enormous rocks and exploding like fireworks. Every time we stopped, I tried my best to take in all the beauty and truly appreciate it, but it was too vast and overwhelming to process all of it at once. I felt that I was as close to seeing Heaven as I had ever been. I couldn't help thinking about Mama, Daddy, and Rita, and how much they would love it here. California might as well be another planet for them, though. Life for them didn't exist beyond the south, and it made me sad for them.

As we drove up to Fairfield, where Kevin lived, I got to see more of the golden mountains contrasting against the backdrop of the unblemished, blue sky. I had fallen in love with California and already felt like I belonged here. The only thing that would make it better was being there with Kevin. Since we lived less than an hour away from each other, I hoped we could see each other every weekend, now that we were both settled in. The closer we got to Fairfield, the more excited I became. I had worn my new outfit, which I'd bought in San Francisco at the first Macy's I had ever seen. It was a lavender cotton shirt that came off the shoulder on one side with a black tank top underneath, a black skirt that stopped just above the knees, and a pair of black tights with tiny lavender hearts on them. Macy's had the most beautiful clothes, and I couldn't wait to be wealthy enough to afford a lot more of them. Everything was so new and exciting for me. I truly felt like Ellie May on the *Beverly Hillbillies*, dragging Jenny around to every new store and landmark I saw. Watching that show growing up, I couldn't have imagined that life could truly be so different from Possum Valley.

Fairfield was a small city not far from Napa Valley, which was also on my to-do list. Kevin's apartment building was nestled in a wooded area near a shopping center. I suddenly felt nervous as we got out of the car. It was around eleven a.m. on Saturday, and my plan was to just show up and knock on the door, hoping he would be home. I knew he would be awake because he had told me he always got up early—and who slept until eleven, anyway? I still had trouble sleeping past six a.m., no matter how late I stayed up, after living with Daddy for all those years.

"Do you think it's OK to just knock on the door, Jenny? What if he isn't dressed or something?" I asked.

"I'm sure he'll throw something on before answering the door," she laughed.

"Are you nervous?"

"Well, yes, a little," I admitted. "I haven't seen Kevin in four months."

"True," she said. "But you've cost him a small fortune talking on the phone almost every night. It'll be fine, I promise."

But it wasn't.

I softly knocked on the door half hoping he wouldn't hear it. The door opened after a few seconds, and a pretty girl around my age with brunette hair was standing there in an oversized shirt. I was sure I had the apartment number Kevin had given me, number 311, but it couldn't be. There was a pretty brunette at the door, and I was standing there staring at her.

"Can I help you?" she asked.

"Sorry, but we must have the wrong apartment," Jenny spoke up. "We're looking for Kevin Murphy."

"No, Kevin lives here," she said.

Just then, Kevin walked up behind her. Behind the pretty brunette that I couldn't stop staring at. Why was there a *girl* in his apartment at eleven a.m. on Saturday, in an oversized shirt? I felt as if I were frozen, unable to think or move.

"Kathy, Jenny." Kevin's voice was notably higher pitched. "What are you doing here?"

Not the welcome I had expected.

I finally opened my mouth, still unsure what to say. "We, um, we wanted to surprise you." And I was pretty sure we had accomplished that. My eyes were starting to well up. I couldn't cry. Crying would only make this horrible situation even worse.

"Girls, this is Brandy." He said too cautiously. "She's, uh…a friend." He looked at her, his eyes desperate.

"Great," I said, choosing to get angry over being the pathetic, crying victim I felt like. "Well, we won't intrude on you and your *friend*, Kevin. We'll just go now."

"And who did you say you were?" Brandy smiled a wide sarcastic smile.

I glared at her, my mountain upbringing almost bubbling over into a screaming, fighting rage, until I felt Jenny's hand on my arm.

"Let's just go, Kathy. They aren't worth your time," she said, as she tugged at my wrist.

"You just got here though," Kevin said, as he walked toward me. "I wasn't expecting you today, but it's fine. It's great to see you. Come in and stay a while."

I grabbed Jenny's arm. "We're leaving now." I had to get away from him before I had a breakdown. I turned and started walking away, Jenny by my side. She didn't say anything. She just held onto my arm as we walked slowly to the car.

"Don't go, Kathy," he called after me. "You don't understand."

But I did. I had been a fool. Tears flooded my cheeks like I had turned on a faucet.

We were in the car before Jenny said anything.

"Come here." She reached over and hugged me. "Are you OK?"

"I can't believe I was so stupid, Jenny," I began. "I should've known he was a player after the incident at Regas. I tried to tell myself I had done the same thing by planning to meet a blind date that night, but it was different for me. You know I'd been planning on writing that personal ad forever, and it meant something to me. He probably has a girl in every town. He made me think I was special, and I fell for it. Let's just get out of here."

Jenny started the car and pulled out of the parking lot. "First of all," she said as she pulled out on the highway, "you are special, Kathy." Jenny got a napkin out of her console and handed it to me. I blew my nose, snot going everywhere. "Secondly, you can do way better than him, anyway. You are so pretty and smart. You're going to Cal Berkeley on a scholarship, Kathy. That is special. You don't need any guy."

But I did. I needed a guy. I wanted one. I didn't want to depend on myself like Jenny did. I wanted the security that a man would provide. Jenny couldn't understand, because she'd never been poor like I was.

"We're apart for four months, and he already has another girl. Why couldn't he have told me? I wouldn't be going to college right now..." Oops. It just came out. "I mean..."

Jenny pulled over and stopped the car. "Kathy, please don't tell me you went to all the trouble to get into Berkeley just to be near Kevin." She looked at me with big, saucer-like eyes.

"Well, Jenny, I...I kind of wanted to go to college, kind of wanted to be near Kevin," I stammered. "I wanted both...you know, like wanting to have your cake and eat it too." I looked at her and smiled sheepishly, knowing she couldn't stay mad at me.

"You are so pathetic." She rolled her eyes. "Why do I hang out with you?"

Then she laughed. She kept laughing until I started laughing too. We sat there and just laughed for several minutes. Only Jenny could make me laugh at a time like this.

Finally, she stopped. "I should've known you didn't want to go to college. You are so crazy, Kathy. You are probably the only girl on earth that goes to a college like Cal Berkeley just to be close to a guy."

It did seem pretty ridiculous when she said it out loud just now. Plus, I was making good grades and handling college life just fine. Maybe I really didn't need a man. At least not right now.

"Sorry I lied to you," I said. "I love you, and guess what?"

"What?" She rolled her eyes again.

"I'm going to finish college," I said. What I said next really surprised me, but I could be so impetuous sometimes, and it usually came back to haunt me. "I'm going to finish, because I really don't need a man. I think I can do this."

"You definitely can, Kathy," she smiled. "That's what I've been trying to tell you."

I suddenly felt a little better, but I could still have used one of Mama's conciliatory hot dogs that she always made for Rita and me when we were sad. I had tried making hot dogs once since we had arrived in Berkeley, but they weren't the same as Mama's.

Chapter 16

THE NEXT DAY

The phone rang again as I was leaving for English Comp I, my last class of the day. I wanted to arrive early because our essays were due. I had just finished mine on the future of genetic engineering late the night before. We had received our assigned topics over a week ago, but I had been putting it off. Genetic engineering was somewhat interesting, but because I wasn't familiar with it, I had to do far more research than I ever had for an essay. When I wrote a paper, I just wanted to sit down and write, not spend hours at the library researching. Luckily, the library stayed open all night, because I had waited the day before it was due to even get started on it. I wasn't optimistic that it was any good. I wanted to get to class early to turn it in, so it would be on the bottom of the pile. Our professor liked to pick an essay at random from the pile of papers and read it aloud, picking it apart and embarrassing the writer, even though his or her name was never revealed. Somehow, it was still humiliating, sitting there in the middle of everyone, knowing it was your paper he was scrutinizing. I had made A's on the previous essays, but I was still afraid of mine being chosen and dissected in front of the class. He seemed to always pick one from near the top of the stack, so I wanted to make sure mine was at the bottom.

I waited long enough for the answering machine to pick up though before I walked out the door. Just as I thought, it was Kevin again. This was call number eight of the day. I hadn't returned any of his calls, and I had promised Jenny that I wouldn't in a moment of weakness. Each time he left a message, I came closer to calling him back because his messages were so sweet and apologetic.

He said he had just been so lonely and couldn't bear another day without me, so he had turned to this girl Brandy for companionship until he and I were able to be together again. It had been four long months, and he had been here all alone in a stressful new job, after all. One message said he couldn't live without me and that he had never met anyone like me before.

"Kathy, it's me again." This message sounded even more sincere and remorseful than the others. "Brandy didn't mean anything to me, and I told her I could never see her again, and I meant it. I will never see her or speak to her again. Kathy, I'll do anything you say, if you'll just give me another chance. I know I don't deserve you, but..." And then he said it. Those three little words that I longed to hear. Those magical words that melted my heart like the sun melts chocolate, and then it's deformed and misshapen and never the same afterwards. "I love you, Kathy." That was it. I shouldn't have done it. Jenny would be very angry with me. I knew better. I would be late for class. But I couldn't resist. I picked up the phone.

"Hi, Kevin," I said.

"Kathy." His voice was so sweet and tender. "Thank God, you picked up. I was getting ready to drive to Berkeley tonight and get down on my knees. Kathy, honey, I am so sorry. Please give me another chance." And that was all it took. He was forgiven. I would finish college as I had promised Jenny, but I needed a man. I *had* to have a man.

* * *

Kevin came to visit me the following Saturday, and we drove to San Francisco. We walked around Chinatown for a while, and then went to Macy's to do some shopping. I still couldn't believe I was shopping at Macy's, my new favorite store. I had never seen so many beautiful clothes, shoes, and handbags. I picked up a pair of Calvin Klein jeans, and Kevin insisted I try them on and model them for him. The jeans were so tight, I could barely walk—or breathe, for that matter—but Kevin assured me that they were supposed to be tight. When I came back out of the dressing room with the jeans in hand, he grabbed them from me and insisted on buying them. He said I looked better in them than Brooke Shields, which made me blush...and smile. After he bought the jeans, we looked at sunglasses. He tried on a pair of Wayfarers, like the ones worn by the Blues Brothers. I told him he looked better in them than Dan Aykroyd. He laughed and decided to buy them too. He was obviously making a decent salary in the Air Force, and it felt good to walk out of Macy's for the second time with shopping bags, plural. It was yet another dream come true for me.

We went to dinner at a romantic Italian restaurant with white tablecloths. But I knew exactly which fork to use when, and I felt like I had it all under control...until I saw the menu. I didn't know how to pronounce most of the entrees, so I ordered some type of ravioli, since I was familiar with that. Of course, my idea of ravioli was Chef Boyardee from a can. That was a far cry from what I had ordered, which was stuffed with what appeared to be some kind of mushrooms and cheese. I just stuffed it in my mouth and didn't ask questions. Luckily, it tasted very good, even though I couldn't tell for sure what it was. Then we went to see the musical *Nightingale*, which was a beautiful love story. It was a fairy tale date for me, where everything was new and exciting. It was such a perfect evening I had forgotten about whatsherwhiskeyname in Kevin's apartment last weekend. None of that seemed to matter now.

We had a wonderful, intellectual conversation about the musical all the way back to Berkeley. Kevin was the only guy with whom I could discuss literary devices like themes and motifs. I had planned and trained for these types of discussions since I was twelve, and I felt like all my dreams were finally coming true. Kevin thought the theme of the musical was money can't buy happiness, but I thought it was that love is the most precious gift we can give. We were both right to some degree, but I thought my interpretation was more romantic (and slightly more accurate). Needless to say, this was my first musical, and I couldn't believe how talented the musicians and actors were. Kevin always opened me up to new experiences, and that was one of the things I loved most about him.

Jenny, on the other hand, was still not fond of Kevin. She was so angry when she had found out that I was talking to Kevin again. I tried to explain to her how that he was just lonely and the girl meant nothing to him, but she called me gullible and said I was letting him take advantage of me. Maybe I was, but I wasn't like Jenny. Jenny was so independent and sure of herself; she didn't need a guy to validate her or to fulfill her life. I did. My plans had included a man for as long as I could remember, and I was too afraid to change them now.

Besides, Kevin promised he would never let me down again, and I believed him, of course.

The next day, Kevin took me to the Golden Gate Park in San Francisco. We strolled hand in hand through the Botanical Garden, where we were greeted with a symphony of colors from a host of trees, plants, and flowers. The bay air was cool and misty as the fog rolled through the park like sea waves. When we arrived at the Japanese Tea Garden, we stopped at the Tea House for a cup of green tea since we were still a little chilled. I admitted to Kevin that I had never tried green tea before, and didn't know that there were houses just for tea. He laughed and assured me that I would enjoy it.

"You are the most interesting girl I've ever known, Kathy," he said, as a young Japanese woman in a kimono very carefully placed a porcelain pot of tea and two small cups with cherry blossoms painted on them in front of us. She was the most elegant person I'd ever seen, gliding across the room, her arms and hands flowing with precision and grace. I was trying to remember if I had ever met a Japanese person before. Maybe at the World's Fair. Kevin picked up the teapot and poured bright green tea into my cup and then into his.

"You're lying," I laughed. "What on earth could possibly interest you about someone like me?"

"Please don't take this as an insult," he said. "In fact, it's more of a compliment. It feels like I get to introduce the whole world to you, as someone might to a foreign student or even a child. Everything is so new and exciting to you. The other girls I've dated have already seen and tried most everything, but life seems to just be unfolding for you, and seeing the world through your eyes reminds me how much I take for granted. I love your excitement and enthusiasm for life, Kathy. It's contagious."

"You must think I'm so naïve," I said, half insulted and half impressed by how observant he was.

He leaned in closer to the table. "You probably are a little naïve, but what's wrong with that? It's refreshing. I get to be the one to show you things and experience them with you for your first time, and I love to see your innocent response. That's it. You're not naïve, but innocent and untainted." He pointed to my cup. "Try your tea, before it gets cold."

Great. Saying I'm innocent and untainted was another way of saying I'm an idiot. Children were supposed to be innocent, not someone my age. I carefully picked up the cup, trying to be very graceful and delicate like our Japanese server, and sipped the tea. It was so bitter, I had to quickly swallow to avoid spewing it out. I was raised on a pig farm, so grace obviously didn't come easily for me. But it was true. I was more like a child that had no training and no experience with life. I had never tried green tea or sushi, never seen a Japanese garden or a botanical garden. In fact, they didn't exist in my world. My life had been all about making a living and helping other people get by. Fun for us was having a day off and sitting in the doublewide, eating a bag of Doritos while watching Andy Griffith reruns or lying in the sun on the redwood deck slathered in baby oil. A park to us was a place with swings and slides, and maybe a lake for fishing and boating, for those lucky enough to afford a boat. We had no idea there were parks with tea gardens and thousands of varieties of flowers and trees from around the globe. There were no five-star restaurants in our world, and no musicals and orchestras. How could two people who live in the same country have such different lives? Even though I had studied books and magazines, familiarizing myself with how rich people lived, I couldn't have possibly known about all the things that people did and drank and ate outside Possum Valley. I really did feel like a foreigner or a child, and for me it was more embarrassing than refreshing.

"Do you like it?" Kevin asked, as he carefully took another sip from his cup.

I wanted to lie and say I liked it, but I was almost certain I wasn't going to be able to finish it without being sick. People in the south drank their tea with sugar, lots and lots of sugar. I looked around at the table, which was bare, except for our teapot and cups. Where was the sugar? Restaurants back home had sugar on the tables for tea, even though the tea already had enough sugar in it to put a person in a diabetic coma. *Sweet* tea. The sweeter, the better. But I wasn't sure if any amount of sugar would make green tea taste good. How did they drink this stuff, and how did it become so popular that there were special houses for it? I thought it needed to be in a burial ground.

"I think it's probably an acquired taste," I smiled. "I haven't acquired it just yet."

He laughed. "That's OK. I thought about having sushi for lunch, but maybe we'll save that experience for another day. There are so many things I want you to try, but we have plenty of time."

I nodded. Part of me wanted to try sushi, but one thing at a time sounded like a good idea, especially when it involved raw fish. I had probably eaten plenty of things Kevin hadn't tried, like cow tongue and pig's feet, but they were always well done. Daddy didn't believe in eating raw meat. And to be honest, neither did I.

When Kevin finished his tea, we walked toward the gift shop. I forgot all about the bitter tea as we approached beautiful miniature trees, flowering bushes, and stunning cherry blossoms surrounding a tranquil waterfall. We stopped on a little curved bridge over a small lake bordered by perfectly manicured plants and looked out at the peaceful scenery. He took me in his arms and kissed me until I felt like I would melt. He took my face in his hands, looking at me deeply with those piercing blue eyes and told me he loved me. The words I had been waiting for, waiting and longing for. I wanted him, I needed him...but as he uttered the words, I became starkly aware that I did not love him. I wanted to like green tea, and I desperately wanted to love Kevin, but neither of those things were true.

"I love you *too*," I said, after a slight hesitation. I didn't love him. But he didn't need to know that. There were many things I loved *about* him, like his good looks, his generosity, his romantic side, and his potential for wealth, of course. And what if I learned to love him? I couldn't risk losing him because I wasn't sure about my feelings for him at this moment. And besides, maybe I did love him and just didn't know what that was supposed to feel like. There were so many variables, and I felt it was in my best interest to buy myself some time by verbally reciprocating his feelings. Besides, who knew if he really loved *me*? He had just recently been with another girl. So, could he truly love me? Love was not my main objective anyway. Let's face it, I was in it for money, not love. I knew that sounded harsh, but Rita was in love with Clyde, and where was that going to get her? Sure, she was blissfully happy now, but what about ten years from now, or even five? Her life would be miserable, like all the other Possum Valley women. Kevin was my salvation from that life.

We continued walking to the Garden of Shakespeare's Flowers. I couldn't believe how enormous the park was, and each section was equally impressive. Inside this garden, a brick pathway led us through flowers and plants that were mentioned in Shakespeare's various works. Kevin told me that weddings were often held in these gardens, which was ironic because as he spoke, I was envisioning myself in a flowing white gown, walking through the poetic garden among the colorful array of flowers toward my future husband. It was truly the perfect spot for a wedding ceremony, for Kevin's and my wedding ceremony. What's love got to do with it, anyway?

Chapter 17

As we drove back to Berkeley that evening, there was an enormous golden orange moon that lit up the sky like a ring of fire. I had heard earlier that we would have a harvest moon, but I had never seen one so bright and beautiful. It reminded me of fall in Possum Valley. The leaves were probably at their peak by now, the yellows, oranges, and reds blazing against the bright, blue sky. The trees were pretty in California, the massive redwoods and the twisted Monterey pines, but I still missed the colorful array of leaves on the maples and dogwoods in East Tennessee. Kevin started flipping through the radio channels, which drew my attention back to him. He looked so handsome in his leather jacket and Levi's. "What kind of music do you like?" he asked. I suddenly realized that we hadn't really discussed music, which was a very important part of my life. How could we possibly be in love, if he didn't even know what kinds of music I liked? He should at least assume I liked Journey, since I had used one of their songs in my personal ad. Kevin continued to flip through the channels, which was beginning to annoy me, because he didn't stay on a station long enough for me to identify the song being played.

"Well, I like the Eagles, Journey, and..." I stopped suddenly when I heard a familiar voice. "I let down my gua-ard, now love's left me scarred," Mike's unmistakable voice crooned, and my heart began pounding in my chest.

"Leave it there," I said. My voice came out just above a whisper, because the excitement had left me breathless.

"You know this?" Kevin's hand lingered on the dial.

I wanted to jerk his fingers away and tell him to shut up. "Yes, yes. Hang on a second." I waved my hands frantically, hoping he wouldn't interrupt the song further. It was Mike. Mike was on the radio. On the radio in San Francisco. I couldn't believe my ears. I had listened to his song a few times since he gave me the cassette tape, and I knew it was good. But it didn't seem possible that someone from Possum Valley could be on the radio in California! I couldn't wait to tell him I heard it. I was so excited tears came rolling down my cheeks. He was so talented. I always knew he was capable of this. I was so proud of him. When the song finished, I told Kevin that it was Mike, singing a song from his new album. He seemed surprised, but not particularly interested. He didn't understand that stuff like this didn't happen to people in Possum Valley. The closest anyone ever came to becoming famous in our community was when two brothers from our church and their wives started a Southern Gospel group called the Singin' Satterfields, and got to perform two nights a week one summer at a music show in Pigeon Forge. The group broke up two years later, when one of the Satterfield brothers had an affair with his next-door neighbor. His wife, Norma, said all that fame had gone straight to his head.

As we drove the rest of the way back to my place, I tried to focus on the conversation Kevin and I were having about his first case as a defense lawyer. He was defending a second lieutenant who had been accused of sexual harassment by a female airman. Normally, this would have interested me, but I couldn't stop thinking about Mike's voice on the radio. This was the longest I had ever gone without seeing Mike. Neither of us had ever been away from Possum Valley for longer than a week. I missed Mama, Daddy, and Rita too. Mama had called some, but I had been so busy I didn't have much time to think about missing them. Suddenly, they seemed so far away. It was Sunday, so Mama would have made roast beef with broiled carrots and potatoes for Sunday dinner. We would have some type of cake for dessert, and plenty of sweet tea, in Mama's blue Tupperware pitcher that she had bought at Jolene's party last year. Mama thought it was too expensive when she bought it, but she later said it was one of the best purchases she'd ever made, since the lid was spill-proof and she could take it with her to church dinners. I had never seen her take it anywhere, but I guess she just liked knowing that she could, if she wanted to. I would have given anything to have a big glass of Mama's sweet tea right then.

When we got back to my place, Kevin walked me to the door. The night air was cool, and I wrapped my arms around my chest as we stood there in the darkness. The low clouds had moved back in from the bay, so there were no visible stars. Kevin pulled me close to him and kissed me.

"Kevin," I said carefully, trying to avoid offending him. "It's pretty late, and we both have to get up early, so we should probably call it a night." It was 11:30 p.m., but I wasn't really tired and would have normally invited him inside, but I felt so homesick that I just wanted to be alone. He kissed me again. "I don't want to leave you," he whispered. I thought about Brandy standing in his doorway wearing his shirt and wondered if I could ever trust him. We'd had a wonderful day, but none of that seemed to matter now. I could've had a good day with Jenny, or just about anybody, in a place like San Francisco.

"We'll talk tomorrow," I said. "I had a great time today, but I'm suddenly tired now."

"OK, Sakura," he smiled. "Until tomorrow."

I watched him walk to his car and drive away before I went in the house. I locked the door behind me and ran to the vanity table in my bedroom and pulled out the cassette tape Mike had given me. The small house we were renting came furnished with pieces that I thought were nice, but Jenny assured me were tacky. My favorite was the vanity table. It was white with an oval mirror attached, and two small drawers sat on top of the table on either side, with three other drawers underneath. I felt like a princess putting on my makeup while sitting on the bench covered in pink silk fabric. I kept important items in the top drawers and my makeup and hairbrushes in the ones underneath. A letter Mike had sent me was in the right top drawer, underneath the cassette tape. I slid the tape in my cassette player and picked up the phone without even thinking about the time. The phone rang twice before I remembered the three-hour time difference between us. It was 2:30 a.m. in Possum Valley. I quickly hung up the phone, hoping I hadn't awakened the whole house.

Mike's voice was crooning on my cassette player as I opened his letter again. The letter had arrived in the mail a couple of weeks ago, and I had probably read it a dozen times since then. I hadn't really missed him until I got the letter, but he had spelled all his words exactly as he pronounced them, and I remembered how genuine he was. It was something that had always annoyed me about him, but now it seemed endearing. He was just himself, and made no apologies for it. I didn't think I would ever miss his extreme Southern accent that had always driven me crazy—but I did. His letter began with *Hello, Darlin'*. He had greeted me that way for as long as I could remember, and I hated it. But when I opened his letter and saw the words, and heard them in my mind, they sounded good. I assumed I was just homesick, and didn't think much about it afterwards. I certainly didn't mention it to Jenny, since I knew she would jump to conclusions and tell me he was my destiny. But tonight, when I heard him on the radio, I desperately wanted to hug him, to tell him how proud I was of him. Tears flowed down my face as I thought about this guy I had grown up with and had always been there for me. I wanted to be there for him now, and I couldn't because of the time difference.

"Hey, I thought I heard you come in." I tried to dry my eyes before I turned around to face Jenny, who was standing in my doorway. I usually spoke to Jenny when I came in, but I had been in such a rush to get the cassette tape that I hadn't bothered to see if she was still awake. "Are you crying?"

"Hi, Jenny," I said, trying to decide if I wanted to be truthful with her. She could usually tell when I was lying, so I knew I should probably go ahead and tell her the truth.

"What did he do, Kathy?" Jenny asked in an angry tone, her eyes wild. "I swear, if Kevin hurt you again, I'm going to strangle him with my bare hands."

"Jenny, no!" I laughed. "This has nothing to do with Kevin," I said quietly, trying to calm her down. "I heard Mike singing on the radio tonight, and it just made me a little emotional, I guess."

"Mike was on the radio?" Jenny eyes quickly changed from anger to disbelief. "Here?!" Jenny was clearly excited too, which made me even happier.

"Yes!" I sprang up from the bed and rewound the tape to the song I had heard on the radio. "He was singing this song. Isn't it amazing?"

"It is really good," she smiled. "I'm so happy for him." Jenny came over and hugged me. "I know you and he were close, and I don't blame you for being excited. This is really big! As good looking as he is, he may become a big country music star like George Strait!"

"He deserves it, Jenny. He's a great guy."

"Too bad you're not interested in someone like him." Jenny pushed the hair away from my face and smoothed it down, as she often did when she wanted to tell me something important. "He is crazy about you, you know."

I felt flushed for a second. "Jenny, you know I've never felt *that* way about Mike. We're just good friends. Besides, Kevin was so sweet today, and you know, he hasn't tried anything with me since that one night back in Possum Valley."

"I hate to say this, Kathy, but that could be because he's getting it somewhere else," Jenny said hesitantly.

"How could you say that, Jenny?" I was fuming. "You don't want Kevin to hurt me, but it doesn't seem to bother you if *you* hurt me. He promised he wouldn't cheat again, and I believe him. You act like he couldn't possibly be faithful to someone like me. Maybe you don't think I deserve someone like him. Or maybe you're jealous that I have him."

"OK, Kathy," Jenny held up her hands signaling surrender. "I'm sorry. I shouldn't have said that. If anything, I think you're too good for him. You know I only want the best for you, and have I ever been jealous of you before? You're my best friend." She walked over and wrapped her arms around me. She was right. She was never jealous of me, no more than I was jealous of her.

"I'm sorry too." I hugged her tightly. "I just need you to support me in this, Jenny. It means so much to me."

"I know," she pushed me back and held me at arm's length by the shoulders. "Just promise me you'll be careful, honey. I don't want to see my best friend in the world get hurt." She looked deeply into my eyes and smiled. I knew she was sincere, and I couldn't be angry with her. Jenny was a real friend, not the kind that only liked you when she agreed with you, or when it was easy or fun. She was the kind that saw all your faults and loved you anyway. The kind that kept your secrets safe and was always there for you.

"I promise," I said. I'm going to go get ready for bed now." I wasn't really sleepy, but I needed some time to process all the thoughts going through my mind.

"Goodnight, Kathy," she said, as she walked toward the door.

"Love you," I said.

She turned back and looked at me, tilting her head. "But maybe, just maybe you've never *allowed* yourself to feel that way about Mike." I rolled my eyes and shooed her away with my hand. Jenny never could stop herself from saying whatever was on her mind. It was obviously a Yankee thing.

I couldn't sleep most of the night thinking about what Jenny had said. She didn't understand my relationship with Mike, or Kevin for that matter. Sure, I was happy that Mike's album was doing well, but we had grown up together. He was like a brother to me. Kevin was the kind of guy I wanted and could fall in love with. He had a prestigious and secure job as an Air Force lawyer. He was well educated, had impeccable manners, and came from a wealthy family. He was everything I was looking for in a man. Mike, on the other hand, had no education and no desire to get one, no security, and was content staying in Possum Valley permanently. Even if I had feelings for Mike, I would be miserable with him because we were too different.

I woke up early the next morning to the sound of seagulls. I was used to waking to a rooster crowing every morning, so it still seemed like a dream that I now lived near a beach. Back in Possum Valley, people dreamed of going to the beach and saved money all year just to go spend a week in some dingy hotel in Florida. Jenny always joked that those kinds of hotels were "no-tell motels," because they were often rented by people having "low-rent rendezvous," as the song by the Amazing Rhythm Aces went. I only knew the song because Mike had liked to play it on his guitar, back when we were younger. *Mike again*. The more I tried to forget about him, the more he kept coming back like an annoying gnat. I got up and walked through the kitchen and out the back door onto the deck.

I thought about the little deck we had on our trailer back home. Rita and I used to rub baby oil all over ourselves and sunbathe on bath towels on the deck. We'd fill Mama's Tupperware pitcher with Country Time lemonade and take the transistor radio and stay out there most of the day, just talking and soaking up the sun. I'd talk about how one day I would be living near the ocean and have the best tan of my life, and she'd talk about marrying Clyde and living on a farm. The Central Coast of California was cooler than I had imagined, so lying on the beach in a bathing suit wasn't often an option. The crisp air felt good this morning though, and I left the door open. The weather in Berkeley was ideal for opening windows and letting in the cool breeze, so the air in our house always seemed clean and fresh. That was a stark difference from what I was used to in Possum Valley, where the air was sticky and hot in the summer, and cold and stale in the winter. The winters weren't as smelly as the summers because Daddy didn't do much slaughtering when it was cold, but they were just as miserable. It was impossible to keep the frigid air from seeping through our thin walls in the trailer.

I had decided against calling Mike. I determined that my initial excitement had made me act impulsively last night, and there was no need to call him. I would write him a letter and congratulate him on his success. *I was obviously feeling a little homesick last night,* I thought. I had never been away from my family, so naturally I missed Mama, Daddy, and Rita, but my new life was in California. Things were much more civilized there; it was truly everything I had ever dreamed of. I walked back inside and flipped on the radio that we kept on the kitchen counter after I started a pot of coffee. Jenny wasn't up yet, but I knew she would want some when she did get up. I never drank coffee before college, but drinking it seemed to be part of the life of a student, since we often stayed up late to study. I had just poured myself a cup when Jenny walked into the kitchen.

"Good morning," she said. She clasped her hands and slowly lifted her arms over her head to stretch.

"I just made some coffee," I said, getting another cup out of the cabinet. I poured a cup for her and placed it on the counter.

"Thanks," she said, as she sat down. "I have a big test today, so I will need this." I never understood why professors liked to give tests on Mondays, since students just wanted to chill out and not think about school on the weekends. My guess was that they enjoyed making us miserable.

I got out the Lucky Charms and poured myself a big bowl. I had fallen in love with the marshmallow cereal the first time I tried it at Jenny's house years ago. Mama never let us have it because it was too expensive, but I had sworn that when I lived on my own, I would buy Lucky Charms.

"Want a bowl?" I asked Jenny, even though I already knew the answer. Jenny usually ate oatmeal with fruit for breakfast, because she said it was much healthier than sugary cereal. I had grown up eating oatmeal, grits, bacon, and eggs, so sugary cereal was like a delicacy for me. I was getting ready for her lecture about my obsession with kids' cereal when I heard it. Mike's song was on the radio again.

"That's it, Jenny." I could barely breathe from excitement. "That's Mike's song."

We sat there drinking our coffee, silently listening and occasionally smiling at each other. She understood that you don't talk or interrupt, like Kevin did, during a song. *It's almost eight a.m. here, almost eleven there. Mike would be gone to work by now. I'll call him this evening.* A letter wouldn't be good enough. I had to talk to him.

* * *

I got to my philosophy class early, so I sat in the back, hoping that I could avoid being called on by Professor Whitson to answer a question. Normally I didn't mind class participation, but when asked a question like why there's something rather than nothing, I usually had *nothing* rather than *something* to say about that. Philosophy class required some effort for me: not because it was hard, but because Daddy had always taught us to work hard and not waste time worrying about stuff that didn't matter. I knew he wouldn't think anything we did in this class was important, and I couldn't get his words out of my head. Plus, it was hard for me to think abstractly. Everything for me had always been very basic and concrete. We mostly talked in class, and our test questions were very abstract and didn't seem to have wrong answers. I had an A in the class because I tried to participate, and I answered the questions thoroughly, mostly writing down whatever came to mind. I enjoyed keeping a journal and learning about ethics and logic, though. I couldn't imagine Daddy sitting around just thinking about thinking, but I decided maybe higher education wasn't for everyone. I missed Daddy though, and I loved him just the way he was.

"The topic today is racism," Professor Whitson said as he walked into the room and laid his felt hat on his desk. He wore the hat every day, probably because he was balding and his head got cold. It's funny how as a student, you sit and look at your teacher each day and scrutinize his appearance, just because he's there. In another setting, I probably wouldn't have given him a second glance, but since he was up in front of me philosophizing three days each week, I had given him a complete makeover in my mind. I thought he would look better if he just shaved his head, since the entire top of his head was bald, with the exception of a few, thin strands that he combed over to one side. The sides and back were thick in comparison, the brown ring of hair around his head creating a donut effect. He was a middle-aged white guy from Portland, Oregon, and he looked exactly how I would have pictured a philosophy professor. He wasn't too bad looking for a middle-aged, balding man, though, and he wore bulky, button-up sweaters over turtleneck shirts every day that gave him that sexy professor look.

I was a little excited about today's topic because I thought the discussion should be very interesting. I knew it would be very different from most of the things I had heard back home, since UC Berkeley students were very tolerant and didn't seem to have a racist bone in their bodies. I thought of Chris and how difficult it was for him in Possum Valley. He probably wouldn't have had any problems here. Professor Whitson began by asking us why racism still existed in the 1980s. Most students gave the same answer that I was thinking, if I had been called upon. Acceptance and tolerance were derived from understanding, which only came from getting to know people. The citizens of Possum Valley just didn't know any black people, and that needed to change for acceptance to occur.

After class, Amy and Jane, a couple of my classmates, invited me to go to lunch with them at a restaurant in town. Amy was an outgoing Asian girl with a sweet smile, and Jane was a white girl with dark hair and glasses. I had talked to them once after class, and I was hoping to get to know them better. I had some time before my next class, so I eagerly accepted, since I really didn't know anyone at Cal except Jenny. After we ordered, the racism topic came up again. We must have been talking loudly or the people beside us were nosy, because a middle-aged man at the next table blurted out, "There's still racism because of all the rednecks in the South." One of the other guys at the table agreed, saying, "Yes, they're an intolerant bunch of hillbillies."

My face turned red. Amy and Jane knew I was from the South, because Amy had asked me where I was from when we talked before. I was certain she could tell I wasn't from around Berkeley because of my accent. I tried to be as inconspicuous as I could, but it was impossible to completely mask my accent when I had only been out of the South for a few months. I had told her I was from Knoxville instead of Possum Valley, because I thought it was close enough, and Knoxville sounded much better.

Amy looked at me. "I'm sorry you had to hear that," she said quietly. "They're obviously ignorant."

"It's fine," I said, wanting desperately to tell the men that I was from the South, and I wasn't a redneck, wanting to defend the people back home and explain to them that not everyone was racist, and many people that were just didn't know people of other races. But I didn't say anything. I just thought about how these men who thought they were so much better than the people back home were being intolerant and judgmental themselves. They were no better than the people in Possum Valley. They didn't know us or understand us. How could they judge us? I realized just how easy it was to pass judgment on a group of people that you didn't understand. I felt a little strange for wanting to defend the people that I had wanted to get away from for most of my life, but they were a part of me. Possum Valley was a part of me, and maybe that wasn't such a bad thing. Racism and intolerance did exist in Possum Valley, but maybe it was everywhere in some form.

Chapter 18

I rushed home that evening to call Mike, as I had planned. I had been thinking about him and his song all day, and I couldn't wait to talk to him and congratulate him. I ran into the house and put down my books. I had homework in every single subject and would be up half the night finishing it, but right then, I just wanted to talk to Mike. *It's four p.m. here, so it would be seven p.m. there*, I calculated. Mike didn't usually work at Seek & Find on Mondays, so I was hopeful that he would be at home. I was a little nervous when I picked up the phone. I had no idea why, since Mike and I had known each other forever. My heart was pounding as I dialed his number, which I had memorized years ago. His mom answered on the second ring.

"Hi, Mrs. Ledbetter," I said nervously. "This is Kathy Fillmore."

Before I could say anything else, Mrs. Ledbetter interjected. "Kathy! It's so good to hear from you. How are you, honey? Do you like it out there, with all the movie stars and celebrities? Mercy, we sure do miss you around here. It's just not the same without your pretty face."

When she finally paused for a second, I responded. "Thanks. It's good to hear your voice. "No movie stars up here," I said. "Just a lot of hippies. I miss everyone there." And it was true; I *did* miss everyone. I just wasn't in the mood for small talk. I wanted to speak to Mike. "I was just wondering if Mike was around," I continued. "I heard his song on the radio out here, and I just wanted to tell him how excited I am for him."

"That's so sweet of you, Kathy. I know he'd love to hear from you, but he's not here. He's promoting his album in Nashville for the next two weeks."

My heart sank. How silly of me, to think he'd just be sitting around Possum Valley when his song was being played on the radio. He was making a name for himself, and probably had girls hanging all over him right now. "Oh, that's great," I said, hoping my grave disappointment wasn't audible. "I'm so happy for him." And I was. A great guy like him deserved all the success in the world. "When you talk to him, please tell him I'm proud of him."

"I'll be sure to tell him you called. He'll be thrilled," she said.

I felt foolish as I hung up the phone. He'd probably forgotten about me already. With all those girls in Nashville, I was probably the last thing on his mind. I went to the kitchen to find something for dinner. I usually cooked something in an attempt to eat healthy, but it was late, and I was hungry. I opened the freezer and took out a carton of rocky road ice cream and got a spoon from the drawer. I sat down at the table and started eating right out of the carton. Jenny and I took turns choosing ice cream flavors, and I usually picked my favorite, rocky road. But right then, I couldn't even taste it. I was just eating. Mama always told me she could tell when I was upset about something, because I wanted to eat. If there were no hot dogs, I would pull out ice cream, peanut butter, or whatever I could find and eat it right out of the container. One time when Jenny and I got into a big argument, I got Mama's canister of sugar and ate it by the spoonful until I got sick. I can't even remember what the argument was about, but I probably wouldn't ever forget getting sick from all that sugar. I was happy for Mike's success, so why was I upset? I just really wanted to talk to him. He'd always been there, had always been a part of my life...*and now he isn't*. He wasn't there for me, like he had been ever since I was a little girl. I looked down, and the ice cream was gone.

When I finally finished my homework, I looked at the clock. It was almost two a.m. It was only then that I realized that Kevin hadn't called me. I hadn't thought of him all day, because of all the excitement with Mike. I was so disappointed about not being able to talk to him that I had thought of little else. It obviously didn't bother me much that Kevin hadn't called, but the more I thought about it, the more upset I became. Isn't that weird how you don't really care if a guy calls or not, but you get angry anyway, just because you think you're *supposed* to be angry? I felt like I was acting a part, feeling nothing but acting as if I did. *How dare he not call me? He'd better have a darn good reason.*

* * *

TUESDAY MORNING

When I got up, Jenny had already gone to class, so I made myself some coffee and went out onto the back porch. It was already after ten a.m., and the sun was bright and warm on my face. I didn't feel like eating breakfast, after all the ice cream (did I mention I ate all of it?), so I just sat there enjoying the cool, foggy morning and the sounds of the seagulls. Back home, I would've already fed the pigs by ten, and would probably be shoveling manure that I had picked up in my truck the day before. Sometimes I felt like perhaps I missed my life back in Possum Valley, but I had decided that I had lived that life for so long, it was just difficult getting used to living a new life. It was so much nicer in California, with so much more to do than in Possum Valley. I couldn't possibly miss my old life. I didn't *want* to miss that life. But I needed to find out what was going on with Kevin. He was the main reason I was here, and if I wanted to stay out of Possum Valley, I needed a guy like Kevin to keep me out after college.

The phone rang just as I had gotten up to get another cup of coffee. I thought it was probably a telemarketer, since we had been getting those calls frequently in the mornings. It was usually someone offering a trip to Las Vegas or a life insurance policy, neither of which I needed or could afford. I picked it up anyway, out of habit, I guess. But it wasn't a telemarketer this time, it was Rita. I knew something was wrong immediately, because she wouldn't call at this time of day; she was usually in school.

"It's Daddy," she said in a tearful voice. "He's had a heart attack, Kathy. Mama got him to the hospital, but they're not sure if he'll make it."

"Not Daddy," I barely got the words out. "No, Rita, not Daddy!"

The tears were uncontrollable. I could barely stand beneath the weight of the news that Daddy might not live. I felt completely hopeless and helpless. I had left him and gone to California, and now he needed me, and I wasn't there.

"You can't let him die, Rita." I was hysterical, and I felt so selfish and so stupid for leaving. What if I never saw Daddy again? That would be more than I could bear. "Don't you dare let him die."

"How could this happen? I asked desperately. "He's only in his forties, and he works all the time. You know he works hard all the time."

"I know, Kathy," Rita said. "I know. Mama wanted me to see if you could come home, you know, just in case."

"Tell her I'll find a way," I said. I'll find the money to get there. I will get there somehow."

"I'll tell her," she said. "We're all praying, Kathy. It's going to be OK. He's going to pull through. I gotta go for now. I don't want to leave Mama alone for too long."

"He has to be OK," I said. "Please, God, please let Daddy be OK."

I hung up the phone and flung myself on the sofa. I buried my face in the pillow and wept, soaking the pillow with tears. All I could think about was Daddy sitting in his old, worn out chair, always talking about needing more rain. Rita and I used to laugh and pretend to do rain dances around him. There was no one like him in the whole world. No one loved manure Monday like Daddy did, and nobody was as proud of their pigs as Daddy was. And nobody was as proud of their Daddy as I was. I loved Daddy. I hadn't realized just how much I loved him until this moment. I had to find a way to get home to see him.

Chapter 19

"When it is dark enough, you can see the stars."
–Ralph Waldo Emerson

Jenny was in class and Kevin was at work. I shivered underneath my bulky sweater, which Jenny had bought for me at Macy's. She said it would come in handy on the cold, foggy mornings. I wrapped my arms around my waist, clinging tightly to my sweater as I lay on the sofa. The house was quiet, and I could still hear the seagulls as they flew by. They sounded melancholy, screeching and moaning overhead. Why had they never sounded this way before? They had always sounded cheerful and lively before, but now, looking out the window at the gray, gloomy fog, their wailing echoes were almost unbearable. I was thousands of miles away at Berkeley, while my Daddy was fighting for his life in Tennessee. I still wasn't hungry, but I had to eat something. I found some of Jenny's strawberry yogurt in the refrigerator, but my trembling hands couldn't force the spoon in my mouth, and I dropped the spoon and the yogurt container on the floor as I fell to my knees and cried. Mama was right when she said I always ate when I was upset, but I had never been this upset before.

I just sat there in the yogurt for a while before I finally picked myself up off the floor. There was yogurt on my sweater, the floor, the cabinets, and even on the wall. How could there have been so much yogurt in that little container? I went to the bedroom and put on a clean shirt, then got the mop and a washcloth and cleaned up the kitchen. I called to check on prices for flights from San Francisco to Knoxville. I had no idea how much it would cost, since my flight here was paid for. The cheapest flight I could find was $408; I was told there were no direct flights to Knoxville. It was only around $300 to get to Atlanta, but Atlanta was over four hours from Possum Valley, and I wouldn't have a way to get home from there. I got an allowance each month, and I had managed to save a little, but I only had $175. I still needed $233. I knew Jenny might have it, because her parents sent her spending money each month, but $233 would probably make it tight for her. I didn't want her to have to ask her parents for more money.

So, I decided I would ask Kevin to borrow the money. If he cared about me as much as he said, he shouldn't have a problem. Plus, I knew he made good money as a lawyer on the base. Obviously, he didn't make as much as lawyers who had their own firms, but he still made more money than anyone I knew. I went to the bedroom, pulled out my suitcase and started packing. I couldn't buy the ticket until I talked to Kevin, but I hoped to be on the first flight out the next day. I had to get home to Daddy as soon as possible. Even though Mama and Daddy had bought the luggage for me shortly before I left, I could still smell the familiar scent of animal flesh mingled with cigarette smoke when I opened my large suitcase. I had always hated smelling that aroma everywhere I went, but today, it smelled different. It smelled more than just familiar. It smelled like home.

The day seemed to drag on forever. After I packed, I called the hospital in Knoxville and talked to Jolene, who had come to stay with Mama and give Rita a break. Jolene said Daddy had been taken to the hospital around seven that morning; it was eight in the evening there when we talked. Daddy was still in the CCU after having surgery earlier that day. Mama hadn't left Daddy's side since he had returned from the operating room. There was a lot of blockage and his condition was still critical, she said.

"I brought my healing crystals," Jolene said in a comforting voice, "and I've spread them all around the waiting room."

That didn't make me feel any better, knowing her history with the crystals, but she did make me smile for the first time since Rita had called to tell me about Daddy, just thinking about her crystals all over the CCU waiting room.

"I'm trying to get the money together to fly to Knoxville tomorrow," I said. "Tell Mama I'll be there as soon as possible, and that I know Daddy will..." My voice broke up, and I couldn't finish my sentence.

"Be OK." Jolene completed my sentence for me. "Everything's gonna be OK," she said. "I can feel it."

"Thanks, Jolene," I managed to utter through the tears.

I put down the phone and looked at the time. It was almost 5:30 p.m., and Kevin usually got off from work around 4:30, so I picked up the phone again and dialed his number. It rang five times, and I was just getting ready to hang up when I heard someone pick up.

"Kevin," I said quickly.

"Uh, hang on just a minute," a female voice said.

I immediately became infuriated. *Again? Another girl, again. Was it Brandy?* It didn't matter who it was. I didn't have time for this. I slammed down the phone. I needed him now more than ever, and he wasn't there for me. That was the last straw. I didn't need his money that badly. Not now, not ever. Just then, the phone rang. I didn't want to answer it, but I knew I had to just in case it was Rita or someone calling about Daddy. I picked up slowly, afraid it might be about Daddy and enraged that it could be Kevin.

"Hello, my darlin'." It was Mike's unmistakable voice. "I had to call and check on you, babe."

Tears flowed down my cheeks as I heard Mike's voice on the other line. The voice that used to irritate me so much sounded angelic at that moment. I felt for the first time all day that everything would be OK. Mike had always been there for me when I needed him, and here he was again.

"I called Rita after Mama told me about your daddy. She said you were planning to come home to see him," he said. "And I want to buy your ticket to get here."

My heart sank. I hadn't even thought about asking Mike to help me with money. He was the one that had always bailed me out of trouble, so it was only fitting that he would want to help me now.

"But I need over two hundred dollars, Mike. You can't afford..."

He stopped me. "I got it covered, beautiful," he said. "I already got some of my money for the album, and I got more comin' from promotions. You don't need to worry about a thing. Just book the next flight and come see your daddy."

"Mike, I could kiss you right now," I sobbed.

"I'm gonna hold you to that, darlin'," he laughed.

"Thank you, Mike. I'll pay you back as soon as I can."

"Don't worry about that right now. Just git here."

I hung up the phone and immediately called the airline. Finally, I felt a little more in control, and I just knew everything was going to be all right. Once again, Mike had been my knight in shining armor. I wondered why that had always bothered me before. Every girl needs a knight in shining armor.

Jenny came in shortly after I had made my flight reservations. I told her about everything that had happened, including my phone call to Kevin's apartment. She hugged me tightly, assuring me she would let my professors know about Daddy, and take care of everything here while I was gone.

"You may have to take emergency leave from school, but I'll let you know. Don't worry about anything right now. But about Kevin..." She stood up straight with a determined look on her face. "I will have *zero* respect for you if you talk to him again. You are way too good for him."

"Don't worry," I said. "It's over." And I meant it this time. I couldn't trust him, and I needed someone that I could depend on when I needed him. Kevin was not that guy, and probably never would be. "I'm sorry for not listening to you before. You were just trying to protect me, and I was so stupid."

"You're not stupid," she smiled. "You'll find someone wonderful that will be everything you've dreamed of when the time is right. But right now, we have to focus on your dad."

"Thanks, Jenny." I said. "Daddy is all that matters to me right now."

* * *

I had no trouble getting up for my five a.m. flight the next morning since I barely slept the whole night. I mostly just lay there thinking about Daddy, and how he couldn't even stand to tell me goodbye when I left for Berkeley. He and I didn't agree on much, but we had a mutual respect that I had for no one else. I guess I just assumed he would live forever. The thought of him not being there, not being there for my wedding, for my children, for me, was unthinkable. Daddy loved the simple things in life, like farming, bacon, sitting on the deck, and watching the sunset. But there were still so many things Daddy hadn't done. I wanted him to come out to California and see the redwoods and the

Pacific Ocean. He couldn't die. Not now.

Jenny drove me to the airport, and I boarded the plane shortly after we arrived. I must have slept most of the flight, because it seemed like I ate some breakfast, took a nap, and we were there. Rita was at the airport to pick me up, and we drove straight to the hospital to see Daddy. It was strange being back home, I mused, as I looked out the window to see the Possum Valley welcome sign, the possum's little fist raised in the air. *There isn't anything like this in California, but it is cool in a way*, I thought. It might not be San Francisco, but it was home.

When we arrived at the hospital, Daddy was still in the CCU, and Mama was with him. Rita asked the nurse to let Mama know I had arrived.

"Kathy!" Mama ran up and hugged me. She looked like she had aged ten years since I had seen her last, her eyes puffy with big, dark circles under them. "I'm so glad you're here." She stroked my hair. "I just can't believe this is happening."

"I'm here, Mama," I said, holding back tears and trying to be strong. "It's going to be OK now."

"He was out feeding the pigs," she said. "And I just happened to look out the window, and he was lying on the ground, right there with the pigs. I knew something was bad wrong."

Feeding the pigs was my job. He had a heart attack doing my job. He was probably working way too hard. What if this was my fault? *Would this have happened if I had been here doing my job?*

Thankfully Mama quickly answered my question. "Your daddy had severe blockage to his heart. The doctor said this was inevitable, and he was surprised it hadn't happened a lot sooner. He said we're lucky we got him to the hospital when we did."

At least I wasn't responsible. I couldn't have lived with that. "Is there any news about his prognosis?" I asked.

"He's not out of the woods yet, but the doctors are hopeful," she said. "I told him you were coming, and he smiled for the first time since this happened. He will want to see you, Kathy. Go on in. Only one person is allowed in the CCU at a time."

I was suddenly nervous. I didn't know if I could stand seeing Daddy hooked up to machines. I walked through the double doors and saw Daddy lying on the bed. Daddy, who was always so strong and full of life, looked helpless and weak, the color drained from him like a corpse. His eyes were closed, and his breathing was strained. A part of me wanted to run out of the room crying, but I knew I had to be strong for him. "Hi, Daddy." I spoke softly, trying to hold back my tears.

His eyes opened. They were the same dark eyes I knew so well, the ones that showed pride for the prize-winning pig at the fair, and disappointment when I told him I was moving to Berkeley. I knew it had crushed him when he found out, but I couldn't stay in Possum Valley just to make him happy. I had to live my life. But where had it gotten me? I was going to college with no plans for the future, and the plans I had to get married had just been shattered by Kevin. Jenny had warned me about Kevin. She told me I shouldn't rely on him for my happiness, because he would let me down. Why hadn't I listened to her? She only wanted me to be happy, and I had put some stupid guy above her and our friendship and above my family. I didn't know which I was worse at, being a friend or a daughter.

"Kathy." Daddy's voice was frail, but I could still detect his excitement. "I'm so glad you're here," he smiled faintly. "I got some pigs that need feedin'." I knew he was joking, but I also knew he wouldn't complain if I offered to take on the job while I was here.

I wanted to hug him, wrap my arms around him and then climb up in his lap like I did when I was a little girl, for him to read me a bedtime story. I loved to hear him read *The Three Little Pigs*, not surprisingly a favorite of his. He was so animated when he read the pigs' line "not by the hair of *my* chinny, chin, chin." I could have listened to him read it all day. I didn't want to unhook any of his wires, so I kissed him gently on the cheek instead.

"That's why I traveled all this way, Daddy. Just because I missed feeding the pigs," I smiled, realizing that he was only joking around to keep us both from crying.

"Good girl," he said. "I knew you wouldn't be able to stay away from them pigs." He smiled more heartily this time, as if my arrival was injecting a little life back into him.

"Don't you worry about a thing," I said, as I looked up and saw the nurse coming.

"I'm sorry, but we need to check his vitals and medications," she said in a kind voice.

I looked at Daddy and tried to smile as reassuringly as possible. "I'll be right outside, Daddy," I said. "I won't go anywhere—except to feed the pigs, of course." I winked at him.

"Kathy," he said as I turned to leave. "It's no secret that I didn't want you to leave, but I want you to know that I'm really proud of you for going to school and getting an education."

I wanted to tell him how much I loved him, but you know how you try to speak when you're upset, but all that comes out is a gasping, sniffling noise that sounds like a dying seal? I didn't want Daddy to hear that, so I just shook my head yes as I walked out the door.

* * *

On the way back home, Rita told me about how hard Daddy had been working since I had left. She wasn't trying to make me feel bad, but she was doing a really good job anyway. When we pulled up to the trailer, Mike's truck was in the driveway. "Did you know Mike was going to be here?" I asked, as I noticed my heart rate speeding up.

"No," Rita said. "I talked to him earlier today. He called to ask me if anybody had been feeding the pigs, and I told him that no one had this morning, but I was going to as soon as I got back from the hospital this evening."

When we got out of the car, I looked over at the pig lot, and I saw the back of Mike's head. I didn't have to see his face to know it was him, and there was something comforting about knowing someone that well. He was tossing feed to the pigs as they grunted and snorted, fighting for each morsel.

"Kathy Fillmore." Mike was coming toward us now with a big smile on his face. "You made it."

"Thanks to you." I ran up and hugged him, and he squeezed me firmly. It felt familiar and right. I had missed him, and I could feel that he had missed me by the way he held me close and lightly touched my hair like it was fine silk. "What are you doing here, though? I thought you were in Nashville."

"And not be here for you and your daddy? I can always reschedule those honky-tonk gigs later on."

"You're such a good friend, Mike." I released my embrace, a little embarrassed as tears flooded my eyes. I quickly turned to Rita. "Will you open the trunk?" She popped the trunk and Mike immediately reached in and got my suitcase. "I could never repay you for all you've done for me, but I'll pay you back for the plane ticket as soon as I can."

"I'm not worried about it." He carried my suitcase as we walked toward the trailer. "Let's just worry about getting your daddy better."

It was a clear day, and the tiered, snow-capped mountains were glistening as I looked out in the distance. The cows looked peaceful and content as they grazed along the rolling hills, and I could hear the mockingbirds and smell the pine trees surrounding the trailer. It wasn't San Francisco Bay, with all the lights and buildings, but it was beautiful, and I felt like I was really seeing it and Mike for the very first time.

We went inside and made some ham sandwiches. It was late, but none of us had eaten dinner. We took our plates into the living room and I turned on the TV, hoping for a distraction, since everything around me reminded me of Daddy. I put my plate on the coffee table and walked toward his chair. Something was drawing me to it, to that old, ratty chair that I had complained about for years. I sat down and put my hands on the chair arms, caressing the taped areas where Daddy's strong hands had been. I could smell Daddy's sweat and cigarettes. It would have disgusted me in the past, but now I wanted to inhale deeper and take in the scent because it was his and it smelled strong and sweet, just like him. I began to cry. At first it was just a couple of tears trickling down my cheeks, and then it was a river running down my face, my head down as the tears fell onto my lap like giant rain drops, soaking my pants. I felt a hand on my shoulder and I lifted my head slightly to see Mike standing there. He handed me some tissues without saying anything. He just stood there with his hand on my shoulder, letting me cry. I finally looked up to see Rita crying too. I began drying my eyes with the tissue. "This isn't helping anything," I said. "What can we do? I feel so completely helpless."

"Why don't we say a prayer?" Mike turned off the TV, took my hand, and knelt beside Daddy's chair. Rita walked over and knelt beside him, and I dropped to my knees to join them. The three of us held hands and prayed silently. After a few minutes, we slowly stood together and hugged. The three of us holding onto each other was comforting, being there for each other, like brother and sisters. Mike had always been like a brother, and I felt a little better after praying with him and Rita, knowing how much they loved Daddy too. I thought about how Daddy used to tell us a story about a spider named Ruby. Every day, Mrs. Walker, the homemaker in the house where Ruby lived, would tear down Ruby's web with her broom, but every night Ruby would rebuild her web. She never gave up, Daddy would tell us, no matter how many times her home was destroyed. Daddy wouldn't give up either. *It isn't in his nature to quit, any more than it was in Ruby's,* I thought.

"I'd better get going and let you two get some rest," Mike said.

"I'll walk you out," I said, wanting to thank him again for the ticket and for praying with us.

We walked out to his truck. He turned around and put his back up against the truck, facing me. "I'm sorry about your daddy, beautiful," he said. "But I believe he'll pull out of this. He's tough."

"Thanks, Mike," I said. "I believe he will too." I spontaneously reached up and kissed him on the cheek. There were so many emotions consuming me, and I felt so much gratitude toward Mike that I kissed him again—but this time on the mouth. This time it was a real kiss, and I kissed him deeply, hungrily, feeling him kiss me back passionately like we had waited our whole lives for this moment. It felt genuine and innocent and perfect, and everything I had ever imagined a kiss was supposed to be but had never felt before with anyone else. I didn't want to stop; I didn't want it to end. But then I remembered I was kissing Mike, and I pulled away. Mike was like my brother. I had just thought how much he was like our brother in the trailer a few minutes ago. *And now I'm out here kissing him like he's my long-lost lover. What was I thinking?* "I'm sorry," I said. "I didn't mean to..."

"Please don't be sorry." He grabbed my hands and held them between us. "That was a moment I'll never forget, and there is nothing to be sorry about."

"But I'm just so emotional right now, and I'm not sure of my feelings. And you're probably dating someone now. I'm sure there are all kinds of girls following you around." I pulled my hands away from him. "I shouldn't have kissed you. I just..."

"Wait just a minute," he said, stopping me. "Are you *crazy*? Do you really think I would give up on you, just 'cause you went off to school?"

"Mike, I never gave you any reason to think..."

"Some things you just know," he laughed. He pulled me close to him. "You're the only one I've ever wanted, Kathy. That hasn't changed."

I couldn't think straight. I had never had romantic feelings for Mike, and I never wanted to lead him on. But now, all I could think about was kissing him again, and again. I felt something between us. Something tangible and real. "Then why are you just standing there?" I asked. "Kiss me."

Chapter 20

TWO DAYS LATER

It was almost time for visiting hours when I arrived at the hospital. Daddy was still in CCU, and there was still no change in his condition when I had left the night before. My positive attitude about Daddy's recovery was beginning to diminish each day that he remained in the CCU. The hospital was old and dark, adding to my gloomy mood. The same Mary, mother of Jesus statute had been in the same spot in the foyer since I was a little girl and had come here to visit Papaw Fillmore before he died. Since Daddy's heart attack, no one had mentioned that his father had died young of a heart attack. It was as if everyone was afraid to talk about how Daddy was about the same age Papaw was when he died. I didn't remember much about Papaw, but I remembered being at the hospital and seeing the Mary statute and the cold, marble floor underneath. It was just as dark and dismal as I remembered, and there were old, somber paintings of Jesus on the cross, blood dripping from his wounds, lining the hall to the elevator. As I walked to the elevator, I thought about how most people visiting the hospital were already sad, and that the gloomy décor didn't help anything. I could've used some cheerful scenes of bright flowers, and maybe a triumphant Jesus standing in front of a radiant, empty tomb. I got onto the elevator and pushed the button for the fifth floor, where Daddy was. The elevator was dark like everything else here, and I decided I agreed with Granny about hospitals. They were horrible, and people just died here.

I got off the elevator with tears in my eyes and walked down the hall toward the waiting room. I saw Mama in there with Preacher Brown from church, so I waited outside the door because I didn't want to interrupt them. The only thing I didn't like about Preacher Brown was shaking hands. I never liked shaking the preacher's hand, because he shook hands with people everywhere he went, and I had a low tolerance for germs. It seemed ludicrous, since I had grown up on a farm and was around pigs and dirt all my life, but I couldn't help thinking about all the people that had coughed into their hands, wiped their noses, and gone to the bathroom without washing. Farm dirt seemed cleaner, somehow. Rita always told me I needed to get checked for having a germ phobia like Howard Hughes. I was worried about it, until I talked to Daddy about it one day. Daddy said I didn't need to see any shrink just because I didn't like shaking hands. He said everybody had some type of phobia or hang up. I asked him what his phobia was, and he told me that he was afraid of letting Mama, Rita, and me down. At the time, I didn't respond to that, thinking he *had* let me down by making me work so hard on the farm. But now I understood that hard, dirty farm work had been good for me because it made everything else I did, like working at Seek & Find Market and going to college at UC Berkeley, easier for me. Farming had taught me how to work and how to survive. I realized that everything I did in life would be easier because I had learned how to be reliable and on time, since the pigs counted on me to feed them, and how to be humble, because shoveling manure is certainly a practice in humility. I was strong and confident because I could grow tobacco and do things that most girls in Berkeley couldn't even imagine. I felt proud of my heritage, and it was a nice feeling.

"Hello, Kathy." I looked up to see the preacher standing in front of me, hand extended of course. "It's good to see you. How's school?"

"It's going very well," I said, reluctantly shaking his hand. I made a mental note to wash my hands when he left.

"Your daddy's looking a lot better today, young lady," he smiled. "He said he was trying hard to get well enough to eat one of Miss Judy's pies. I had a feeling your daddy wouldn't forget he was due a pie."

I laughed. "Now, that sounds like Daddy."

"I'm praying for him, Kathy." He patted me on the back. "He's going to pull through this."

"Thanks, Preacher," I said. "I believe he will." I felt a little better, knowing

Preacher Brown was praying for Daddy.

I went to the bathroom and washed my hands, then went to see Daddy. He looked much better than the day before, and he told me the doctor said he might get to move out of the CCU the next day if he continued to progress. "I gotta get outta here and get back to the farm. I got a ton of work to do."

"That's great news, Daddy," I laughed. "But Rita and I will be taking care of things on the farm until you're ready to get back out there."

"We need rain, Kathy," he said. "I don't think it's rained the whole time I've been in here."

I never thought I'd be happy to hear Daddy talk about rain after hearing about it my entire life, but right now, it was music to my ears.

"You'll have to get back to school soon, won't you?" he asked.

I hadn't even thought about school for the last couple of days. As much as I liked Berkeley, I wasn't in a hurry to get back there. "We'll see about that," I said, adjusting the cover around his feet. "You're my only concern right now."

I stayed with Daddy until he fell asleep. The color was coming back to his cheeks and he looked more like himself, the man I loved and admired so much. "God, please don't ever let me take my daddy for granted again," I prayed.

Mike was in the waiting room with Mama when I got back. I hadn't seen him since the other night when we kissed, and I had tried not to think about him and what had happened because I didn't know how to process it. I knew I was very emotional because of everything that had happened with Daddy and Kevin. I still couldn't believe I had kissed him, and how good it felt. But was there really something between us after all these years, or was I just scared and confused, looking for someone to make things better?

"Look who stopped by, Kathy." Mama looked at me with knowing eyes as if she was aware of the kiss. And maybe she was, or maybe I was being paranoid. But it was entirely possible that Rita had seen us from the window. She hadn't mentioned it to me, but if she saw us, she had probably already blabbed to everybody.

"I just heard the good news. I'm glad your daddy's doin' better." Mike smiled his warm, sweet smile, the one I'd known all my life but was suddenly different. It was as if I knew him like my own brother, but I saw him in a completely new way, not as the childhood friend he had been but as the amazing man that he was.

"Yes," my heart fluttered. "It's great news." I had a strong urge to run over and hug him, to kiss him as I had before.

"Why don't I take you lovely ladies to dinner?" He didn't take his eyes off me.

"The two of you go ahead," Mama said, looking at me and grinning. I still wondered if Rita had said something to her, but I didn't care. I wanted to be alone with Mike. "I'm going to stay here with Larry."

"Are you sure?" Mike asked, his eyes still glued to mine.

"Yes, but you and Kathy should go," Mama said. "She probably hasn't had a decent meal since she got here."

"I won't be long, Mama." I gave her a kiss, and Mike and I walked to his truck.

"Thanks," I said, as Mike helped me into his truck. He had one of those big trucks with a sideboard that you had to climb into.

"Are you OK?" he asked, as I got settled. He had always been chivalrous. Not the kind that was polite to women because he wanted something, like Kevin, but a true gentleman that was raised to treat women like ladies. It was a nice quality, although it hadn't meant much to me before. We drove to the Cream of the Crop Café near the hospital. It was known as one of the best local places to get home cooking. I had never eaten there, because I thought I got enough home cooking at home. But I had missed all Mama's home-cooked meals while at Berkeley. I had been eating fast food or frozen entrées, which were great in the beginning, but got old quickly. The restaurant was nice inside, with wooden floors and shelves filled with preserves and canned goods along the walls. Red and white plaid tablecloths and little vases of daisies adorned the tables, giving the place a downhome feel. The waitresses looked like pioneer women with long-sleeved red tops covered with tiny white flowers and long, flowing navy skirts with white aprons. Their hair was pulled back in buns, and they had little shawls around their shoulders. Even though the restaurant mostly appealed to tourists coming through Knoxville on their way to the mountains, I found it very charming and regretted not having eaten here before. I thought about the farm, and how pretty it had looked earlier. Nothing around here had changed—but maybe I had, a little. Our waitress brought us a big basket of homemade biscuits with plenty of butter and preserves. I ordered chicken and dumplings, fried apples, and sweet tea. I hadn't had sweet tea since I had left, and it tasted even better than I remembered. I thought about the tea house and the bitter green tea that Kevin and I had there. I wondered why we didn't have tea houses here in the South to celebrate the delicious sweet tea that everyone loved so much. They'd probably be much more popular. When the waitress brought my plate, I wanted to cry the food smelled so good. I had always liked chicken and dumplings, but I didn't remember them being this good, either. Mama called them comfort food, and now I understood why. Sitting here, eating chicken and dumplings with Mike across from me, I knew everything was going to be all right. *I'm home*, I thought, as I drank a long, cool sip of sweet tea.

"About the kiss, Mike," I began. I had to tell him how much it meant to me, how much he meant to me while I had the nerve.

"Please don't tell me it was a mistake, Kathy," he interrupted. "I'd waited for that kiss for most of my life. I've never hidden how I felt about you, and I think you felt something too. I think..."

"Mike, wait." My turn to interrupt. "You didn't let me finish. I was going to tell you that I *did* feel something. Something I've never felt with a guy before. Since I was twelve, I thought I knew what kind of guy I wanted. Now I realize the guy I wanted may have always been right here."

Mike's eyes were teary. He didn't cry. He was like Daddy, not the kind of guy who cried. And to be perfectly honest, I didn't really want an emotional man. Maybe it was because of Daddy, or maybe it was because I grew up in the country, but I liked a tough guy, one that could handle his emotions along with everything else.

"I can't believe this is finally happening. You're the love of my life, Kathy. You're my..."

"Lady?" I grinned. He always had a song for everything, and I couldn't resist beating him to the punch this once.

He smiled. "That's it. You're my lady." He reached across his plate of chicken-fried steak and took my hand. I felt a charge all through my body. I was his lady.

* * *

TWO WEEKS LATER

"Daddy!" I yelled at him from the kitchen window. "You're supposed to be taking it easy!" He had only been home from the hospital for five days, and the minute we turned our heads, he was in the barn. The doctor sent him home with strict instructions to rest for a couple of weeks, and change his diet forever. He was going to be a difficult patient, but I was determined to keep him with us for many more years. He walked in and sat down at the kitchen table. "You're breathing hard, Daddy. You're overdoing it," I said.

"I'm fine," he said. "I just walked to the barn for some fresh air. You and Rita are doing such a good job, I don't need to *do* much of anything."

It was true that Rita and I had been working hard to keep everything going, but we were getting plenty of help from Mike and Clyde too. Mike and I had been inseparable for the past two weeks. It was like I had just discovered a gold mine that had always been in my back yard, and I had been too busy looking everywhere else for it. I told Mike that, and he said I was worth the wait. It used to annoy me that he always said and did the right thing. What was wrong with me? Who doesn't want that? I guess you have to be away from something (or someone) to truly appreciate them. I hadn't seen him today, but he had called me earlier and said that they had called him into work. He would come over after dinner, when he got off. I missed him already, and couldn't wait to see him. But I had plenty to keep me occupied. The farm chores were keeping us busy, and I still had to decide what I was going to do about UC Berkeley. I had been gone for nearly three weeks, but I had no intention of leaving until I was sure Daddy was going to be OK. Now that he was doing better, I realized I still was in no hurry to go back. Maybe everything I really wanted was right here.

"Kathy, will you go down and get the mail now?" Daddy asked. "I'm expecting something, and it should have run by now."

"Sure, Daddy," I said. I didn't know what Daddy could have possibly been expecting. Maybe hospital bills. The sky was a brilliant blue, and the mountains still had a blanket of snow on them that blended into the sky, making it impossible to tell where the mountains ended and the sky began. *Only God could've painted that picture*, I thought. There wasn't any mail for Daddy, just Possum Valley Press, our free weekly newspaper. It mostly had ads for used cars and farm equipment in it, so it was well read in the valley. Maybe Daddy was looking for a new plow or a new bush hog, as if he didn't have enough old equipment laying around. I started walking back, and there it was. I don't know how I could've missed it on the way down.

Marry me, Kathy was written across the roof of our barn in big, white letters. I couldn't believe it. *He must have done it last night*, I thought, stunned. It had to take him quite a while, to get up there and paint it in such huge letters. *A month ago, I would have been utterly mortified to find this red neck proposal on our barn, but now, it's the most beautiful thing I've ever seen.* My heart raced, and I ran all the way back up the driveway to the trailer.

I was out of breath by the time I got back. No one was home but Daddy. Mama had gone to the grocery store, and Rita was at school. "Daddy," I said, trying to catch my breath. "Did you see the barn?" Daddy's face gave me my answer. He was beaming.

"Do you really think I walked down to the barn this morning for my health?" He smiled. "I went out there to see what that boy had done to my barn."

"So, you knew." I walked behind Daddy's chair where he was sitting and wrapped my arms around his neck. "I'm so happy, Daddy." I leaned down and pressed my cheek against his head. "I'm so happy that you're back here in your old, ratty chair where you belong, and I've finally found the guy I've been looking for."

He took my hands and kissed them. "Well, if it took me having a heart attack to get you two together, I guess it was worth it," he laughed. "But next time, don't be so stubborn. Hospitals are no fun."

I squeezed him tightly. "I love you, Daddy." At that moment, I loved everybody, the mailman, the pigs, you name it.

Chapter 21

"A man travels the world over in search of what he needs and returns home to find it." –George A. Moore

The knock on the door was no surprise. I could tell from the way he knocked that it was Mike: a rapid tap from someone eager to come in. I went to the door, my heart beating audibly in my ears, heat rising up from my gut to the top of my head. Now I understood how couples in Possum Valley could move into trailers on their parents' property. It seemed so simple now. They were in love. And now I was in love; if Mike wanted to live in a van out in the driveway, I would do it. *(Let's hope it doesn't come to that, on second thought).*

I opened the door to see him standing on the stacked cement blocks that we used for stairs. He burst in before I could invite him and lifted me off the floor, twirling me around until I was dizzy. "I love you, Kathy." He put me down and looked in my eyes. "I always have, and I want you to be my wife. I know we're young, but we've known each other all our lives. We don't have to get to know each other, and our parents know each other, and..."

"Shut up." I couldn't wait any longer. "I'll marry you. You didn't have to climb up on a barn to ask me, you know."

"You deserve my best," he said. "And that's exactly what you'll always get."

I knew he meant it. How could I have ever been so stupid, to fall for someone who treated me so badly (Kevin) when Mike was here all along? I was obviously one of those people who liked to learn things the hard way.

"Congratulations, kids." I just remembered Daddy was still in the room. "Mike already asked me for your hand in marriage," he said. "I told him he was asking for a lot, wanting to take you away from me." He looked at me and smiled. "But I think you'll be in good hands with this young man." It felt good to know Daddy approved of my choice in husbands.

"I'll take good care of her, sir," Mike said. "Now, why don't we go feed the chickens and pigs?" He took my hand and we walked outside.

* * *

We walked inside the barn to get the feed, the barn that Mike had climbed on for me. He pulled me to him and gently kissed my mouth, my throat. "You've made me the happiest man on earth, Kathy." His mouth was on mine again. I felt so wanted, so loved. I thought about how Mike had never tried to come onto me, or take advantage of me the way that Kevin had. He had just patiently waited for me, because he believed I was worth it. He made me *feel* worth it, just as it should be. Girls shouldn't feel pressured by guys into doing something they aren't ready for. All girls deserved to have a guy like Mike, a guy who made them feel special, appreciated, and loved. Why did girls settle for less? Why had I settled for less? The price for a rich guy was too high. Why would I ever consider being bought by someone, when someone else found me priceless?

"I'm happy too, Mike." I kissed him softly on the lips and brushed the back of my hand against his cheek. "I just can't believe it took me so long to realize how I felt about you. You've always been there for me, giving me candy, getting me out of trouble, making my birthdays special..."

"I'll always be here," he said. "And I want to make you as happy as you make me. I have something else to ask you, and I want you to know that this is your decision. You mean more to me than my music, more than anything else."

"What is it?" I had no idea what he was talking about.

"I don't want to keep you from getting an education, if that's what you want," he said.

I hadn't even considered any of that. The education never meant much to me, and still didn't. I would need to have a job of some sort, though, since I wasn't marrying for money anymore.

"I'm sure I could get a scholarship to finish at the University of Tennessee," I said.

"True." His voice was shaking a little, as he took my hands in his as we stood there in the barn, forgetting about feeding the animals. "But how would you feel about finishing school in Nashville?"

"Well, I might be able to get into Vanderbilt, but I don't know about scholarships," I said. "But why would I do that with UT right here?"

He squeezed my hands, his damp with sweat. "Because I've been offered a record deal in Nashville. They're offering me two million to sign. You won't need a scholarship. I could pay for your college, wherever you want to go."

I couldn't speak. Tears streamed down my face as I fell into his arms.

"But will you be happy living in Nashville, Kathy?" he asked. He was serious. He was seriously asking me if I'd be happy living in Nashville with two million dollars, when I was willing to live in a van with him an hour ago. I felt so stupid. It was only when I stopped worrying about getting away from home and getting rich that my life fell into order. I could have saved myself so much time and effort if I had taken the path of least resistance, and just allowed myself to see what was right there in front of me—instead of searching for something that wasn't there.

"Mike, I'm so happy for you." I finally found the words. "You deserve this, and I would love nothing more than to be a part of it, and everything you do from now on."

"OK, Kathy," he said. "But there is one more thing you'll need to do to be my woman." He had a sly grin on his face.

"I'll do anything," I said.

"You're going to have to kiss a frog in the mouth," he laughed.

Mike never forgot anything. It would probably annoy me in the future, but for now, I loved that he remembered my favorite color and every other little detail about me. Kiss a frog in the mouth. Yep. I deserved that. "OK," I said defiantly, hands on hips, "but you'll have to sing, 'When a Man Loves a Woman' at our wedding."

"You must have read my mind," he said. "How could I not sing *our* song at *our* wedding?"

Chapter 22

MAY 14, SIX MONTHS LATER

"Love isn't something you find. Love is something that finds you."
–Loretta Young

"You're up next," Fannie said to Rita as she poked her head into my bedroom where Rita, Jenny, and I were waiting. Fannie had planned the whole event, and had done everyone's hair, of course. I wasn't as nervous as I thought I would be. Mike and I had been inseparable for the past few months, and our relationship was as effortless as breathing. We talked about old times and looked forward to the future together.

"Love you, sis." Rita said, as she was leaving the room.

"Love you too," I said. She was my bridesmaid, and Jenny was my maid of honor. They had on yellow chiffon dresses with three flowing ruffled tiers at the knee. I asked them if the yellow was too much, but Jenny said she was so happy I was marrying Mike that she would wear a cardboard box, if I wanted. Rita agreed, of course. I felt like Cinderella in my long, full white dress with a fitted V-neck, sequined bodice, and long sleeves that puffed up at the shoulders. We were overdressed for our wedding on the farm, but Mike and I wanted to be married on the farm, and Mike wanted me to have the long, beautiful wedding gown I had always wanted. He said from now on, his life's purpose was to make all my dreams come true. I certainly couldn't argue with that.

"Your turn, Jenny." Fannie said. She adjusted Jenny's bra strap, which had slipped out from beneath her sleeveless dress. Jenny came over and hugged me tightly. "I'm so happy for you, Kathy. You and Mike make the perfect couple."

"Thank you, Jenny," I said, pushing her toward the door. "Now get out of here, before you make me cry and mess up my mascara."

I looked around the room as I waited for the signal from Fannie. Fly strips still hung from the ceiling, and my old binder that said "How to Marry a Rich Man" was still on my dresser. The last thing I ever planned to do was to marry someone from Possum Valley, but God had dreamed a bigger dream for my life that was always there for me, just waiting for me to wake up and discover.

"It's showtime, gorgeous!" Fannie ushered me out into the hallway, where Daddy was waiting to walk me out. I was so used to seeing him in blood-stained shirts and jeans that I barely recognized him all dressed up in a tuxedo. He looked strange, but it was a good strange. I held back my tears as I thought of how close I came to losing him just a few months ago.

"You are beautiful, my sweet girl," he said as he held out his arm like a knight from a fairy tale. "If that boy ever does anything to hurt you, I'll kill him with my bare hands, you know." Now that was the Daddy I knew.

"Of course, Daddy," I laughed. It was a little scary walking down the make-shift stairs from the trailer in my dress, but I had on sneakers underneath. I hiked up the dress in the front and Fannie held it up in the back, and we made it down with no incident. When I finally looked up, Mike was standing there beside his daddy. Our eyes met, and my knees became weak, as my heart skipped a beat. He was more gorgeous than I had ever seen him, and I felt like the luckiest girl in the world. I stood by Daddy as Mike sang our song, coming and kneeling in front of me at the end.

"I know exactly how he feels, 'cause baby, baby, I am a man." I could only think about him as a twelve-year-old, kneeling in front of me all those years ago in Joe's Pharmacy. It made me laugh and cry at the same time. When he finished, the guests erupted in cheers and applause. I looked out at our guests for the first time, seeing Mama looking beautiful in the new, yellow dress daddy had bought her.

And Chris.

Jenny said she was bringing a date but wouldn't tell me who it was. I couldn't believe my eyes. Chris had come all this way to be at my wedding. There was no hope for the mascara, as tears cascaded down my face. But I didn't care.

Nothing could spoil this day.

We walked next door to the empty lot for the reception that Jolene and Mama had worked on for weeks. The old house where Heath and Henry lived had been torn down, and only the cherry blossom trees I had always loved remained. It was a beautiful spot, and Chris being there where the people had lived who had such hatred toward him seemed like the perfect revenge. Mama and Jolene had placed hay bales all around for seats, and we had a big table piled high with every kind of pork imaginable: pork chops, pork loin, ham, and all sorts of things wrapped in bacon. Chris and Jenny walked over to the small table for two where Mike and I sat, pretending to eat cake (we were both too nervous to actually eat), and Mike stood up to shake his hand.

"We haven't met before, but I've heard a lot about you," Mike said. "Thanks for coming."

"It's my pleasure," Chris replied. "You have a special lady here."

No one talked about the cross burning or about Chris being different. Everyone was kind and treated him like he belonged. And even though I knew that perhaps some people were just being polite for my sake, I thought it was a start. A year ago, someone would have said something about Chris being there, but now I felt Jenny and I had planted a seed of acceptance that would hopefully grow over time.

"May I have everyone's attention, please?" Fannie yelled as she stood on top of a hay bale. "Kathy is going to toss the bouquet, so all you single girls gather around."

I stood up and turned around, tossing the bouquet high into the air over my head. I immediately turned around to see Jenny holding it, with a surprised look on her face. I looked over at Chris, and his eyes were fixed on Jenny with an enormous smile on his face. I didn't know what might happen between the two of them in the future, but what I did know was that life was full of surprises, and sometimes our wildest dreams couldn't compare to the beautiful reality that God has planned for us.

"And now, this song is dedicated to the bride and groom." I heard Clyde's voice, followed by the sound of the Righteous Brothers' recording of "You've Lost That Loving Feeling." Mike took my hand and pulled me close as we began dancing across the field. The whole crowd once again erupted in cheers and applause. I felt like a celebrity, but the truth was that I had married one. And there went the rest of my makeup. I couldn't stop smiling or crying. I must have looked frightful, but I never knew it was possible to be so happy. Maybe I had always loved Mike, I thought, as I looked into his blue eyes, but all I knew for sure was that I loved him now.

I never imagined in a million years that I would end up coming back to Tennessee and marrying Mike, but I read somewhere that the best journey takes you home. And even though I had to kiss a frog or two along the way, I'm glad I found my way back.

Acknowledgments

Sam: Thanks for being the first to read my book and the only one to listen to all my crazy ideas! You are the love of my life. End of story.

Zach and Jacob: You guys are my sunshine. No matter how old you get, I will always be your mom and will always love you. P. S. Don't forget to eat your veggies and drink plenty of water!

Jan-Carol Publishing: Thanks for giving me a shot!

Readers: Thanks for reading!

Thanks be unto God for his unspeakable gift. II Corinthians 9:15

Questions and Topics for Discussion

1. How does Kathy (whose character is set in the 1980s) differ from girls of her age today?
2. What are the similarities in Kathy and girls today?
3. Would a more independent, self-confident girl want to marry Mike, Chris, or Kevin? Why or why not?
4. Would girls today care if Mike was financially successful or not?
5. Are guys different today than they were in the 1980s?
6. In what ways were Kathy and her sister, Rita, different? Which one did you resonate with more?
7. One of the themes in this book is that there are many types of prejudices and they exist everywhere. Do you think most people agree with that? Why or why not?
8. How did Kathy change as she came of age at the end of the novel?
9. Were you happy with how the book ended? Why or why not?
10. Have we as a nation made progress in race relations since the 1980s?

About the Author

Joy Ruble is originally from Knoxville, TN. She is a former high school English teacher and has written for various newspapers, including *Northwest News* in Albany, GA, where she was a staff writer and columnist, the *Knoxville News Sentinel*, where she wrote as a guest columnist, and a community newspaper in Monterey, CA. She currently tutors high school students in grammar, writing, and SAT prep. Joy lives in Knoxville, TN with her husband, Sam. They have two sons, Zach and Jacob Ruble. Joy's passions are playing tennis, reading, traveling, and spending time with her family.

You can learn more about Joy at:

Gettingjoy.com and on Facebook / Joy Ruble

Coming Soon

Joy is currently working on her next novel, *Only the Beginning*, which takes a humorous look at three 50-something year old high school girlfriends learning to deal with aging parents, divorce, and empty nests. When they reconnect at their 35-year reunion, they realize how much of themselves they've lost over the years and decide to do something radical to regain their identities.

CPSIA information can be obtained
at www.ICGtesting.com
Printed in the USA
JSHW041510250420
5296JS00004B/17